AN

Robert Wallace is the pseudonym for Robin Wallace-Crabbe, who was born in Melbourne and now lives in the mountains south of Canberra, New South Wales. A writer and artist, he has had two novels published in Australia: *Goanna* and *Feral Palit*, which received the enthusiastic support of the novelist Patrick White. Robert Wallace has written three Essington Holt thrillers, *To Catch A Forger*, *An Axe To Grind* and *Paint Out*, all of which are published by Gollancz.

AN AXE TO GRIND

by

Robert Wallace

GOLLANCZ CRIME

Gollancz Crime is an imprint of Victor Gollancz Ltd
14 Henrietta Street, London WC2E 8QJ

First published in Great Britain 1989
by Victor Gollancz Ltd

First Gollancz Crime edition 1990

A CIP catalogue record for this book
is available from the British Library

ISBN 0-575-04768-2

Printed and bound in Great Britain
by Cox & Wyman Ltd, Reading

*for K who chops the works philosophically
and D who works his chops in the woodshed.*

'When you have succeeded in something or other, quickly turn your back on it, and enter a new adventure.'
Raoul Dufy

Chapter 1

'Apparently, like Trotsky, the old lady took a lot of killing, Essington, a frightful lot of killing.'

'What's so strange about that?'

Gerald Sparrow looked over the table at Dawn, at her angry face.

'That she was hard to kill?' he asked her.

'Exactly, that a woman would be any harder. I've read medical studies, lots of them, proving conclusively that women are biologically tougher than men.'

'Not disputed, Dawn,' said Feathers; that's what we'd always called Gerald Sparrow: Feathers. No doubt Dawn could have come up with some ideological objection to that as well. She hated it when I called Karen 'Bluey'. 'Karen, why do you put up with it? He treats you like you're some kind of child. You've got a name you know.' The Great Dane I called Desdemona. I'm sure something could be made of that.

Bluey, the name, I liked it. It sort of grew, nobody chose it. Maybe it was the terrible track suit she wore that fixed the colour into my subconscious—electric blue with 'Idaho State' silk-screened in yellow across the chest. But as far as I could recall the name evolved as a contraction: Karen . . . Ren . . . Wren, then Blue Wren . . . Bluey.

It was best to think of Dawn as sent by God . . . a kind of punishment. He or She or It had looked down upon us—Karen and me—and thought: 'There's a couple getting along just too well, putting life out of balance.' So we were sent Dawn Grogan who was only too aware of Karen's golden beauty.

Feathers looked to me for leadership. Maybe he was still a bit hung over from the flight—twenty-seven hours. He had got in last night, into Paris, that is. Then flown straight on down to Nice first thing in the morning. Normally it was the other way round with us. Normally Feathers led.

Funny fellow really, secretive, evasive. He liked to draw things out, like the story of the lady who got chopped up. Giving a little at a time, leading us on.

We were sitting on the terrace. Through the eucalyptuses the blue waters of what scientists claimed to be the very polluted Mediterranean glistened in an illusion of purity. Each of us had an aperitif somewhere between mouth and marble-top table. Mine was pink, Karen's was pink, Feathers' was pink—all drinking kir. Dawn was facing a beer. Beer was the people's drink. Dawn seemed to like 'the people', so long as they weren't men.

'Anyway, whatever, she was killed?' Karen was interested in the story.

'Butchered with an axe. A most terrible sight. I mean, it was only a murder but the circumstances were sufficiently awful for the national press to take it up.'

'Ghouls!' judged Dawn. Desdemona snarled. She'd taken a set against Dawn.

Karen and I were getting married in the morning and there we were chatting away about this old lady getting chopped up at Millbourne on the New South Wales central plains.

Rebecca came to the bay windows; just stood there waiting, letting me know that lunch was ready. I led the way inside.

'You seem to have settled into this new life. Genetic, do you think? Written on the chromosomes?'

Feathers had been a kind of father for me despite the fact that we were the same age. It hadn't been so long ago that he'd more or less given me five thousand dollars to clear debts. Now, with my aunt Eloise Fabre dead and me the closest relative, an only nephew, I was a lot better off than comfortable. Yet still the same old me; a scunge at heart. Though now scungyness sat uneasy. Big house out on Cap Ferrat, Rebecca and Renardo keeping the real world ticking over. Me, I swam a lot, had tried fishing without much luck—were there fish out there or only plastic bags? Mostly I just sat out among the *crème de la crème* like a shag on a rock. Truly on a rock because that more or less was what my end—the lighthouse end—of Cap Ferrat was: a great big ragged rock with a bit of dirt in the hollows best suited for growing the eucalyptuses of home.

Yet, with riches thrust upon me, I was bored out of my wits.

Karen, an altogether superior being, had got herself going after a while. She noticed first up that when you changed an Australian dollar into a French franc there wasn't much you could buy with the result. Then she found that things were even worse for the occasional Chinese national who ventured onto the soil of Western Europe. Therefore, she figured, the trick might be to import stuff that didn't cost too much over there in China into France. The French love buying nice things, they will pay the world for them.

'But Bluey, we don't need the money. We've got money!' I would spread my hands: 'Money we have!'

'Not the money, Essington, it's the challenge.'

She sensed that we needed something, something to do. Both of us.

I always had the intention of becoming a painter. Suddenly, with nothing to stop me—I could have bought my own gallery—I realized I didn't have the drive.

Anyhow, silk was what Karen was into. That was how we scored Dawn. Theoretically Dawn did the stuff at the China end, but for the last four weeks she had been helping—'consulting' is what she called it—while Karen set up her shop on the Rue de France, Nice. Where once there had been a 'Galerie de la Renaissance': all unforgivably *el chico*. Born in New Caledonia out in the blue of the *Pacifique Sud*, Karen had the advantage of fluent French. She did the negotiations; come to think of it she did the lot. I supplied the capital; otherwise I seemed no more occupied than before. Except for fending Dawn off.

Immediately after lunch Renardo drove Dawn and Karen to Nice in time to open for the afternoon trade. It was the height of summer. Most of Paris and a lot of Holland, Germany, Switzerland and England had jammed themselves into the Mediterranean coastline. Everybody clasping their little plastic cards. Karen had the card stickers obscuring the front window. Pretty they were, after their fashion.

They sold silk by the metre, by the mega metre; silk as beach wraps, silk as bathers, silk as T-shirts with stripes, with zigzags. There was a new line—here I had done a bit to help—of reproductions of designs by the early French moderns: by

Matisse, Dufy, Derain, Braque. All pirated with subtle changes. They were selling like hot cakes.

'Silk, Essington,' Karen had said: 'it's a goer. Everyone loves silk, the romantic feel. The way it's made, its history . . . silk routes from China. People think of silk when they think of things like frankincense and ivory.'

'I've never thought of frankincense in my life, Bluey. I don't even know what it is.'

'Come to think of it, neither do I. I'll ask Dawn. Dawn'll know.'

'She would.'

'Come on, Essington. She's the way she is.'

'Oh, I don't mind the politics. In fact I quite like the idea of her sitting out there on the terrace being waited upon while she snipes at the . . . what is it? . . . "the hegemony of the bourgeoisie". What could be more bourgeois than buying and selling, for Christ's sake? No, Blue, what pisses me off is that she's got a thing going for you.'

'Not to worry, Essington. You're safe on that score. I like he-men.'

That was about as nice a way as anyone could describe a big solid fellow going to fat in his middle forties, who'd been broken to adulthood on the cattle stations of the Australian outback. They'd called us jackaroos. We were more like labourers. Only if you were a jackaroo you weren't expected to hold out for the award wage.

Gerald Sparrow and I, womanless, wandered back out onto the terrace for a bit of sit and sip. The dog came too, she liked to make sure I was in good hands.

'Anyway, you can't say I haven't lined you up with a bit of skirt?'

'Money hasn't bought off your coarse streak, Essington.' Feathers was a senior partner in the law firm, Richards and Partners. It used to be Richards and Temple, but Temple had retired hurt. Feathers had a long bony face and the coldest blue eyes. He looked every inch the clergyman's son that he was—almost the preacher's. I'd said to him a few years back: 'You're really the priest, aren't you? Only Caesar's priest.' And he replied: 'Actually the servant, Essington.' But then the desiccated smile gave the game away.

'Feathers, you never had a chance to finish your story. The lady chopped up with the axe.'

'It's a story that should interest you; and it's got links somewhere over here, I believe. In fact, Essington, I was hoping to prevail upon you to offer a hand. But I run on.'

Very formal, Feathers, liked the sound of his own voice. A disease of lawyers, teachers and, of course, the clergy.

'As I told you, Oula Strossmayer was cut to ribbons with a small axe. There was evidence, so the police say, of a long and terrible struggle. She lived, had done for quite some time, in a large house on the outskirts of Millbourne—cattle and sheep country mostly. A bleak town, nothing to distinguish it from hundreds of others. At one end a signpost telling you that you should drive at sixty kilometres per hour—this of course holed three times by frustrated spotlight shooters returning empty-handed.'

Feathers was going to tell a tale; it was in his nature, nothing omitted.

'At the other end a sign saying that you can speed up again. That's on the off chance that you ever bothered to slow down.

'Between these signs are two thousand souls, give or take a few. It has two hotels to keep the population watered, a sort of combined club complete with golf course, a ragged line of shops and, of course, three churches: the Anglican, the Roman Catholic and the Uniting—you may not have kept up with the Uniting Church, Essington. That's a curious, I should have thought unholy mixture of Methodist and Presbyterian. And, my God, didn't they argue about real estate when they were coming together.

'All in all not a very likely town for Oula Strossmayer to choose as her final resting place. Oula Strossmayer was not—how should I say?—an entirely typical Yugoslav refugee from the turmoil of the Second World War. She was not a woman of the soil.

'Since your own heroic farming days, Essington, the composition of the Australian town has changed. I dare say that the same is true here in France. The contraction of markets, of returns, the problems of global overproduction have led to a

11

drift of population towards the cities. Yet, at the same time, there has been a compensatory movement out—idealists, conservationists; people ill-equipped to deal with life as it is lived. Millbourne, I am led to believe, has its fair share of these people, and, it follows, a craft shop, art groups, reading and discussion societies.'

'Global overproduction!' I objected. 'People starving everywhere!'

'They're not in the market-place, Essington, never have been. But back to the craft shop.

'This sprang up long after Oula Strossmayer first settled into the big house on the edge of the town. Once, I believe, the house had belonged to a farm bordering the little grid plan that city surveyors so inappropriately drew up in the nineteenth century every time the natural pattern of settlement was recognized as having established the nucleus of something. This strange woman had gone out into Australia, a deeply xenophobic Australia, and settled by buying the town's grandest house—for next to nothing, I might add; I've looked at the records—and moving in.

'She did not win friends but neither did she try to influence people. She concerned herself with herself, or so it seems. Living a lonely life, tending her garden—she was a very keen gardener—and until age forced her to neglect it her garden was a source of some civic pride. They claimed it as their own, but not so its creator. At the time of her death it was a jungle at the far end of which there lived a potter. He occupied what had once been shearers' quarters, cut off from the farm along with the homestead and its three or four acres.

'I gather the potter had a wife—in the broadest sense of the term—and a child. He made little jars, ceramic jars, and filled them with jam which he bought in large tins; the sort of tins ordered by canteens, hospitals or prisons. This he decanted, covered with wax, the regulation gingham, elastic band and hand-written label. They got by. That's the sort of level, Essington. I don't think he would have made a wage but no doubt it supplemented the dole. Perhaps he worked at something else as well.

'So this "craftsman" discovered Oula where she finished up, half in and half out of an unused chook run. The trail of blood led back to the house where upended furniture, breakages and the rest told the story.

'Although by all accounts she led a lonely, an isolated life, after her death there were countless witnesses to her warmth, her humanity, to her education, her sense of culture. Things that had been locked up within her since 1947 when she bought Woolabar—that was the name of the home, Woolabar—fake Aboriginal—an extension of that which comes from the sheep's back.

'Essington, all this is ghastly enough. The papers had their brief fling and then it was dropped. That was where I came in. Old Richards was a native of Millbourne. We don't have a Richards at Richards and Partners. We don't have a Temple either—thanks to you I might say.'

'But you do have a Sparrow.'

'We do indeed. A rather elevated Sparrow with Temple gone into retirement.'

I had unwittingly come into conflict with Temple not so long ago. The conflict had proved a public embarrassment to the man and he had been convinced that he should retire for the good of the firm. Actually, it had been my aunt who was the cause of the problem. I had simply picked up the pieces after her death.

'Really too elevated,' Feathers continued, 'to be concerned with the will of an old Yugoslav woman, no matter how she died. The details are being handled by one of our secretaries. It's all very straightforward if a little upsetting for the population of Millbourne. The house and money are to go to a Father Down, who is a bit of an outsider in the Roman Catholic Church—he argues the cause of urban Aborigines. Oula Stross-mayer intended her house to become a retreat for distressed Aboriginal youth. This could be a mistaken intention but it is the clear intention. And there's the money to do it in the property and in the form of a painting by the French artist, Raoul Dufy.'

'A Yugoslav woman living in Millbourne, New South Wales, with a Dufy hanging on her wall. You're having me on, Feathers.'

'No, indeed, I'm not having you on at all. That is the situation.'

'Well, it makes a droll tale.'

'A tragic one, indeed, a tragic one. And a fraction more complicated than I've indicated.'

'More complicated?'

'I know I'm a bore, Essington.'

'Hardly a bore.'

'No, I know I am. In fact I've spent years perfecting the art. I'd be disappointed if you didn't agree.'

'OK then, Feathers, you're a crashing bore.'

'Thank you, Essington, thank you very much.'

Chapter 2

The grill gate slid open and Renardo returned in the Citroën Estate that had come with all else I'd inherited.

'If I wasn't a simple man, Essington, I'd feel bitter that one of the least deserving of God's creatures should be so amply and so unjustly rewarded for a life of . . .'

'A life of . . . Feathers? What would you say I'd composed it of?'

'Words fail me, Essington. I'm sure I really don't know.'

'Blessed are the pure of heart.'

'You really couldn't have been thought to qualify in that department.'

Feathers had expressed a desire to walk. So we walked. A track led down from opposite Aunt's gate—I could not get used to thinking of it as my own—to the *Phare*, the lighthouse, from which it formed a spectacular walk in either direction: towards Beaulieu or towards the ancient village of Villefranche now overbuilt with blocks of holiday apartments. We made for Villefranche because from that side of the cape we could see the United States' warships moored in the harbour. They added a businesslike aspect to a too-pictorial view. The dog couldn't believe her luck.

'So what are the complications of the Strossmayer woman's death?' I asked. I was a shag that was coming down off its rock. At the sea's edge stone was washed by unusually large waves rolling in and causing problems for people who liked to sunbake on the odd flat surface; the air was filled with spray. There was a stiff breeze. I had to raise my voice.

'Well, Essington,' Feathers shouted back. 'Firstly, the police have so far been unable to tell why she was killed or if anything was stolen. The Dufy painting . . . I never really cared for Dufy, did you? Slight.'

Feathers liked paintings. He was a collector. In what now seemed to be another life I had, from time to time, managed to furnish him with nice little pieces that I had picked up at Sydney and Melbourne auctions. He had always known just what it was he wanted. No, quite the connoisseur.

'Very badly mauled by imitations, I'd have thought. If you get away from the idea of a Dufy and actually look at the work itself, particularly his early work, it's quite a different story.' I had to stick up for a local, a Niçois hero. 'He was buried up there near Matisse'. The sea crashing on the rocks behind us— we had now turned the corner into the sheltered *rade*—was the sea Dufy had celebrated with his intense, oh so French, ultramarine blue.

'The Dufy painting?' I urged him to continue.

'It wasn't there. Luckily, I should have thought. It stood a good chance of being damaged even if it wasn't in line to be stolen.'

'So if they were after the Dufy who would have known about it?'

'There are two possibilities, it seems to me. Her few friends—some 'alternatives' around the town—and the good Father Down. It's reasonable to suggest that they would have seen it, though not known its significance, its value.'

'Father Down would have been told,' I suggested. 'She must have discussed her plans with him—the house as a sanctuary.'

'I should have thought so.' Feathers agreed but added nothing more. We were following the path around a cove. There were the remains of a concrete swimming platform about fifty feet below us and a grill gate giving access to steps leading up to a quasi-Moorish villa above. Part of the path had slipped. Feathers, never a sporting type, was hugging the shore side closely as we crossed this marginally treacherous section. He was careful to look up, not down.

'Vertigo?'

'It gets worse, I find, with age. My mind goes.'

He had gone white. We sat down on a little rusted bench nicely placed beside a rubbish bin. Here the path was wide enough for people to pass. A helicopter was warming up on the landing pad of the nearest destroyer. Desdemona barked at it.

'You said two possibilities, what's the other one?' I urged.

16

'Oh, yes. Well, if it wasn't friends, or the good Father, then it could be a man who claims to be Oula Strossmayer's son, Milo. He called himself Milo Strossmayer. He's challenging the will.'

'And did he have the painting?'

'Good Lord no. It's with a rather earnest young couple who live in Surry Hills, Sydney. It seems that Oula had it taken down there for safe-keeping. My God. It's pretty here, Essington. It's . . . how should I say? . . . filmic.'

'Too much so, after a while. It feels a bit overdone . . . almost too—well not perfect, that's not the word but . . . it's a smug landscape. Cocksure.'

'Maybe that was Dufy's problem . . . he couldn't improve on it. I've often thought that artists need scruffy subjects. That's the Sunday painter's first mistake, to choose such lovely scenes.'

'Why would she send it away? Was that long before she died?'

'Question one: I'd rather not enlarge on that at this point in time.' Feathers giving me a squint at his mysterious side. 'Question two . . . not so long.'

'You're the brains, Feathers, always have been. You know me, I'm the old Essington: lots of muscle and a bit thick up top.'

'If you say that often enough you may get to believe it.'

'She got rid of the painting. To do that she must have had a reason. You don't keep a painting like that with you all those years and then send it off to anyone, let alone to . . . to who exactly?'

'What you mean, Essington, is "to whom", surely.'

'This couple in Surry Hills. How do they get to be so thick with Mrs Strossmayer?'

'Not Mrs Strossmayer, it seems, Miss.'

'Or Ms. That'd be Dawn. She'd insist on Ms.'

'It appears that Oula Strossmayer has quite a history and this couple have been intent on discovering what it is. They were interested in a film, I believe. In making a film of her life.'

'Jesus, that'd be gripping. What were they going to call it? *Forty Years in Millbourne, New South Wales*? You'd have a great première at the Millbourne Mechanics' Institute. Do they run to a Mechanics' Institute?'

'Her life before Millbourne. As you would have known if you had been a little more aware, Essington.' I don't know why I'd put up with Feathers all those years. Admittedly, he had flown half-way round the world to come to my wedding . . . which was going to be a non-event anyway.

He continued: 'In Australia, after years of neglect, a new generation is realizing that migrants have something to add to our culture and to our life. Something a little deeper than folk dancing: real lives, their stories.'

'So this nice young couple were into Ouna . . .?'

'Oula!'

'OK. Were into Oula for her story and, it seems, for her Dufy. If an old lady has nice friends like that she wouldn't need any enemies.'

'I think, Essington, it should be possible to see what they were doing in another light.'

A couple of joggers passed, from their thick thighs I would have thought officers from the ships. They had a 'buddy' system. They were only allowed out in pairs.

'And what light's that?'

'Oula Strossmayer was worried about the painting. It seems there were threats. They took it off her hands for safe-keeping.'

'So, if the police know all this, they must have the killer, if not now, soon.'

'They do know. It's through the police that I'm in a position to provide you with all this stimulation. The point is that the threats came from outside Australia. They came from Entrevaux.'

'From Entrevaux!'

'That's right.'

'But that's up in the mountains behind here. That's on the road to Sisteron.'

'Exactly.'

'And I thought you came to see me married.'

'I did, Essington.' Feathers stood up. He spread his arms in a theatre of generosity. 'I did . . . and then I thought that I could . . .'

'Kill two birds with one stone.'

'Your words.'

'No they're not, Feathers, and not too appropriate for a wedding.' But then I laughed. Feathers had always been the same. And there had been lots of times when his double-handed generosity had kept me in food and lodging. Still, there was no end to the depth of the man: secrets within secrets within secrets.

I wouldn't know if it was a form of banishment. If it was, the minister at the English Church in the Rue de la Buffa didn't seem to mind. His face was tanned, he was not a man under pressure, even with the street throngs of his fellow countrymen and women who had come down for the summer.

We were on familiar terms already. He had buried my aunt on one of the few cold and blustery days that the eastern end of the Côte d'Azure permitted itself.

It was me who had decided about marriage. I guess it was a possessive gesture. Karen had no objection despite the belated interference of Dawn who could have taken a PhD on what was wrong with the wedded state in the late twentieth century.

A curiously lonely feeling inside the church. We had one extra guest—an elderly woman seated in the back pew. Other than her, us. The English Church was, at the moment of our being brought together by God, the least crowded place in Nice. The car attracted interest, parked in the yard outside the Presbytery. Renardo had brought the yellow Bentley Continental, Aunt's joy, now a collector's item—passers-by in their sloppy summer clothes would have thrown confetti and rice on it for itself alone. We, the wedding party, they ignored.

Dawn and Feathers, attending us, looked an odd couple indeed. Feathers delighted in sartorial elegance, the perfectionist in him governing choice and application down to fine details. With a different head he could have been a male prop in a French perfume ad. The gloom of a severe blue double-breasted suit was only broken by the too perfect handkerchief, the dots of gold at his cuffs.

I guess self-expression would be the word for Dawn's outfit. She had applied a bit more gel to her spiked hair adding, as a feminine touch, a sash of gaudy silk, an offcut I assumed, holding up trousers of distinctly masculine cut. She looked a lot like a young Lisa Minnelli.

Rebecca cooked lunch and after that it was going to be back to battle stations: Dawn and Karen at the shop; me and Feathers pottering around, him telling me about life.

'Why can't you get someone in to look after the shop?' I asked.

'Because she likes it. You can't spend your life stuck out here.' I made Dawn aggressive. I didn't try, I just did.

'But it's my wedding day.'

'Just a formality. You had your wedding months ago. Cripes, what's it to be now, a sentimental groom?' She turned to Karen, put a protective arm around her. 'Aren't men the pits?'

'Karen Holt—' that was her name of a couple of hours—'are you going to put up with Dawn's bullying on our wedding day?'

She looked terrific, Karen, but very unFrench despite a New Caledonian father. We'd tried to get them over for the ceremony but they couldn't be buggered—either that or it really put him out that a daughter they had given up as a dead loss should finish up on her own two feet. I guess you could have described her as chic punk—her soft features painted to become the mask of a doll, long eyelashes that might drop down the instant she was laid horizontal.

Karen wasn't stupid, she knew what was going on and she was enjoying my awkwardness in the situation.

'Essington, it is only a wedding.'

Dawn looked triumphant.

'I never really saw what was wrong with doing nothing.'

'Crap, you didn't.' Karen snapped and then softened by what must have been a wounded look. 'Oh, Essington.'

We walked out into the garden, Karen and I; Feathers had seemed uneasy, caught in a first matrimonial squabble. Dawn was looking shifty.

Once we were alone I said: 'I'm sorry, I know I'm being a pain in the arse.'

'No Ess, it's Dawn that's the pain in the arse. Only we're stuck with her and it's just for a couple more weeks.'

'But she won't let you go, and she's at me all the time.'

'Where's your sense of humour? It doesn't matter, Ess, it doesn't matter at all—Dawn's Dawn.'

'I keep on fearing some feminist plot, I suppose—you two against me. Unequal combat.'

'Can't you see it's funny—Dawn, you, me? We're a classic comedy situation.'

'It's funny for you, you're the prize. Me, I'm the one who stands to lose.'

'No you're not, Essington, it's me that loses. Because it's my choice and I chose you. Don't be a bore and make me regret it, will you?'

It was like being in Australia out there. You could smell the eucalyptus on the air—only no koala bears. We walked back to the house and to an impatient Dawn.

'Come on, we've got to open up.' They ran down the stairs to where Renardo was waiting by the Citroën. Karen winked over her shoulder.

The ever discreet Feathers emerged from hiding. 'The young wife,' he said with a faint smile. Karen was twenty years my junior, always would be, but right at that moment I was the closest I would ever be to twice her age. I'd never thought of it as a problem, me being forty-seven, till Dawn had landed on our doorstep. Up to that moment she had been no more than Ms D. Grogan, an essential link in our silk trade.

'It's not like I'm ancient or anything.'

Feathers just smiled.

'And I'm not in a mood to take interference from you. Dawn's about all I can handle. So let's get off the subject.'

Feathers was not in a position to moralize. His romantic life consisted of trips to the Philippines, the Mecca of the paedophile. That was Gerald Sparrow's other life—or so they said. It turned out to be only one of several, if it existed at all.

It was an unwritten agreement that Renardo, and Renardo alone, drove the yellow Bentley. It was compensation for wage slavery though, from his glum and slightly stooped demeanour, you wouldn't have thought that anything could be a compensation for anything.

He didn't smile, Renardo. Rebecca, his wife, she was the sunshine in their life and capable of spreading some rosy glow over mine as well. The wedding had made her sad, very sad indeed. She and Renardo belonged to the region; they were the true inheritors of the eastern Côte d'Azure, more Italian than French. They expected ceremony at weddings, births and deaths—surely these were great moments in each individual existence, things worth celebrating.

To Rebecca, life with Aunt had seemed dull enough. Now with my anti-wedding I was following in this strange Australian tradition of eschewing ritual.

A few days earlier she had taken me to task in her rich southern accent—I had caught the same rolled 'r's, the long 'a' sounds. Rebecca had been my language teacher before Karen came along with the New Caledonian French learnt in child-hood and shoved into a compartment at the back of her mind during a healthy Australian adolescence.

'Monsieur 'olt,' Rebecca had demanded, 'rather you live as you live now than that you mock marriage in this way.' She had disapproved of us living in sin.

'I don't mock anything, Rebecca. It's what we want and, anyway, who is there to invite?'

It hadn't occurred to her that we expatriates were essentially lonely people. It would no sooner enter her head to cut family ties than it would to fly to the moon.

'In Australia, Rebecca, we celebrate non-events—it's the way of the Antipodes. The land of the kangaroo!' Then I held up limp arms, hands flapping on my wrists and hopped across the kitchen's terracotta tiled floor.

She shook her head over a steaming pot of bouillabaisse. 'A land of animals and barbarians,' she judged.

Chapter 3

Rich but carless I sat with Feathers at the Bar Plage behind the Villefranche beach. If he looked good in his formal get-up, Gerald Sparrow was the total ocker casual, in mid-thigh length, cotton gaberdine shorts and long socks. More like a daring young front-bencher in the Queensland Parliament than the sophisticated professional on a Riviera holiday. The bits of him that stuck out were freckled and going a very nasty red in the mild sun.

Bar Plage was run by Renardo's nephew. They knew me there, smiled upon me, we swapped pleasantries. The waiter, a more distant cousin of Renardo's, had a cut mending just below his eye. He was the family's boxing hope but looking pretty puny in baggy floral shorts and a Sad-Sack Hawaiian shirt. I'd never seen him in anything else.

Once or twice I'd thought to ask for a chance to go a few rounds togther. I used to be quite a hand at boxing though a hothead once hit. I guess he'd have killed me, though if he did, it would have been David felling Goliath. If I had held his face in a glove he couldn't have connected. Not a chance.

So there I was on my wedding day getting just a fraction plastered on the local rosé while chewing the flesh off the little local olives with my old school pal, Feathers. Desdemona just fitted under one side of the table.

'So who the hell would be sending threats all the way from Entrevaux to Millbourne, Australia? It sounds fantastic. Or is it the result of the information explosion we read about? The global village? They say that's what it is now.'

'That's what I don't know.'

'You're going to find it hard at this end. I mean, you don't expect to whip up to Entrevaux, do you, stand in the town square, shout questions, have them answered? They all know it's illegal to threaten people and really bad form to have

23

threatened somebody who subsequently has been found cut up with an axe.'

'I'm the lawyer, Essington. I don't need lectures on Caesar's realm.'

'So what do you need? What do you hope to find out?'

'I'm not exactly sure. I think you, in your bull-headed way, misunderstand my visit. Would you believe, I came here because of friendship? I'd be here getting abused if there were threats from Entrevaux or not. Since I'm here, it would be strange, even negligent, not to follow up what there is to follow.

'There is a will making a bequest that is bound to prove less than popular with Millbourne's civic fathers. Almost everybody in the country who holds land is frightened by Aboriginal land rights or has used land rights to give vent to their pre-existing racial hostility.

'Not only is the will likely to be unpopular but it's challenged by a claimant, a would-be son—though there is no evidence from Oula Strossmayer's papers, such as they are, that she has any surviving relatives at all. And then the Strossmayer woman is brutally murdered . . . after being threatened.'

'By somebody from Entrevaux? Did they send picture post-cards with nasty words written all over them?'

'No, letters, letters written in English, on a typewriter.'

'And how did they come to you?'

'Well, they didn't, I haven't seen them. They were passed to the local police by Oula.'

'And the police?'

'The police did nothing. There was a drive against marijuana around Millbourne at that time and the police claim that it was all they had the personnel to handle. Unfortunately, Essington, to the law, she was just another old foreign lady. I got the impression they considered her a trifle mad. The local sergeant couldn't understand what she was saying, that's what he said. The law is not quite the same for those of foreign birth—a prejudice that could be helped.'

'Wants to be.'

'Tribalism, ancient as rock.'

'Should have vanished by now.'

'Well you will be unsurprised to hear that it is alive and well in Millbourne, New South Wales. Which was, by the way, "Tidy Town" 1983. They're still proud of that.'

'Big deal . . . you mean they pick up papers?'

'They did on the day of judgement 1983.'

'The papers but not the threatening letters.'

'You must realize, Essington, just how isolated this old woman was. I'm sure there are many others like her . . . in their mid-seventies. If this Milo fellow really is a son he would be fifty years old. She had few documents. It seems that most of her paper life was lost either during the war or in the confusion ruling directly after the cessation of hostilities. Somehow she managed to bring the Dufy with her; strange that, getting it through. How she did it I wouldn't have the least idea. But she managed it.'

'Rolled, I'd imagine. If it wasn't too big there wouldn't have been much problem, carrying it rolled and wrapped in old newspaper.'

'As you may know, Yugoslavia had a terrible war, the more general horrors of which were multiplied by inter-racial strife. The Ustase were a vicious and notorious pro-German Croatian group. I've read in the accounts of a British army officer dropped into Yugoslavia to co-ordinate the resistance that the Ustase collected eyeballs as trophies, carried them in their kitbags.' That was the sort of stuff Feathers read, war books. And he liked to wax a touch philosophical: 'Curious, when you stop to consider the horrors of modern Africa . . . it's not so long ago that Europe was given over to much the same kind of thing. World War Two was, in essence, an inter-tribal conflict that got out of hand.'

'With a little help from their friends, Feathers. There was some goading along the way, from the big powers.'

'Since when have you been majoring in Yugoslav history?'

'Since never, but even slow old me picks up a thing or two.'

'A thing or two like what, Essington?'

The waiter approached, wearing an expectant look. I ordered a couple of black coffees. Feathers wanted an ice-cream—he'd been watching a boy at our adjoining table who was mining for the three coloured balls under their mountain of cream. Funny the secret sides to a man . . . and the self-awareness of

25

children—I was certain the boy was playing at holding his attention.

'A thing or two like the stepping up of the hunt for war criminals . . . questions asked of the English, of the Australians; Klaus Barbie causing a lot of people sleepless nights up there in Lyon. Now old Demjanjuk, the Treblinka man, bringing it all back to battered witnesses for the prosecution. I think, Feathers, there's still a residual capacity in the grey matter.'

'Point taken.'

The coffee came and the ice-cream. Was that a wink Feathers passed between the tables. He'd always been secretive, rather publicly so, seen to be clandestine; that was the Sparrow line, that was how he got his thrills.

'I hope it's not teaching you to suck eggs, Essington, just to provide a tiny bit more detail.'

'There's a dab of ice-cream on the tip of your nose.'

'Thank you.' Unabashed he wiped it clean.

'It was a very confused situation, Yugoslavia. The Italians buttering up the Croats, the Ustase—their Fascist wing led by Ante Pavelić—the German speakers. Certain Croatian regiments poised to go over to the Germans in forty-one and sabotaging the nationalist military resistance. Catholic Church against the Orthodox and then, among the resistance, bitter feuds—Mihailović's Chetniks going partially over to the Axis forces in their struggle against Tito's Communist Partisans. The Orthodox Church, aligned with the Communists, balancing Catholic support for Croatian pro-Nazi forces. A mess, a total mess.

'And then peace, the umpire blows the whistle, it's over. But still a lot of shouting to come.'

'That's when the migrants started spilling into the new world.'

'Exactly . . . many simply wanted to forget. Others wanted to make sure nobody would remember. Still others, a marked minority, settled into exile planning their eventual return, their final victory.'

The boy was finished. He wandered off at the heels of a mother but not without flashing Feathers a last enigmatic smile.

'This old woman, Oula, it's reasonable to imagine . . . in

1945 she would have been part of that great wave of the displaced who surged back and forth over the face of Europe trying to shake off histories, to gain new ones—people compromised one way or another, or simply broken. All desperate to prove that they had had no connection with the vanquished German armies or their network of puppet governments.

'They put their names on lists, those who could not or would not go home. Depending on the vetting you got a new life in a new world. If you had really cooperated with the Nazis maybe you got Haiti. If you were fairly clean you got to the USA. Australia fell somewhere in the middle. If you were valuable but embarrassing you got anonymity and South America.'

'We got our fair share of Croatians though.'

'We did indeed. But there's no evidence to connect Oula Strossmayer with them. Nor were all Croats of one mind. Leo Mates, a Croat, was a prominent member of the post-war Yugoslav Government. Tito ran it, he was a Croat.

'Whatever her past, there was nothing to be proved. Of course, that's something they all played on. Suddenly, in a new country, you could present yourself as anything. A baron in distress, a great humanist thinker whose works had been destroyed, anything.'

'And what did Oula Strossmayer present herself as?'

'Nothing, as far as I can make out, absolutely nothing. She was just a woman, another nondescript woman who'd managed to survive.'

'Well, what about the other couple?'

'Which other couple, Essington?' Feathers was getting very red indeed. I led us to another table, now vacant, shaded by bamboo blinds laid out over a grid of rusted steel. The Bar Plage was not up-market—those wishing to hit the high spots gave it a fairly wide berth.

The waiter returned with a bowl of water for the dog who was submitting to a lot of sniffing from a small, shaggy fellow with a bow tied around his neck.

'You said there were a couple of film makers in Sydney who wanted to do something with her life.'

'Oh them. The Griffins. Very close about the whole business. I talked to them once and they didn't add a thing. They seemed to think I was trying to pirate the material.'

'But the police . . .?'

'That's how I got onto them, through the police. No, they didn't get anything out of them either.'

'You must have seen the Dufy.'

'Seen it . . .? I've got it in my office at the moment.'

'You've got it. They handed it over?'

'No option. They had no rights to it at all. Nothing in writing. She just gave it to them for safe-keeping.'

'What was to stop them keeping on keeping it safely?'

'Nothing at all, only honesty. Some people do suffer from it, Essington. They read of her death—like I said, the papers made a bit of a thing of it—and then they contacted the police. I held the will—I finished up with the painting. The executor, Father Down, had nowhere to keep it since he despises property. Doesn't even have anywhere to keep himself, to rest his saintly head. Not altogether unlike yourself, Essington, not so long ago.'

We wandered along to the end of the beach, past the blue plastic water-slide with its shrieking, descending children, arms and legs waving. Past the boule ground where the wise-looking old—a curious deception that—hunted the kitty with metal balls. We climbed the steps that led us along the railway until we could turn down the Boulevard Charles de Gaulle in the direction of the lighthouse. Light cloud from Africa was drifting north.

'Feathers, how do you know the chap who lived in the shearing quarters potted commercial jam?'

'What a curious question, Essington. Why do you ask?'

'It just seemed to be an incongruous detail.'

Feathers looked a trifle embarrassed.

'I mean, did you see the tins stacked around the back of his shed? Did you see him opening them and spooning the stuff into his studio-fired pots? What?'

'I bought a jar, Essington, if you must know. I stopped off at the Millbourne Craft Shop and bought myself a pot. They looked so nice. And, in fact, it's true, when I was looking around the property I did happen upon a stack of big jam tins . . . what would they be? Litre, maybe two-litre. And then when I tried the stuff next morning all I had to do was put two and two together.'

'Clever fellow.'

'Crook, I'd have thought.'

'I didn't know you'd become a jam connoisseur. Is that in place of wine?'

'No, Essington. As well as.'

A strange painter, Raoul Dufy, a man who perfected the trivial touch. Terribly French in a way. If you do a tour of the private galleries of Paris the thing that strikes you is the French resistance to difficult art. They positively prefer the slight, the easy pictorial trick.

For me, Dufy is the definitive French artist right down to his preference for that colour of lapis lazuli that art snobs who are totally out of touch like to call 'French' ultramarine. The interesting thing is that he was right in there at the start of it all. When Matisse, Braque and Derain were being abused by critics for their raw and mildly random use of pure colour, when they were being called 'Fauves' or wild beasts, Dufy was in there too, being just as ill-mannered. That was up to 1906. Then he went angular along with his mates, looking at and learning from Paul Cézanne who died at that time from what my mother would have termed 'catching his death'. That is the way the story goes—he got wet painting outdoors. So, inspired by the just-dead Cézanne, Dufy joined in at the very start of cubism, producing, in 1908, green and ochre landscapes with a strong geometric structure. But by late 1909 he was already heading for the flippant style that made him famous and which turned him into such a pernicious influence. He developed a system—later defined as 'line over open colour'—in which, just as it says, he smeared in an abstraction of bold colour areas and then drew the subject over the top so that subject and colour do not exactly overlap.

He drew beautifully with a light illustrator's line. He was a wonderful decorator. And left behind a couple of handfuls of fine works. That is a lot more than is allotted most mortals.

Perhaps his best paintings were concerned with music, like some of his post-World War Two violin studies or his early, just post-cubist still lifes of a bust of Mozart. Dufy loved Mozart.

You could have knocked me over with a feather—Feathers did just that. The photo of Oula Strossmayer's Dufy was not a photo of prancing race horses or of the swaying palms I had expected. It was a 1910 Mozart bust with a worked cubist space, a lot of white, black and grey and, in the foreground, where he had drawn in a violin and a piano keyboard, an expanse of full-bodied vermilion.

'But that's worth a lot of dough, Feathers.'

'I rather suspected as much. Blessed are the poor at heart. Oula couldn't have known its true value. Surely she couldn't.'

'I wouldn't have thought so. Nobody could—not till now, till this moment. The art market has gone crazy. Prices are astronomical. Close to twenty-three million pounds for a Van Gogh: Japanese buyer . . . cheap for them with the yen so high.' I knew about these things. Feathers knew I knew. Not only did I, by the grace of my dead aunt, have quite a collection all of my own, but, in an earlier existence, I had tried to live by buying and selling minor Australian works. That was after I decided my future wasn't going to be on an Australian farm— well, life decided that for me, I couldn't afford a farm to have a future on.

Now I followed the market with interest. Some commentators felt the new boom reflected a lack of faith in artificially high stock market prices. These had risen against the pundits' economic predictions. The theory now was that the winners wanted to stick their ill-gotten cash into something that could ride out a crash. Art was the fashionable answer. Art, because so much of it was already stashed away in national museums, was in short supply. That is what they say markets are, supply and demand.

Of course that's not quite true in reality. They are supply, demand, and a hell of a lot of fiddling.

Chapter 4

Entrevaux was once a border town. Now it's full of big-eyed escapists. Maybe a bit like Millbourne, New South Wales. Only difference is that Entrevaux would be a lot better looking. Two mountains meet at a narrow gorge which is the valley of the River Var, an easy place to fortify, to guard. High up on one side there is a seventeenth-century citadel linked to the town by a fortified walk. You enter by a drawbridge, now permanently down. In the narrow streets it is possible to buy little jars of honey or hand-knitted jumpers, or jam—no sign of tins stacked around the back. Outside the town the modern world has set up camp—supermarket, car park, the office of a real estate company—where once the Romans had built. Entrevaux gets one star in my Michelin—that is a fairly low score. Me, I might have gone for two or at least one and a half. Michelin do not stoop to halves. Also, according to Michelin, it's got a doctor, a pharmacy, a hotel, you can camp there; there are trees near by, fishing and nice walks.

A great place in which to sit and write nasty letters to Australia. While Feathers and I ate endives rolled in ham and baked in an egg custard, sipping through a carafe of wine tasting as though it had tried desperately to become sherry, I was tempted to go over the road and buy a handful of pretty postcards to poison pen everybody I used to hate. Now I was rich I found I didn't really hate them enough. Funny thing that.

Renardo was polishing dust off the Bentley and making quite a hit with a bunch of kids who were hanging about in the car park waiting for God to make them big enough to get the hell out of the place down to Nice, about an hour's drive away. I didn't send him off to play chauffeur, it was just that he preferred the role. He was chatting to the kids while making sure they kept their fingers off the gleaming paintwork.

'Bet you Dawn's dive-bombing Karen at this very minute.'

31

'God, you're coarse, Essington. A fitting punishment if she were.'

'Punishment for me or for my bride of one day. One day! Do you realize that? Makes me feel like the hero in a tragedy.'

'I'm not sure tragedies have heroes, Essington. Victims I would have thought. And usually victims of their own madness.'

'And there she is at breakfast, putting in the groundwork for an extension of time. "Two weeks won't be enough". Crap it won't.'

'I'm sure things will work themselves out. At least they both seem to agree with your suggestion that they have someone for the shop.'

'Oh great. Then we can set up our *ménage à trois* while the money rolls in. Paradise.'

'Might depend on what sort of employee you get.'

'Right Feathers. The old legal mind. Maybe I should do the interviews.' We sat, silent. I was enjoying the warm clear air, the crisp definition it gave to rock outcrops and the foliage of stunted trees.

'What's your next Strossmayer move? Go over into the car park and shout out—what was the name?—Milo. Scream out, Milo! Maybe a notice in the church, you could try that; why not, they're bound to be good Catholics.'

'I'm thinking, Essington, thinking.'

'That's it, a notice pinned in the church and Milo comes down off a mountain, like Moses.'

'The question is, did the threats and the challenge to the will come from the same source?'

'Not his mother. He wouldn't chop up his mother with an axe. Not even in Millbourne, they wouldn't go in for that kind of thing.'

'Have you seen Millbourne, Essington?'

'Can't say I have.'

'Reserve opinion then, dear boy. Reserve opinion.'

When Feathers reached down inside himself and dragged out a 'dear boy' you could rely on something a bit steely to follow. So Millbourne was where you'd chop up your mum. I wondered, did that put land values up or down?

'There isn't a lot in chopping up your mum if you haven't got a chance of inheriting. Milo was claiming against the will,' I probed.

'He is. Not that I think he has much chance. The simplest thing would be to steal the painting. Quicker and surer than a legal challenge, wouldn't you have thought?'

'Did he know she had it?'

'Impossible to say.'

'He could simply have gone off his chomp arguing with the old girl.' Me, I went off my chomp—I had a flash point—I knew all too well how civilization can fall away under pressure.

'That's possible, but why the threats? By all accounts they seem to have been part of some plan, calculated to unsettle. And they'd been sent from so far away.'

'What did the police think? What did they say when you were chasing up the threats?'

'Well, not much at all. They were indirect. I would have thought ill at ease and, having been caught out, covering their tracks I shouldn't wonder. The way I see it is that they ballsed it up. Failed to take the matter seriously. Proved themselves so inefficient that they managed to lose the letters after the woman passed them across. All they finished up with was a record of the name and the Entrevaux postmark in the Duty Book. That was the only lead, Milo Strossmayer and the town.'

We paid our bill and headed over to Renardo who was settled into earnest conversation with one of the scruffy band.

'Mind you, Feathers, the threats, they could have been mailed by someone passing through.'

'I realize that. But there were, I'm told by the Griffins—the film hopefuls—four separate mailings, widely spaced out in time. They are the main source for all this information. In fact they say Oula received the unwanted mail over a period of months.'

'Still, somebody who passes through. If you went from Nice to Geneva this is one of the routes you'd take. Certainly from Nice to Grenoble it's the normal one.'

It was really a life mask Renardo wore, playing the role of chauffeur. On a previous occasion he had proved himself to be a man of standing and power in the local community. I had no idea how wide his influence spread. He had little trouble keeping the kids interested but he waved them away on our approach. He looked to me for directions. I had already given him a vague idea of what I thought Feathers was looking for. The trouble was you could never quite know with Feathers. And you couldn't know at all with Renardo. If the hills were teeming with poison-pen Croats and he knew it, he'd only tell you if you found the right question or if you were in real trouble. Great in a scrap, Renardo.

'Perfectly pleasant little town. Was it for keeping people out or letting them in?'

'The fortifications? I don't know, Feathers. This side of France kept on changing hands, so I guess it was for both.'

'Or it depended on your point of view—which side was inside, which out.'

We were sitting in the car. I was waiting for a decision from Feathers; Renardo was waiting for instructions from me.

'Rather annoying, these business hours.' Feathers observed. It was one-thirty, nothing would open again before three-thirty—that was French civilization. Dawn had called it a contradiction in terms, 'French civilization!' She was particularly affronted by television advertising which she considered 'hopelessly sexist'. Dawn was a sort of feminist Khomeini. She believed that if she believed something all the world should follow, and to hell with pluralism—pluralism was a bourgeois wank.

I didn't have a thought. We just sat. Feathers looked like he was thinking, his Adam's apple moved up and down—that's how you tell.

Renardo sat, features set, the picture of gloom. He worked on it in the mirror, I was sure. Just stood there for hours trying the mask of a funeral director. God had given him the basics for the part: grey skin, long nose, long flat cheeks, great bags under his eyes.

There was the real estate office with 'closed' on the door. But in real estate you never let a sale slip through your fingers. I went over, rang the bell. A man emerged from the house part of the building, made no sale but gave me some information: like where to find Yugoslavs up in them there hills. Information extracted gently so as not to arouse too much interest. Mostly I talked like one keen to move into some French real estate. He could live in hope that I'd return the following week clutching a chequebook. He would have known about foreigners—even your average Yugoslav—they fell for *La Belle France*. The French, they fell for France too. You don't find armies of French buying up old farmhouses in England or the United States.

'Curious thing, Yugoslavs going to France to rebuild an old farmhouse,' I said.

'More what you would expect from a nation with less history, higher prices or no sun,' Feathers noted after I had brought him up to date with the local land-sales gossip.

'Let's take a look, Renardo. We've come this far. As long as the car can handle the road.' I had no idea what I was letting myself in for.

The landscape was stunted oaks clinging to the surface of limestone mountains; low, drought-resistant shrubs filled gaps between trees. These were legumes mostly—I knew that from my farm days—feeding nitrogen into the limey soil in which they thrived. We followed the river upstream while the Digne train, a jaunty, yellow, one-car affair, trundled along beside us. Day-trippers waved at the outrageous car more than at us and, I guess, at the joke of the vehicles' twin yellowness. At the Pont des Cornillons both river and railway passed beneath as we turned north around a great wall of rock protruding out of the land-scape's face. A little further and we crossed the Var again, turned into a side road, the D902, and followed the multi-course river bed up in the direction of the ski resort, Valberg.

'Fabulous country, Feathers. In November you can swim in the morning and be skiing in the afternoon . . . it's a dream for that minority of Europe's three hundred million who make it up the ladder.'

There were stone houses dotted here and there either side of the river, some half ruined, some half saved, few totally saved and quite a number absolutely beyond repair. I wondered at the waves of romantics, particularly the British, who must have bought one of these piles of rubble as a grasp at sunshine only to be defeated by the labour of it all and by rapacious local tradesmen.

Castellet-les-Sausses was a concentration of semi-ruins with rocks holding Roman tiles in place. There was nobody around, our Yugoslavs could have been writing their poison words in any of the thirty or forty lofts or cellars. There was no bar. A goat bleated at us from her chain. Nothing else uttered a word. In the Bentley we must have stood out enough to attract attention—but no, not a movement.

'Well?' Renardo demanded.

'Well?' I asked Feathers.

But he just clung to the leather strap hanging at his temple and considered the situation. He was looking snappier today. The trip being business, he was clad in one of the many Sparrow suits. This time a natty little number cut out of lightweight grey worsted. How he handled the temperature I had no idea—the car predated air-conditioners.

The goat got sick of the new object thrust into her landscape, put head down and continued the search for nutrition. Pity she wasn't created a rock eater. I had heard stories of goats devouring a Standard Vanguard that might have been no more than underhand attacks at the quality of post-war British steel. People will stoop to anything.

'It's clearly just a question of asking.' Feathers was clinging to lawyer's mastery; the trained mind in control. 'That goat indicates something. I gather the creature must drink.'

'Only occasionally. The dew would be about enough to keep it going.'

'You and your rural wisdom. Surely the more sensible course would be to water the creature. Look, did you see that? A curtain moved. I'll go and ask.'

'You can't speak the language.'

'Indeed I can't. Essington, would you mind?'

How could I refuse this innocent who had crossed the world to exploit my good nature, even if I failed to understand why he was pushing so hard, so far?

After a very long pause a surly woman answered my knock. In her hand she held a rope attached to the collar of a snarling German Shephard.

'Hello, madame.' Very correct, empty hands by my sides.

She looked me up and down.

'I'm looking for a Yugoslavian family that I believe live hereabouts. Strossmayer. I have some good news for them, from Australia.'

'Ah, Australia,' she said. 'French Kiss.'

When I was a lad a French kiss had not been what this aged woman of the soil was telling me about. And then it clicked . . . the French challenge boat for the Perth America's Cup. Weather-beaten folksy peasant that she might have been, at heart she was a simple television freak like all the world.

The dog snarled again; I wondered if it watched *Lassie*.

'Yugoslavia,' I repeated, hoping to wipe *French Kiss* from her mind.

She shook her head slowly.

'*Étrangers* . . . from Eastern Europe, madame.'

'*Bulgarie*?'

'Not me, madame, I'm from Nice.'

She shook her head. 'Not Niçois, not you,' she said. 'You're a foreigner, I can tell.'

Pride showed in her eyes. She wasn't going to be fooled. The dog took a lunge at my kneecap. Fuck Feathers—manipulative bastard.

'I am a foreigner, madame. I have come up from Nice to find some people from Eastern Europe. I have news for them.'

'I am not an Arab, monsieur. This is my country. We have defended it. Now we give it to the Arabs! The Arabs do not defend France.'

'Neither did the French, Madame,' I said, keeping a close eye on the dog. 'Perhaps the Arabs would have done a better job.' I smiled, bowed, retreated to the car. Maybe the courtesy confused her. She kept hold of the dog. Thank God!

'Next time you ask.'

Feathers blinked at me through the open car window—an owl awoken before dusk. Then we both looked at what was striding down the dirt road—a man in khaki cotton shirt and trousers which hung loosely about his thin, wiry frame. His face was deeply tanned, hair greying and swept back from a broad forehead. He had strong cheek-bones and chin. He was walking directly towards our preposterous car; a smile played on his lips.

'Here we go,' said Feathers. 'A local, most likely.'

The man let the webbing bag slung over his shoulder drop to the ground. 'Hello.' An American accent.

I got out. Feathers stayed inside, sitting up in the back seat like a Soviet diplomat searching for a picnic.

'Lost?' I was asked.

'Looking.' We stood about equal height, and I am tall. The smile continued to play about his lips.

'Say that again.'

'Looking,' I repeated.

'Australian,' he exclaimed. 'You're Australian, aren't you?'

I shrugged. 'And you . . . American?'

'Canada.'

'Essington Holt.' I announced, holding out my hand.

Here he paused. 'Matt,' he said finally. 'Matt Smith.'

'Pleased to meet you.' We seemed to shake forever. He kept on smiling. 'You live around here?' There were a lot of unlikely people stuffed into France's southeast corner.

'Kind of half-time.' He tilted his head to one side as though to consider my appearance. 'Lost,' he repeated, but not believing it. He checked out my companions.

'Looking for someone.' Come straight out with it Essington: 'For a Milo Strossmayer. A Yugoslav, I believe.'

'Yugoslav!' He was thinking, twin lines shot up from the bridge of his fine nose across his forehead. 'Strossmayer,' he repeated. 'Milo Strossmayer you say.' A good head for names. 'What do you want with the guy?'

Feathers, who had been listening in, now poked his head out the car window. 'A legal matter,' he said.

'Legal, you don't say.' Feigned lack of interest. Matt took a couple of steps towards the car, addressed the legal mind direct. 'You Australian too?'

Feathers nodded.

'I could have picked it. Beautiful country they tell me, I've got family out there myself.'

A lonely man, I thought, wants to talk. Then he opened the car door, said that he believed he might be able to show us the house.

There was quite a bit of twisting and turning till, obeying Matt's every command, we arrived where the road all but petered out on one side of a tributary of the Var. We were high up above where the water ran rapidly over big stones. Half-way up the slope on the far side there was an ancient but restored stone building perched on a shelf and accessible by means of a steep narrow track. Behind the building there was a face of rock rising to where the stunted growth feathered the line against the sky.

Matt Smith had been trying to find out what we wanted with this Strossmayer, asking about the 'legal matter', and the good Mr Sparrow had avoided answering the question. Now we were all sitting prim and proper in the car. Renardo making a display of being bored behind the wheel he adored.

'Looks deserted to me,' I said. 'Is this the place?'

Matt didn't reply. Instead he was staring at Feathers. It wasn't till much later that I realized our guide must have been attempting to work out our true purpose. Most certainly he couldn't have calculated on what happened next. A car door was suddenly flung open and Feathers, grey worsted suit and all, was sliding and hopping down to the running water. Then he was stone-leaping across—a regular mountain goat, vertigo notwithstanding.

I was dumbfounded. Matt was out of the car, shouting, but not at Feathers, in another direction, down along the bed of the river. And he was running with not so much as a 'pleased to meet you' flung over his shoulder. Nor was it written on his face. My reading was that the Canadian wasn't pleased at all.

The old Holt brain was working to keep up with the coming and going. Renardo, the only constant, sat and stared at the top of the steering wheel.

Some time after Matt Smith had rounded a bend and slipped out of sight, Feathers was knocking at a bleak-looking door. He stood back, hands on hips, waiting. Then he knocked again. What, I wondered, could he posibly be doing? What did he want? Expect? And what was our recent guide on about? Who'd he been calling?

Renardo kept on sitting, staring ahead as though one of life's little comedies was not being played over there to his right. He reached to his side, picked up and put on the chauffeur's hat that Aunt had seldom managed to prevail upon him to wear. He tilted it forward. It was to keep out the glare and most certainly not for the form of it.

'Cooee!' Feathers let fly with an Australian bush call, hands cupped around his mouth to form a megaphone. He replaced them on his hips. He turned slowly, examining the surrounding country. I followed his gaze.

Nothing, just trees, rocks, water and sky—the huge clear sky.

Out of the blue he did the most surprising thing I had ever seen from Feathers—he tried to open the door and then a window on one side of it. That was all he could reach. Next he descended the stairs and tried a smaller door leading into a basement.

The world is divided into those who will happily invade the privacy of others and those who will not. I belong with the latter; I am constantly amazed by my opposites. I would never have suspected Feathers of the behaviour to which I was witness. I was horrified. Renardo too—he flashed me a look. I decided to bring Feathers back. Before I got out I asked Renardo to keep a look-out. If anything went wrong I told him to take off, cruise about; we'd find him. You could see he did not approve—the crass Australians offended him.

As I walked to the river Feathers was working on the lower door. It was quite a climb—a hell of a one for a sedentary worker like Feathers. By the time I reached the house he had got in.

'Hang on,' I shouted. 'You can't barge in.'

But by then he was trying a bunch of keys on a second door inside.

I wasn't going to follow him. I looked back at Renardo, the image of dejection, standing beside the yellow car.

Feathers got the inside door open. 'Either come in or go away, you're in the light.'

I stepped back, my eyes panning anxiously over the landscape. I could hear a car a way off—nothing unusual in that.

From inside, from where Feathers was, scraping, an occasional heavy bang, the sound of boxes being moved.

'Feathers! For Christ's sake, get out of there.'

When he emerged he was holding a machine pistol—I knew what it was straight away, I'd seen them in *Columbo*, on the telly, just under a week before.

Chapter 5

The face was set, it was an expression utterly new to me. I was watching another Sparrow, a bird of a different feather, a being he had kept concealed. It was an unnerving experience—after all, we had known each other as children, had been through school together, stayed in constant touch since then.

Suddenly it was as though he had stepped out of a painting in the Australian War Memorial, maybe out of one of its glass cabinets or dioramas—the sandy hair, pale eyes, Adam's apple, slightly receding jaw—an image from antipodean war mythology.

Other things dropped into place. I remembered his interest in the battles that formed Australian myths; how he, and he alone it seemed to me, took Anzac services seriously. On the eleventh hour of the eleventh day of the eleventh month—Armistice Day—it was Feathers who stood straightest, most silent . . .

That hill, that house, they were his personal Gallipoli.

All that had bored me then; it bores me now. But Feathers was some kind of addict. Holding the machine pistol he was serving someone, something, a higher cause. It wasn't legal work he had undertaken at Entrevaux.

But who was he working for? What was he doing? Something had driven him to such uncharacteristic behaviour—was it a sense of duty? We are a weird species we humans, really weird the things that get us to tick.

But Christ! What would they have thought at Daks or Aquascutum or Ermenegildo Zenda or wherever if they had seen the smart suit powdered over with dust, as it was?

'What have you found, Aladdin's cave? For God's sake, Feathers, let's get away from here.'

'Essington, you don't find something like this and turn away. We've responsibilities in the face of international lawlessness.'

'That's when you do turn away; it's called judgement.'

'Come inside then, see what you'd really call it.'

So I went in—softhead. I cast a final glance around the hills and trees to see whatever I could see. Flying high over the valley were two great hunting birds—symbols of something. Higher again a big plane full of people trying to leave themselves behind. It was making a white line on blue fading out at one end.

No human beings anywhere, only Renardo pissing against a stunted tree.

Maybe again a car sound from far off, blending with the gurgle of river water.

So stupid Essington went in, into the dark. I blinked, hated the sense of dust, of the millions of mould spores floating on damp air.

The boxes of munitions were beyond the second door. One lid was off, that was the machine pistols. What was in the rest only a dealer could know—just stencilled letters signifying death, marked out over backgrounds of grey or brown or khaki.

Instantly I knew it was big, too big for me, too big for either of us. Yet Feathers was making notes in a little pad. He was writing down the numbers. Curious that, he'd go down on his knees just to make sure he got it right. Why was this Sydney lawyer getting it letter-perfect up in the mountains of eastern France?

'Feathers, we ought to get out of here. It's a trap: the way in is the only way out.'

He nodded, but only because he'd heard my noise. He was more concerned to get the details down. Obsessive thing, the legal mind. But what Feathers was doing didn't strike me as being altogether legal—not even in mind.

I walked back to the open door to scan the landscape. The birds and the aeroplane were gone to wherever such things go. The river continued to splutter as it hit the rocks—quite a wrestle to get that water back to the sea in the height of dry summer. Renardo was the only radically transformed feature in the scene, he was shouting, waving his arms about, pointing. But the eyes of the middle-aged man are not the most finely tuned instruments in this imperfect world. I had to adjust to the light—several seconds passed before I saw, or at least before I registered, the punchy-looking four-wheel drive pulled up down beside the river with three men getting out. They'd come up some track—maybe a back track to the main road, one that would be under water when the rains came.

'Feathers! Visitors! Get out of there.'

Maybe it was my voice tone, more likely he'd finished. Out he came. This time empty-handed. Me, I felt too empty-handed. The contents of the four-wheel drive were scrambling up looking hotheaded and big and fit and dangerous. Looked like the Canadian, Matt, had called up his pals. That track was our only way down.

Renardo was much too far away, even with the shotgun I knew he kept in the boot. He was handy. He'd helped me out before, he had the right (or could it be the wrong?) connections. But he was carrying a lot of years, there wasn't a way he'd be able to scramble down, over and up—he knew that too.

In desperation I made a 'take off' gesture over the valley hoping Renardo would understand. Then I turned to Feathers and shoved him ahead of me up the apparently unassailable slope at the rear of the house. Of course, in France, everything has been climbed at one time or another by fancy lads dressed in Lacryl tights of pretty scarlet or yellow so they look good on film dangling at the end of a rope. Climbed also by little people who hid in rocks while tax collectors and army recruiters or simple honest plunderers moved in from north, south, east and west. The whole landscape is secret tracks, small caves, big caves, holes in the ground. You've just got to find the way.

So I pushed Feathers up in front of me, figuring that even if they wanted to the chances were they wouldn't shoot, not after the driver of a big yellow Bentley sloper had seen them, knew what they drove, where they lived. I shoved Feathers up what could almost have been cut foot-holes in a face of rock. Nobody was going to have built that house there centuries ago without creating a way out, a back door.

Good at getting us into trouble, the legal Sydney mind wasn't so good at leading the way out. He was terrified. His feet slipped, he scrambled and slid and crawled—an inelegant ascent. Me, I kept him at it and paid heed to what was down below. I guess I'd appointed myself head kicker. There wasn't any way a pursuit could go around us; or at least that was what I hoped.

The four-wheel-drive boys went into the house first, taking a look at what we could have seen and maybe picking up some weapons so they could keep us from telling the world. If once we got to the top it was going to be a jog through the mountains, then we could forget Renardo, our witness, who now sat in the car, reluctant to push off.

It wasn't so far to climb, not as far as it looked, not if you didn't glance down. We soon reached a higher shelf and ran along this to where it became a rocky track still climbing between scrub and stunted oaks. Feathers was making good time now that his natty little Florentine stitched slip-ons had more surface to grip. He had that bone-and-sinew build that the long distance runners boast, although I think the sinew had gone limp after desk years at Richards and Partners. He was starting to do all right. Long strides uphill, moving away from Essington who was a heavy lad, even in good nick—kind of clumps of muscle that didn't like to go anywhere too far too fast.

We made it to the ridge well in front, though by a diminishing margin. There was still a track: Feathers headed off along it. On one side the earth had shifted dramatically a few million years ago leaving a sheer drop. On the other side, just a long, scrubby, rising slope. He kept on, never looked down.

I glanced over my shoulder to see the opposition's lead runner not all that far from biting off my ear. That action—looking round—brought me down. I tripped on God knows what part of mother nature and sprawled full length under the weight of someone who was instantly barking incomprehensibilities at his comrades. They sent the strength on after Feathers. Me, I was left to a single captor. Their mistake. Long distance running's one thing, survival another. I was a survivor, life had already taught me that out in the Australian bush. And even up and down the enchanted streets of the Côte d'Azure's fishing villages.

I just lay there. He had dropped down heavy on me, knocking all the air out. He had an arm under my chin pressing against my windpipe. His other hand grabbed a bundle of greying locks and pulled back a head that could, with one bovine stare, bring out all of Karen's maternal instincts in a flood.

'What are you?' A thick accent. But no Frenchman this.

I was lifting my body as best I could. Bringing shoulders and chest off the ground, going with the pull.

'What you doing here?' I stayed silent. How could I answer? The forearm on the throat was starting to choke me: it was enough just to breathe.

He didn't keep me down. He liked pulling me up, backwards. I liked going. He must have come close to kneeling behind me; my back was feeling like it would break clean in two somewhere down near the coccyx. I could sense his muscle force as though it was my own, part of the Holt nervous system. It was like we were a two-headed beast. So I could feel when, just for an instant, the grip slackened, as though the arm on my throat was my own. I swung my shoulders hard down to the dirt, thrusting forward with my legs as I rolled. I slid around in his grip, bringing an arm up as I turned. I was away.

I had felt something not so nice, kind of heavy and flat, pressing into me as we writhed locked together. If he got that out—goodbye Essington. But he only had two hands and needed both. I had two hands as well.

Big he was but no talent for that kind of stuff. Maybe just a shooter. Certainly stupid. He'd push all one way, nothing reserved. Next time he shoved hard I went with his momentum. He knocked himself half out when his head hit the ground, losing the neck grip. I elbowed him across the temple. As he rolled under the blow I brought a knee into his groin, hard. He let out a howl. When he opened his eyes he was staring into the muzzle of a 9mm pistol. He blinked.

I was on my feet. He half rose on bunched knees to meet a full upper cut, something to slow him down for a bit. Then I took off after Richards and Co's missing partner.

I met him coming up towards me, very much the worse for wear. They'd given him a thumping, the bastards. Feathers wasn't up to that sort of thing—anyone could see that.

They did not meet me. I was just a little off and to one side, flat in the undergrowth. The men walking at Feathers' back suspected nothing. They appeared happy in the thought that I was a lot closer to base being hugged to death by Boris.

What to do? Ambushing was a new game for me. I half wanted to start shooting—Feathers had taken a real pasting. But the pistol I had retrieved with the big hole for a barrel—it would blow a person to pieces at close range, a great big chunk of lead tearing through flesh and bone. I couldn't do it, I just couldn't shoot.

So I said: 'Stop!'

They stopped, turned. As they turned their hands moved. I fired. The bloody thing kicked like a mule but I must have looked convincing. Their hands stayed still.

I held the gun as I'd seen cops do in the movies and pointed it at one broad Slavic head. 'Lift your hands up.' Each word slow and clear. Up went four strong, thick-fingered hands. 'OK, Feathers, search them.' I kept the barrel pointing at the vulnerable-looking cranium. Feathers pulled a handgun out of each jacket—must have picked them up at the house: they wouldn't need them for shopping, not in historic Entrevaux.

Feathers had stepped back, well clear; he too held a gun on our captives. It struck me how absurd he looked, and then that maybe I looked silly as well. But this bizarre thought was balanced by the knowledge that the men at whom we were pointing pistols were real, probably trained, certainly danger-ous. Where was Matt Smith lurking? How about the other one out there who'd be groggy perhaps but untethered, between us and home. I got Feathers to come round to my side. He did that without losing aim, slow and steady despite the blood smeared over his face; he had a nasty look around his pale eyes. At the dawn of time when brown eyes first saw blue eyes they must have scared them shitless. Feathers' looked like beams were projecting from each iris. Was he smiling through the blood? Schoolboy dreams of heroic acts?

Me, I was working out how we get back alive—all of us, without any shooting. And I was supposed to be the mad dog, the aggressive, the crazy!

I said: 'Walk.' Like lunging a horse in a yard. And they walked. A gun was as good as a whip. They walked nice and steady and right into Boris as he came along, shambling, hands holding his great abused head.

Truly, I reckon it was Feathers' mad look that got us back safe and sound. None of the three captives looked scared, not

46

even all that rattled, but I think they were worried about Feathers, didn't know what he might do with eyes like that.

Even down the rock face to the house where Goldilocks had broken the chair, slept in the bed, eaten the porridge, they kept steady. They gave no trouble. It unnerved me, it was as if they still had a trick up their sleeves; only I couldn't work out what it was. Unless, maybe the tanned Canadian, waiting, with more troops. I didn't want trouble, I felt ambivalent enough as it was. The three bears had a right to anger, it was justified.

Renardo had gone, perhaps that was just as well. They'd already had all the opportunity required to connect us with the car. God knew what Renardo was planning at that moment; whatever it was he was doing it out of sight.

We forced the bears on down over the river to their four-wheel drive. I instructed them to stay there, to sit tight. I'd leave their vehicle on the main road; they would have to walk to pick it up.

We offered no explanation for our behaviour.

Neither did they—it was love you and leave you, without much love.

We drove all the way back to Entrevaux—not so far really. No sign of the Bentley till we hit the town itself. There it was, standing out like a sore thumb, a beacon in the car park. Beside it Renardo, and around him a small band of people gathering. I knew he had connections, but that far afield? A couple of the men held shotguns. They were natives, all of them, bred from the region's ancient stock—a people in their own land.

I edged our stolen wheels right up beside the Bentley, shoved Feathers across from car to car then broke into the group of would-be saviours Renardo seemed to be recruiting.

'Why on earth did you do it?' Karen was incredulous. We were arranged around the dinner table, Dawn wearing her 'what else would you expect' expression. Rebecca had removed the soup plates and placed on the table an earthenware baking dish in which slithers of calf liver still sizzled amid chunks of bacon and sliced tomatoes. The food had improved since the death of Aunt who had been a stickler for 1930s Australian–English cuisine, the worst of both worlds. Not only improved but, with my encouragement, the service had dipped a fraction towards the peasant. Me, I was a peasant by ancestry and by inclination. No need to send off to one of those smarmy organizations which will, for a fee, prove your connection to Lord Such-and-Such. They'd be crazy if they didn't light upon a happy start, wouldn't they, business being business. And mathematically, the way I look at it, everybody has to be well connected in the end. It's all a matter of how far back you can spare the time to go.

Me, peasant stock all the way back to Adam—I was the exception. Thus the great natural irony of a childless aunt with countless millions. Well, I guess you could count them, and maybe they don't measure up too well these days against the sea trunks of money made by inside traders, cocaine importers, arms dealers and restaurateurs.

Everybody has to keep going up because the plumbers are heading full speed in the same direction—buying yachts, sea-front apartments, islands in the South Pacific.

So, being a peasant, I'd tended to encourage peasant presentation, made me feel at home, and it made Rebecca flower as an artist—things in earthenware bowls are what she is good at, those and great big fish with their opaque eyes asking a final question.

'Why on earth did you do it?' She had asked the question of Feathers who was now scrubbed up with face showing touches of grazed red and blue bruise.

'Why should I not have done? They are criminals, gunrunners.'

'Reagan's a gunrunner . . . it's accepted practice.' Dawn entered the fray. 'Anyway, you wouldn't have known the guns were there if you hadn't broken in.'

'I had to, to prove it.'

'God save us!' she emptied her glass. For a body who didn't approve of things Dawn really managed to go through a lot of my Sancerre—at heart a boozer but never a drunk. That made me warm to her a little. A boozer can't be all bad. And she was giving Feathers a tough time—in the circumstances I approved of that as well. Just stop playing for Karen, Dawn, I thought, and we could get along all right.

'If you don't know what's in there, why the hell do you want to prove that what's in there is . . . oh bugger it, it's crap. Like, of course, anything that's there has got to be there.'

'That's philosophy,' grinned Karen who was picking away at the bacon and tomato—she didn't like offal. ('I'd say, 'But it's just a word, "offal".' And she'd screw up her nose. 'I don't care what it is . . . it's not muscle; it's the filters and things.')

Dawn was dogged: 'So they were stashing guns . . . your words. What if they'd been stashing yoghurt, say?'

'Then I would have found hundreds and hundreds of little jars, wouldn't I?'

'You couldn't sell them to Iran.'

'These weren't for Iran.'

'I never thought . . . I just said it . . . like, "Iran".' Dawn ended sentences querulously.

'But they could be bound for somewhere.'

Karen and I were rolling eyes at each other, enjoying the mumbo-jumbo contest.

'That's like saying they were there because you found them. That they're going to go from there to somewhere just because they exist.'

'But I didn't say that, Dawn. I said I had to break in to prove they were there.'

I intervened. 'So you had your suspicions, right?'

'Correct, Essington.'

'We were after poison-pen freaks, not gunrunners.'

'Not exclusive catagories.'

'To go straight up and take a look because you believe the owners are Yugoslavs . . . you're some kind of xenophobe?' Usually, it was in her nature, Karen just couldn't be bothered. She had something against the speculation that so much conversation tends to become. When she did join in the trick was to duck. 'Anyway, the crime rate around here, it's amazing, isn't it, Essington? They use grenades, machine guns, the lot—just for hold-ups!'

'A male-dominated society . . . the Latins . . . the Godfather code.'

'But Dawn,' Karen countered, 'How about the Virgin? I mean, in Australia "virgin" is . . . well, a term of abuse. But here the Virgin Mother, she's as important as Christ.'

'It's obvious why. She's a goddess because all men want . . .'

Dawn didn't actually say what they wanted to do. 'Just a sex symbol in disguise.'

'They do go in for heavily armed crime, Feathers.' I said. 'Maybe you could have broken into half the houses we passed up there in the mountains and found the same thing.'

'Not on that scale. That wasn't a cache, it was a mini-arsenal.'

'Whatever it was, where does it leave Raoul Dufy?' I asked. But instead of hearing the answer I turned my attention to Dawn's and Karen's continuing argument about the Virgin till it petered out and we all fell silent.

'You know about these things, Feathers.' I assisted.

'Guns? Why should I?'

'Not guns . . . the Virgin Mary. Through your father.'

'Oh! In the Church of England we don't go much on Mary. John the Baptist, yes . . . the Virgin, no.'

Feathers' father, the Reverend Sparrow, had been a minister. He had actually squandered his life on the poor in Chippendale, right next to where the good Father Down presently attended his suffering Aboriginal flock.

'John the Baptist!' shrieked Dawn. 'That's a nasty little story, that is. One way or another the church has done a lot of harm to women.'

'And little shreds of good, here and there.' Feathers forked out another slice of liver and then another and then another. You would have thought he had worms, skinny like that.

'Me,' said Karen, 'I like the Virgin. When I visit churches I light candles to her. She's a nice idea.'

'And pray for what?' Dawn asked.

'Pray for? Me? I pray for . . . I wouldn't have a clue. I just sort of pray for being, for light.'

'For The Light?' Feathers looked relieved now that the conversation was off guns.

'Just for light. No capital letters.'

Dawn and Karen were off early to interview applicants for the shop job. They had more than they could possibly handle, mostly unsuitable. There was a lot of unemployment and poverty just under the glitter of the southern surface. Not as bad as in the north where the collapse of old-style heavy industry had taken jobs out by the bus-load; but it existed, unemployment was a reality. Particularly among people out of the French colonies. The French have a clever system. If you call a colony a colony they are quick to point out that it is in fact part of their republic. Yet if the people from that part of the republic come in droves to France they shout 'France for the French' and start to vote for the National Front, a neo-fascist party. *C'est la vie.*

There were a lot of North African applicants or that is what it seemed from the names. Dawn, despite her ideological purity, wondered if they would be good for business. Me, I said, 'Dawn, one thing is for sure, they look good—complexions like silk itself, beautiful dark eyes.' I was getting to like giving Dawn a little bit of hell. Now Karen was joining in on the side of the Virgin I felt that the tide could be turning.

We had music going, Feathers and I. One of my first acts had been to buy top-of-the-range sound gear to stack on top of Aunt's outmoded Grundig in its rosewood box. In a world trading away from quality minute by minute maybe the worst casualty has been music. Synthesizers took the mind out of it. Anything they can do has to be more regulated than hand and mind co-ordination—they make the bagpipes sound varied by comparison. I was filling the day with Thelonious Monk's brilliant improvisation. His *In Walked Bud* complete with Art Blakey's Jazz Messengers surrounded us, high fidelity. Feathers hated that. He preferred the music of Chopin and Ravel played by people with Eastern European names. I like that too but there was a lot of pleasure to be had from keeping him unhappy.

'If you knew the guns were there, Feathers, why all the talk about art?'

'More or less impossible to explain.'

'You could try, as a wedding gift. You realize you didn't give us a present?'

'I am the present, Essington. From the other side of the world.'

'To work!'

'What do you mean, "to work"?' he asked.

'You came here with some idea stuffed into that head of yours; it was a coincidence that I was getting married.'

'Terribly unfair.'

'But true.'

There was a jug of iced water sitting between us on the table. We were out on the terrace looking across to the house next door where my friend, Clyde Warner, had once lived. It made me sad, that house; it was less than a year since I had found it empty, ransacked, only hours before the police discovered Warner's dead body in Nice. It looked even sadder now with its new owners who couldn't move without blow waves and buckets of scent and lacquer and powder and gold chains. They were Swiss. Madame walked as though a sculptor had left his chisel up her arse. I never saw her out of high heels.

'Tell me, Feathers, how did you know to look? It's not the sort of work a lawyer does, is it, to look for guns? Sell them perhaps—look, no. Surely you can fill me in, you owe that to me.'

I could feel the debt in every movement: torn muscles in my back, a shoulder that didn't work properly. The hot sun was doing some good but the pains would stay with me for days. At my age tissue is slow to heal.

'I don't like to point it out,' I kept at him, 'but you could still be up there, maybe in one of those boxes by now. You realize that? So, tell me. Perhaps there aren't any Raoul Dufy paintings at all, no old lady in Millbourne, nothing, just men and guns.'

'Well, I do admit you have a point. I suppose I don't know where to begin and that's because I should not begin at all.' That was the truth of it, it was hush-hush, under the carpet.

'You must expect to pay something for my protection, Feathers.'

'In a sense I have used you. I felt bad at the start about that.'

'So there are no paintings, no Oula Strossmayer?'

'Oh yes there are—or with Oula Strossmayer I should say, rather, "there was", different tense.'

'All that and guns as well? So . . .?'

'Essington, will you promise not to say a word, not to anyone?'

He was looking very serious now—looking like a judge about to pronounce the death penalty. 'It's all out of my dark past, when we left school, Essington, you and I . . .'

Chapter 6

'I left a year before you, remember? Vocational guidance, they called it.' I could still recall the shame attached to leaving before your education was completed.

'What did they suggest, Essington? "A healthy outdoor life?" They said the same for Yelpie Townsend, didn't they? Now he's a psychiatrist on Macquarie Street, treating the best of Sydney's nervous breakdowns.'

'That may be so but I think they were pretty right with me.'

'Your mother believed them, as I remember. When you disappeared into the bush; she wanted that, didn't she? And I went on to university. At that time, Essington—you might not remember—but at that time there was a lot of patriotism. Now, alas, a thing of the past. We were all more British then. I recall buying a Harris tweed overcoat; sweated to death in the thing but I wore it—a gesture to the Empire.

'At that time national security was paramount and it was up to us, the next generation, to step into the war hero's shoes—there were two ex-fighter pilots among my lecturers. The Cold War was raging.'

Mr and Mrs Next Door were preparing to climb into their dart-shaped red Ferrari. I had timed them before—at least half an hour from indication of intention to take off till departure. She was in a kind of lamé number and white stiletto-heel cowboy boots that sparkled in the morning sun as though stitched with diamonds. He'd just taken up a stetson large enough to drown pups in its crown.

'While you were listening to your fighter pilots, Feathers, I was circling some dusty ring of bleached timber rails with a horse at the end of a rope. We didn't need fancy ideas out there, we had what looked a lot like life.'

'Yet it was an illusion, Essington, a rustic illusion. The future did not lie in that direction, in your world of plaited leather and elastic-sided boots. But that's another story, one you learnt the hard way. At Sydney University I was approached by a fellow student to see if I was interested in . . . well it was hinted . . . the security of Australia.'

'A load of garbage! Feathers, I'd always looked up to you, you know that? Now you tell me you fell for that.'

'I fell for it then, if you must put it that way, yes indeed I did. I believe in it now. I hope I'm a fraction wiser, a fraction more selective, but the national security—certainly. And why not, Essington? What's wrong with that?'

'I can't start now, it would take me too long to tell you.'

'Whatever you like to think, there are jobs to be done, there must be people to do them. The long and the short of it is that I took up the challenge, and not at all lightly. I admit it appealed to a romantic side of my nature but . . .'

'Tell that to Dawn.'

'I knew what I was doing—a lifetime of commitment.' Thelonious Monk constructed the last chords of 'Purple Shades', the needle lifted off the record and left us in a silence that lasted for some time.

Eventually I asked: 'You're still part of the set-up?' Feathers nodded. 'Part of an organization that attacks tourist hotels in the middle of Melbourne as practice—scaring the tripes out of rooms full of aged, globe-trotting Americans? Who bribe burnt-out junky pimps to infiltrate religious sects? Who mace each other as a form of sexual foreplay?' I was listing some of the more recent gaffes of the Australian security services. 'Feathers, are you crazy?'

'I can't see that it's crazy to protect one's country.'

'That's what you were doing up at Entrevaux? The French Secret Service sink conservationists' boats in New Zealand, you raid French mountain lairs! You're all part of an international élite of weirdos.'

'If I'd known you'd react like this I would never have attempted an explanation . . . out of friendship, mind you.'

'It was friendship, Feathers, that made me save you from the gunrunners, remember that, won't you? That's what you nuts need, always have needed, some poor dummy to come in and clean up your mess. Irangate, Feathers! You're part of one of those kinds of set-ups; only you're in kindergarten—that's a grade below the CIA.'

'Try to forget your headstrong prejudices for a moment, Essington. You're speaking as though locked into a perpetual 1960s, left-liberal revolution—a movement which was in fact little more than a mask for Communist aggression.'

'You believe that? You, my friend all these years, thinking such Boy Scout thoughts? You amaze me.'

'And you me.'

We were getting heated. I had raised my voice sufficiently for Mrs Next Door to swing her head around as she took from the Ferrari a basket she had deposited there five minutes earlier. Crunch, crunch, crunch, over the gravel, Mr Next Door walked stiff-legged in imitation of Clint Eastwood, carrying his contribution to their day.

'I don't give a damn if you like it or not.' Feathers shouted. 'I am still, as it were, connected. That is what got me involved in the whole Strossmayer business.' His tone became secretive, confidential. 'It is felt, in certain circles, that there are old wars being fought on Australian soil—Croatian guerrillas are training in camps scattered along our south-eastern seaboard, north and south of the national capital, Canberra.

'Essington, you may be relieved to hear, it is not just the idiot Left that concerns us.'

'Us? Who exactly is us?'

'That's something I would prefer you not to ask. If it is any satisfaction to you, I am right out on the fringe. Apart from anything else my work doesn't allow much time to fulfil my obligations. I simply do what I can.'

'It's ASIO,' I said, naming the most prominent of Australia's security organizations. 'Of course it has to be ASIO.'

'Why must it be? There are other groups, you know. Less vaunted but they exist.'

'I'll stick with ASIO.'

'But you can't talk about it . . . understood?'

'No, Feathers, I won't tell. But please permit me the occasional laugh.'

'Laugh as much as you like. As I said, somebody has to do these things—we're a national necessity.'

'Either that or you're not.'
'As you like, Essington.'

As the red Ferrari hurtled down the hundred or so metres of
drive to prop at the automatic gate of what, next door, was
now called 'Rancho Grandee'—the *Dallas* influence on the
economic sector of European life—Renardo was obliged to
walk down to where Desdemona was already snarling and
leaping at the grill gate. He admitted a bunch of agitated
policemen bristling inside a deep-blue Renault sedan.

Sure instincts caused him to walk rather than make use of
the gate switch up at the house. Renardo was practised at
slowing down the law. He knew his stuff: even at the gate he
pretended difficulty with consummate theatrical skill. The men
in blue looked determined to take revenge on someone—I
could read a policeman at a hundred paces even if Feathers
could not.

My relations with the police had been cool for quite some
time. I had brought a dislike of uniforms with me from
Australia. Is this divided world also divided into those who do
and those who do not get along with the officers of the law?

During the shenanigans of the previous year I had been
protected by the presence of a lawyer friend of Renardo's—I
had assumed he was a friend, it cost an arm and a leg. All that
was now past. Past but not resolved in the minds of the lads at
the *préfecture*. And Monsieur Claude Chevet, advocate, had
taken off to Portugal for the summer in company with all his
grandchildren.

I watched Renardo hurry up behind the advancing car
gesticulating wildly with his free hand while clinging to the dog
with the other. But the visitors were parked and out before he
could catch up, luckily still restraining Desdemona. They
advanced on the door, two men in uniform and a couple in
what maybe they thought served as a disguise: one, a mustard
suit; the other, linen jacket and crushed, dark-blue cotton
slacks. This latter, the most casual of the quartet, sported a
blue shave showing through skin as translucent as that on a
child's portrait by Sir Joshua Reynolds.

'Monsieur Holt?'
'Right.' I was giving them nothing.

The man in the mustard suit I had encountered before during the extended inquisition that followed the death of Clyde Warner, my one-time neighbour. The men in uniform were, I guessed, for effect—they had guns on their hips and fixed expressions probably learned from the television screen. The role, that's what attracts them to such a socially unpopular profession in the first place.

They formed a half-circle a pace outside the front door. Renardo stood at the bottom of the steps beside the gleaming Bentley. His back was to us, he was facing the lighthouse, looking out to sea, he was panting.

Feathers had vanished, retreated into the enormity of the house.

'Would you mind answering a few questions?' The man with the blue shave seemed the expert on the problem of foreigners, maybe just of rich foreigners. This foreigner could tell that the question was really not a question, it was an instruction.

My French was just up to it. Between Karen, Rebecca and Renardo they had made a pretty good job of it. I could comprehend a lot better than I could speak but as long as people tolerated my random drifting into and out of tenses, then they could keep up.

They wanted to know where I had been yesterday.

'Entrevaux. Know it?'

Sure, they knew it. Don't be a smart arse with them.

Why did I go there? Because I had a friend staying and I wanted to show this friend a bit of *la Belle France*.

And where was my friend now? You wouldn't get police this restrained, this polite, in Sydney.

She was in Nice with my wife. Well, in fact, I just bit back on that: too clever by half. 'Inside—I think he's sleeping.'

They would like to see my friend also.

No problem. Why didn't we all come inside and sit down? I caught Renardo glancing over his shoulder.

We bundled ourselves into the first reception-room—still exactly as Aunt had arranged it. More Empire revival than anything else, I guess you'd call it, but elegant and the individual pieces were real.

My interlocutors sat where indicated, on the edge of the seats as though ready to spring up the instant the ancient wood showed signs of giving way. There's a lot of wood-worm in France; they are used to legs falling off things.

'Coffee? A drink? Would you like something to drink?' I rang for Rebecca.

'We are not here to be entertained.' Blue Shave had English and, from the way it sounded, loads of it. Suddenly his three mates seemed out of it, outclassed. Nothing quite so fancy in this world as a lot of languages.

'Not entertained, then what?' I asked.

'Informed . . . by you and by your friend.'

'Then I'll fetch him.'

Rebecca arrived at the door.

'Perhaps this lady could bring him.' Blue Shave had shifted into French. He gestured to where Rebecca stood looking not at all surprised.

Because, I guess, they are only mortal, wealth keeps the police in check. In France, in England, in Australia, I knew from experience that if I'd been in a bed-sitter stacked with dirty pots and pans this lot would have started by breaking my knees.

I asked Rebecca to fetch Feathers, finding myself wondering if Richards and Partners held the end of strings long enough to reach across the world to the Côte d'Azure.

'You went on a sightseeing tour?'

'Wonderful country,' I said. 'That's the prettiest bit of all, the road up through the mountains.'

'In your old yellow car? Very conspicuous . . . well known here on the coast.'

'Officer, I know it's flashy. It came with this house, a collector's item. The two are inseparable, house and car. Very few were built with that body, rare.'

'Is that so? How very interesting.'

'Anyway, what's wrong with taking a drive?'

He looked at me, expressionless eyes, smile playing on his lips. 'Nothing—your papers?'

Still no Feathers. I left them to play pat-a-cake and trotted upstairs to my room to fetch the Holt calf-hide wallet. When I returned they were in a huddle, Mustard Suit and Blue Shave. One of the uniformed gentlemen was looking out of a window, watching Renardo. The other was at my elbow: he'd stuck there up the stairs and down again.

'It seems, Monsieur Holt, when there is trouble you are just a couple of steps away.' The man in the mustard suit nodded as though he had understood.

I had to admit it, there was some truth in what he said.

'What did you do in Entrevaux?'

'I told you, sightseeing, looking about. That old fort is fantastic, and the fortified walkway.'

'You visited houses?'

Feathers entered.

'My friend, Gerald Sparrow, advocate, Sydney, Australia. Monsieur . . .?'

'Assistant Commissioner Betti.' Blue Shave introduced himself and followed it up with a perfectly cordial handshake.

'Garoud,' said the man in the mustard suit keeping his mitts to himself. Rank and file were left out of the pleasantries.

'And what brings you to France, Mr Sparrow?'

'The marriage of this, my oldest friend, Mr Holt.'

'Oh, really, congratulations.' Betti and I shook for a second time. I smiled, batted my eyelashes a little—life, the rich voyage through time.

'Your passport, if you please.' The smile was gone. Betti held his hand out to Feathers who fumbled about inside his jacket. He had got himself into a suit, he rarely got himself into anything else. Out it came, passport with stamped visa and all.

Visas were terribly important, France was tightening up on illegal immigration—the price she paid for her landscapes, culture and civilization.

'Thank you.' The passport was handed back. They love it, everywhere in the world, petty officials making mere mortals nervous. But I wasn't feeling nervous, quite the opposite, I was working on temper control.

Betti pressed on: 'May I ask you a personal question, Mr Sparrow?'

'Indeed, go ahead. I can't promise an answer.'

'But of course, who can?'

'The Lord,' Feathers offered that like a gift. 'I dare say the Lord.' For a second Assistant Commissioner Betti looked doubtful, just for a second.

Then he asked, 'How did you receive that wound on your face?' A graze from the temple to the cheek-bone. Not to mention the eye.

'An embarrassing question, Commissioner. But I'll endeavour to answer it.'

'He fell down,' I said.

'In truth, a clumsy act.' Feathers pretending confusion. 'Not the kind of thing to which I'd like to own.'

'Would you admit to falling down while entering a house?'

'I most certainly would not.'

So our gun hoarders had not felt squeamish. They had gone straight to the law—maybe the law were their mates.

I looked at Feathers. He wore the expression of a person following a snail race with no money on.

'I suggest that it did happen, Mr Sparrow,' insisted Betti.

'Suggest on my friend.'

'I would say that you drove out of Entrevaux in the big yellow car, the two of you. That you stopped outside a house, an old restored house perched above a river: you climbed up to this house, broke in and stole certain things.'

I had fixed my gaze on the two uniformed men who, unable to follow the conversation, were now circling the room respectfully examining its contents. Aunt had been a substantial collector. Money lifted out of Australia late in the Korean War wool boom when graziers bought Rolls Royces as paddock pick-ups. Wise old woman, she had got out at the top. The art all those sheep's backs converted into was the surest of hedges against diminishing values. The best of the collection was upstairs. Here the police were staring at little drawings by Boucher, Claude Lorraine, Jean-François de Troy and a pastel portrait by Maurice Quentin de Latour. They seemed to like the Boucher best—Pan diving onto a wood nymph whose face wore a welcoming expression; a plump wood nymph, her body a fraction out of style in our modern world.

'Did we indeed?' Feathers' face said nothing. Betti addressed Garoud at close quarters in French. He asked to be excused, they went outside.

'A thief! Essington, I come to your wedding and these, your new compatriots, accuse me of bring a thief!'

'Not my compatriots. They wouldn't be even if I wanted them to. It's not so easy to turn French.'

Betti led the re-entrance—he was bossman. 'The accusation is that you have stolen pictures.'

'Pictures!' Now Feathers was doing a Scarlet Pimpernel imitation.

'Two drawings. You, Mr Holt, you have been involved in the art trade here in the past, I believe?'

'Not really.'

'That is not what I am told,' the Assistant Commissioner said. 'The police have already talked to you at length about these things.'

'But they were wrong and they dropped it,' I said.

'And you are a collector,' he gestured at the drawings on the walls.

'My aunt's, she was a collector.'

Betti translated the exchange to Garoud.

Feathers puffed up his thin frame, his face reddened. 'Officer, I came here, as I have said, for a celebration. We are not thieves. Neither of us steal. I do not need to steal. Mr Holt does not need to steal, that is self-evident. If Mr Holt wanted a drawing, two drawings, a dozen drawings, I happen to know he is in a position to buy them.'

'That may be so. But why then does his friend need to run a shop?'

'My wife!' Perhaps that was the first time I had said 'my wife' in my forty-seven years on earth. 'She enjoys it, it is an interest.'

'To own a lot of property does not mean it is so easy to live.' Betti gestured, arms akimbo at the ceiling. 'All this is very expensive—just to keep it.'

'And Mr Holt is very rich . . . very rich indeed,' Feathers explained.

'That may be so. Yet I am told that together you have stolen two drawings by the artist Raoul Dufy.'

'Raoul Dufy!' Feathers spluttered. 'Raoul Dufy! . . . *c'est incroyable!* I don't even like the stuff. Trite!'

Chapter 7

Great stiff-upper-lip play—all the pigskin, tweed and flannel of an Anglophile youth had been Feathers' preparation to deal with life. Not to mention the brogues now cast aside to be replaced by snappy little Italianate numbers. Maybe he'd developed ingrown toenails and needed softer leather.

If we hadn't had the smooth Commissioner Betti I felt we would have been miles in front. Still, it was encouraging to find them so far off the mark—where there're mugs there's hope.

Betti insisted on us going to the *préfecture* to continue our chat. Under fire from Feathers he admitted that they had no intention at that moment of laying charges. He wanted more information, that was all. Was he trying to be pleasant?

It is a curious process, French law. I only half followed it. Most of what I knew was the result of my becoming addicted to the sensational case of a woman accused of tying up her four-year-old son and drowning him. Something about the woman's face had captivated the media and Mr and Mrs France. That, and the fact that during the investigation various members of the family started to shoot each other. What had struck me was that at its best, French justice was a very open investigative system. At its worst it was at least as nasty and closed as the law anywhere else—Sydney included.

Feathers was happy enough about going with Betti. We offered them a lift but they insisted on calling for another car. When it came to them wanting Feathers to ride with Betti and me to go along with Garoud we objected. That would have been step one in an interrogation process—before that we would need French lawyers, the lot.

So we rode along together, Betti in the front and us two foreigners in the back. Garoud came along behind. By way of conversation Betti started in about Australia's objections to French nuclear tests in the Pacific and then he was off on a tangent about current French policy in New Caledonia. I had opinions about these things but I reckoned the trick was not to voice them.

By the time we piled out at the *prefécture* in behind the airport, down beyond the far end of the Promenade des Anglais, Betti had got himself quite worked up politically and ideologically—he was a fervent patriot.

We entered through the swinging glass doors, single file; clip-clopped along the tiled corridors till we came to a stop at an unmarked door; we went in. We were alone, just the three of us—Garoud and his uniformed mates had gone on with our driver: maybe rushing for lunch.

We sat one side of an empty desk top, Betti took up position on the other. The walls were blank, there was a telephone, that was all, and a high, horizontal slit window telling us that the sky existed. It was the sort of room you could hose down.

'This isn't an office, it's a torture chamber.'

'Down, Essington,' said Feathers, still fixed on his Pimpernel role.

'Now it is an office,' smiled Betti. 'So?' he asked—but it wasn't a question. 'We are alone, just the three of us. Now we could talk the truth for a change.'

'We have.' I was becoming proud of Feathers.

'Have we indeed? Would you like some coffee, a sandwich?'

I said, 'I'd like to leave right now if you don't mind.'

'You are free, let me assure you of that. Go when you like. I can talk to you anytime. But why not now, while we are together? It is so much more convenient.'

'Talk about what, Assistant Commissioner?' Feathers asked.

'About what happened.' Then he started his spiel. Told us how the trouble with bureaucracy was that you can't tell who's lying, how a particular type of person does well inside public life and a lot of them are mendacious. But then, here and there, a human being makes it through.

Could Betti have been that human being?

'You could be recording,' I said.

'Absolutely right, I could be taping this, but I'm not.'

'How do I know that?'

'You don't. What you should know,' Betti continued, 'is that I can make things difficult, even impossible for you. You

64

understand? The democratic freedoms have limits. They are, as I'm sure you, Mr Sparrow, advocate, must know . . . they are illusions. They work only as long as we leave the mirrors in place. Otherwise . . .'

'Otherwise?' I asked.

'I leave that to your imagination.'

'So, what do you want? That we tell you the truth . . . again!'

Feathers was frowning. More at me I guess than anything else—my indignation was winding up.

Betti said: 'First let me tell you my position, that might help. A sandwich surely? Coffee perhaps?' He called for them over the phone—two coffees and a tea, he was having tea.

The gist of Betti's message to the world was that things were not so bright in the state of France—maybe we weren't being tape recorded. Then it trickled through that the Assistant Commissioner was about as Anglophile as a French patriot could bring himself to be. I started to cool down, lost my sense of persecution.

'We have problems everywhere,' he said. 'But particularly here in the south. In this region the *Front National* has considerable support as perhaps you, Monsieur Holt, have observed. This party appeals to bigot nationalist feeling—its view of a nation is narrow, dangerously narrow. People forget history quickly. A real quasi-fascist power emerging in France would have been unthinkable ten years ago. Too many remembered the mistakes, the excesses of the Second World War. Now people are confused, perhaps things have become too complicated for thought.'

'Maybe they have,' I concurred. 'But what about the Algerian War period?'

A tap on the door, a tray was brought in by a woman tottering on impossible heels. Betti chose to ignore my query about the French historical memory.

'Within our force,' Betti continued, 'these problems are reflected, particularly here in the south where the *Front National* receives quite a share of the vote. A lot of votes. Therefore they have their supporters in the police force—as everywhere we are a mirror of society.'

I had read the press reports, especially those referring to the area around Toulon and Marseille—police shootings of Algerian youths; their support of rightist thugs; high-ranking officers attending the funeral of *Front National* groupies who had blown themselves up with their own bomb.

'So?' I asked through a mouthful of *baguette* and sliced ham.

'So I am interested in houses filled with weapons up in our hills,' said Betti.

'Weapons!' Feathers exclaimed. 'I thought it was Dufys.'

'A complaint has been brought to the police that you stole art works from the house of certain individuals. Garoud is investigating this complaint; it is difficult, you are not French nationals. A certain lightness of touch is required. We came to you because of Garoud's investigation. I am more interested in the men who made the complaint.'

Feathers' eyebrows shot up, 'So you are not actually part of the police?'

'We have our sections.'

'Why would I have anything to do with guns?' I asked.

'Why else would you enter that house?'

'I wouldn't enter any house.'

'One of these men has been treated by a doctor at Entrevaux for a broken jaw. They claim the blow was inflicted by a person who went into that region in a yellow Bentley. They can produce a witness, a man who got a lift in that Bentley.'

Matt Smith, I thought. One of their own.

'A yellow Bentley means you, Mr Holt.'

'Or my driver, Renardo.'

'Not likely, under the circumstances.'

'Why?'

'It simply wouldn't make sense. The doctor is one of the people I have been watching. Entrevaux is an area I have been watching. I have reason to believe that certain foreign nationals are using the terrain of that area for training—Croats, I am informed. These people had representatives at the recent Far Right political conference in Greece. You might remember there were demonstrations against that conference in that country; services were withheld by unions.'

'Yes, I remember.' I looked to Feathers, his face was a mask, a bruised mask.

Betti pressed on: 'These people are assisted by some police

in this area—part of a secret political agreement, a pact against Communism, against non-Europeans, finally against democracy.'

'I wish you luck if you intend to break the pact,' said Feathers. 'But I saw nothing . . . I broke into no building . . . as for broken jaws!' He shook his head in a mime of disbelief.

'So, you will not co-operate?'

'Of course I will. I'm sure my friend, Mr Holt, will co-operate as well. We would both be on your side. The politics of these people are abhorrent to me. But what can I say? I saw no guns. I wouldn't steal Dufys if I was a thief. Matisse, yes—Dufy, no.'

Later I found the Dufy theft accusation a puzzle. The only explanation seemed to be that it was a form of communication—perhaps a threat. Certainly it established the Australian connection.

We were back beside the Rancho Grandee by mid-afternoon, resting under the tall eucalyptuses wafting their nostalgic perfume on hot pink-tinted air. It was the colour of light around Nice that brought opalescence to building surfaces and by contrast forced the sun-baked blue of flaking shutters to jump out as a pattern of dancing rectangles.

The neighbours had returned. Their poodle was pissing on the Ferrari's wheel rims. Bully for it. Desdemona chose to ignore the toy dog's yapping presence—a giant's aristocratic disdain.

The police driver who returned us safe and sound had not said a word all the way, even in the long minutes of traffic jam around the Old Port while a television crew made a commercial for something nobody wanted. Nice is a beautiful town, it grabs me. And like a lot of beautiful things it is rock hard. The previous Christmas it was the only major city in France whose civic fathers refused to allow the establishment of a 'Restaurant of the Heart'—a fancy name for soup kitchen.

We were over-polite to the driver as we got out, thanked him a lot and I thought he caught the irony. He looked like next time he saw us he might try for a kill. Taking off, the car left rubber on the road—it was only public money, public rubber.

Feathers disappeared upstairs for a nap.

I felt in need of distraction. I had not exorcized any of the demons that had been running up and down the tracks of my system while the law had taken me in hand. I headed back through the thick of Nice traffic to the Rue de France in the Citroën brake. I parked about a million miles away from the shop, underground, surfaced on foot then headed for Karen, her world of silk and Dawn.

It's a lot of fun walking around Nice in summer—you can play 'pick the nationality'. The sun is a magnet. The genuine Niçois, the locals, are completely outnumbered. The price of the high-rise apartments thrown up all along the coast tends to exclude the young who just don't have the money. It's an old crowd that throngs the streets.

The silk shop was packed. It wasn't so big anyway and the tables on which the bolts of cloth were stacked took up the space; those and display models draped in the more striking print fabrics. Dawn was at the back earnestly talking to someone I took to be a job applicant. Karen was measuring out a gaudy length for a serious couple who were making extra sure of full measure—actually it was a design I had assisted in adapting. They shut at seven, that would be in two hours. Nothing for me there. I said I'd be back, got a screwed-up nose in reply, then re-entered the crowded street. People go great distances to holiday where they can walk up and down streets as crowded as those they have just quit. Truth is most of us like being packed together, even like complaining about it. Experiments on rats do not apply.

The traffic hardly moved; horns blared, tooted, honked. Just along the road a couple of *clochards* sat, feet surrounded by empty plastic wine bottles. They, at least, had had a pretty good day.

'Monsieur Holt?'

I looked around and found myself flanked by a couple of what could be taken for the local lads. Serious, they were. Police off duty? The idea flashed through my mind then I discarded it.

I faced the biggest of them. 'Could we have a word?' he asked, in French.

'Depends . . . what about?'

'You'll find out.' It had a hard ring to it. I looked down, the one who did the talking was poking something at me behind the cloth of the pocket of his loose seersucker jacket.

'Wouldn't be a banana, would it?' I joked, forcing myself to laugh out loud. He was looking pretty relaxed, as though all you had to do is point a gun and the world would open up. Still laughing out loud I kicked him in the groin like a full back putting the ball into play, then spun and head butted his mate in the face—almost the same movement. A deafening bang— he'd had a finger on the trigger! There was no room to move, not on the footpath, not on the road. We were packed like sardines. A woman screamed. I kicked the gunman again, fetching him a glancing blow to the head as he was messing about on the ground. People froze all around but nobody tried to help; they didn't know who to help. I dropped my knees onto the gunman's chest, thrust a hand into his pocket, grabbed the pistol but dropped it when I saw the cause of the scream. Someone else was screaming now. Things had happened so fast. The man I had head butted had fallen straight backwards, he'd gone through a window; he was half in and half out of a boutique. The glass he'd broken hadn't all fallen at once, a piece must have hung up there for an instant, adhered to the frame, then dropped. Heavy stuff, plate glass, he was badly cut and bleeding all over Kenzo summer prints.

A wave of noise, a mixture of fear and disapproval, perhaps a bit of horror, swept through the crowd. What a crazy thing to do—use a shooter in such a crush! But it was not the time for me to judge the actions of others. I ran back to the silk shop pushing people as I went, weaving and shoving.

The agitation stayed down the road, around the smashed window. I stood for a second outside Karen's shop looking from the mayhem I had left to the careless activity among the silks. I was thanking the Almighty for life, drinking it in, the sensation of being, while the adrenaline worked its way back down to a manageable level.

I was alive.

But as I stepped through the door I was pitched forward by the impact of a gunshot. Consciousness vanished in the falling or when I hit the floor.

*

Outside the window there was space and then walls filled with windows and beyond that more walls, only smaller and with smaller windows. Far, far away in the distance, craggy mountains against the azure sky.

A thumping pain in my head. On one side of the bed a man in a uniform. Karen, ashen-faced, on the other. Her eyes had sunk inside puffy folds of flesh.

'Ess.' I realized she was holding my hand, I could feel her fingers. I managed a little smile.

'Where's this, Bluey?'

'It's the hospital, Ess.'

'But where?'

'Nice, Ess, Pasteur.'

'And the other visitor, Blue, did he bring flowers?'

'An Assistant Commissioner Betti put him there. We talked about it, Ess . . . not to worry.'

'Got a mirror?'

'A little hand one.'

'Could you let me use it? I'd like to see myself, take a look at the mess.'

'There's no mess, Essington.'

'Give us a look anyway.' I held it up. I looked like the Picasso drawing of Apollinaire . . . a cross between the wounded and a turbaned Sikh—I tried out comic faces.

'Don't make me laugh, Ess. Jesus, I've been crying for hours. I thought I'd crack.'

I must have dropped off to sleep. Next time I woke Karen was still there with Feathers standing behind her. A nurse was where the policeman should have been and a doctor was doing something to my arm.

I woke again in the dark. There was just the policeman, only he didn't look the same. He sat. I lay. Who was like a cat? Who like a mouse?

Then there was sun pouring in the window and Karen was with Renardo. He was standing respectful at the foot of the bed.

'Remember my aunt, Renardo?'

'Madame Fabre, yes monsieur.'

'In the hospital at Monaco?'

70

'In the hospital.'

Karen looked brighter. Apparently the bullet had slipped along one side of my thick skull cutting a little groove. When you stop you can never tell if it's at the right or the wrong moment. But now I knew that when I paused before going in the shop door I had been right. An instinct had saved me from death. There had been a third man—my attackers' fall-back position.

Late afternoon the police guard transformed itself into Assistant Commissioner Betti of whatever branch he liked to claim. He was looking at ease, relaxed. I noticed that he was going bald quicker than I remembered. To compensate for thinning at the front his black hair curled in ringlets at the back, above and over his collar.

'A slow learner, Monsieur Holt.'

'There's nothing to learn. It's not clever that somebody shot at me.'

'But what a pity you couldn't trust me.'

I looked at him long and hard—trying to make sense of him, sense of everything. He returned my gaze straight and even, no avoidance. I'm one of those people who believe that you can read a person. I'm always wrong but I still like to believe—I guess I reckon it's all we've got since language fails ninety-nine times out of a hundred.

'OK, what do you want me to say?' I asked. 'But take it easy, Essington's not a well boy.'

'Essington?'

'That's me, Essington Holt.'

Betti laughed. 'Extraordinary . . . E for Essington . . . Essington Holt . . . very aristocratic.'

'Hardly.'

'So tell me about it, Essington.'

Later, when I considered, I realized the cleverness of Betti's playing with my name. It established a familiarity, we became like friends. I told him about it, about most of it anyhow. Like all the stuff at the Entrevaux end. Maybe it was the drugs that loosened my tongue. When I had finished he called the policeman to sit on guard. Was he afraid of me getting out or of someone else getting in? And I said they'd got it wrong, Gerald Sparrow was their target, not me.

*

Back at Villa du Phare I was sitting up, dull-eyed but well enough to enjoy being fussed over by Karen and Rebecca, each in their different ways. Feathers journeyed north to Geneva as soon as he decided that I was only playing possum. No doubt Richards and Partners had plenty of parcels of clients' money doing lots of anonymous things up there in Switzerland. Or perhaps he just wanted to go boating on the lake, watch the swans gliding, stare down into the water's deep clear prism. I don't think the Swiss dump into their lakes. After what they dump in the Rhine there's not much left over. The Rhine is Switzerland's effluent drain.

I had my bed placed so that I could watch Mr and Mrs Next Door, the urban cowboys. Neighbours are addictive. I felt I couldn't live without those two.

Desdemona developed the habit of standing at the foot of my bed, staring at me; did the turban puzzle her?

Betti returned. Big smiles. Lots of 'How are you now, Mr Holt? Aren't you looking better!' Neat little bows for Mrs Holt as though she was suddenly a total surprise. Then big indications that he'd rather talk to me alone. 'For everybody's sake, it is safer that way.'

So Karen tiptoed out. There'd been a hell of a lot of tiptoeing since I first woke up. I was longing for the fall of a heavy foot. But not from Betti, nor did it come; he was very softly softly.

'I can hardly remember what I told you . . . must have been the drugs.'

'It was enough. It was good. Only you should have told me earlier.'

'Or not at all. Anyway, now I've got a couple of questions. They keep on coming up.' But right then, at that moment, they vanished. I sat, trying to capture them, to think.

'Questions like who shot you?'

'That's the obvious, but not the one I lost . . . OK, who shot me? And the others, the first try, who were they?'

'There is a man in hospital. He has a gunshot wound in the stomach . . .'

'A what? How could that be? He went through a window . . . one of them.'

'Correct. He lost a lot of blood. And he has a gunshot wound.'

'Jesus!'

'Your fingerprints were on the gun.'

'You don't have my fingerprints.'

'I put them on a little plastic strip while you were in the hospital.'

'So you think I shot that guy? You're wrong. You know that, you're wrong.' I was starting to shake, it was unnerving stuff and I was still weak.

'I don't think that,' Betti said. 'I know what happened. The man who went through the window is an officer of the police. He is also a member of Charles Martel.'

'Who's he when he's at home?'

'Charles Martel? A French hero; he led the army which turned the Saracens back at Poitiers in 732.'

'I wasn't even born then.'

'Charles Martel is also the name of an anti-Arab organization flourishing down here in the Midi—semi-political, semi-terrorist.'

'More of your *Front National* boys?' I asked.

'Extremists of that organization. Across the south these hatreds are well established. The coast, the perched villages on the hills, the ports . . . a history of fighting Arabs. The Massif des Maures, stretching from Toulon to St Raphael, is named after them. Right up to the eighteenth century Arab pirates brought terror to the coast. Our wild horses are descendants of their pure bloodstock. Perhaps the people—of course the people. Myself.'

'So they're a little close for comfort?'

'That's correct. In a sense we are the French Christian Arabs. Well, some of us. It is often the case that conflict flares between peoples who are too alike. In politics the Left fights itself, bites its own tail. I have talked with the man who fell into the window. There was another man whose fingerprints are also on the gun. I suspect that he too is a police officer, now he has disappeared.'

'The man who shot me? He'd been watching the shop.'

'They all had, all of them.'

'Well, is he in the police too?'

'I've no idea. I could not get any information about him.'

'That's right,' I said. 'I remember my question. What about the Dufys? Why Dufy, for Christ's sake?'

'Why not? I don't understand.'

'Betti, are you being straight with me?'

'Straight?'

'Are you the good guy you're playing? Sure, you'll say yes; still, I just want to hear it. Like they say . . . "once more with feeling".'

'All I can do is repeat what I have said already. Of course, it is essential that the police force does not become a quasi-military shield for the far Right of our politics—for any political extremist position. If it does then we are finished. Yet this is not so unthinkable in France. In 1960, as you pointed out at our first meeting, there was a military revolt against the government . . . against a conservative government. You see, you are more likely to get conflict between shades of political opinion than between their opposites. At that time it was General de Gaulle who faced mutiny. Now we have a conservative government, ironically it thinks of itself as Gaullist. People who voted for it, certain of those people, that is, hoped that it would destroy the trade unions, export the non-European population. Of course this has not happened. Yet the government needs the votes. The *Front National* has a certain power. A difficult situation, unstable.'

'You're on a clean-up drive, Assistant Commissioner, do I understand that right? Tell me, is it official what you do?'

'Entirely official, yes. And, I'm afraid to say, scarcely possible.'

'But you have some effect?'

'A little.'

'Well . . .' I searched about in my mind, in my head, under the bandage. I liked the bandage. 'Well, what about Dufy?'

'That was the accusation they brought against you.'

'I know, I know that, but why Dufy?'

'I don't understand.'

'And there was another thing,' I said. 'The guns . . . did you find the guns?'

'Guns?' he repeated. Could he have forgotten Entrevaux? Betti went for the enigmatic look, sucked his cheeks in, made like a junior Mitterrand. His eyebrows went up. He was playing games, French games, police games. He was playing now you see it, now you don't; now we talked about it, now we didn't.

'You don't remember guns?' I asked. 'It was you who mentioned them, brought them up.'

More eyebrow raising but no consciousness going with them, well certainly not mine.

'So we don't really know anything. Could it be . . . what was his name? The man in the suit?' I stumbled.

'Garoud.'

'Yes, that's the one. Could it be he knows some answers?'

'I think we both have a lot more to say, Mr Holt. I don't want to tire you. Your charming wife would be angry I think.'

I realized after he was gone that I was not much wiser about anything. But maybe the Assistant Commissioner wasn't much wiser either. Conversation fills in time, it's entertainment. What I wanted was something positive—I needed to know. Still, I had stuff to think about, lots of it.

It was clear that Betti was fishing, following an intuition. The guns had taken him by surprise, me mentioning them. Also he appeared to have no idea about Feathers' affiliations. But maybe then neither did the people who'd taken a pot-shot at me. Somehow—it must have been God punishing the innocent—I'd stepped into the firing line, become private enemy number one.

Maybe I should have taken to crime like half of life's success stories. That way people might have given up on trying to have me shot. Or I could have joined a secret service, become a spook.

Chapter 8

I was the martyr for the nuclear family. I had given of my blood so that the wife should stay home with the husband. The timing worked well. Dawn had selected one Farah Mohame with whom to play shops. Not that the shop had been Dawn's idea in the first place. But she was the business brain—that had emerged clearly enough—and she didn't get bored. Karen, she regarded the shop as a way of adjusting to having nothing to do—Karl Marx: 'Freedom is the recognition of necessity.' . . . Or was it Walt Disney? One of the greats, anyway.

Whatever freedom is, Karen had it; yet still she searched for some necessity.

'Takes training, if you're not bred to it like the Royals.'

'What about Lady Di then?' she asked.

'She breeds.'

'But they farm them out . . . like in China, I bet.'

'Maybe we should have children.' I said it for something to say.

'To solve the problem of what to do? You wouldn't want to admit that to your kids.'

'Oh, I don't know. They say the maternity hospitals in New York fill up nine months after winter power breakdowns. Nothing for it but to dive between the sheets . . . no light, no nothing.'

'Essington, we're not like that, we've got everything. It's weird.' But her mind had moved on to other things. She shut the door, stepped to the window, closed the shutters. She was into song, a forties ballad. Keeping the voice low, husky.

'Strip . . .' her lyrics '. . . the man needs distraction.' And off came one of our very own printed silk T-shirts. A pirouette.

I half recalled the tune—was it Billie Holiday?

A chorus-line kick. 'Strip . . . a woman needs reaction.'

She stood, legs and arms akimbo, an apricot line of briefs

just a shade lighter than her sun gilded skin. She ruffled her hair between tapered fingers, growled, then leapt to just out of reach at the end of the bed. Desdemona sprang up snarling.

'Down!' I called to the dog. 'No excitement . . . doctor said,' I appealed to Karen.

She stood above me sliding the briefs off like the heroine in a soft-porn movie. Then hauled back the sheets and slowly, with quasi-medical precision, prepared the patient for love.

Later, lying there in the shutter-slatted light, Karen's head on my shoulder, bandage rakishly askew, I said, 'Those old musicals . . . they've got a lot to answer for . . . was it Rita Hayworth?'

She rolled over, crouched above me, breasts brushing hairy chest. Just before we kissed she whispered the answer . . . 'No,' she said, 'Rin Tin Tin—what a body!'

Over lunch I asked, 'Why Farah Mohame?' It was Dawn who'd been keen not to rock the Niçois racial boat.

'You should have seen her, then you'd understand.'

'That's sexism at its worst, Karen.'

'No it's not, Guillaume.' (Guillaume, that was Apollinaire's name. Only he died of his head wound.) 'It's desire. Nothing wrong with desire.'

'After she's been ripping me to pieces with that tongue of hers?'

'She had nowhere else to put it. Now, with luck, she's got Farah.'

'Farah's not one of your Australian sunshine girls. They're very hung up, those North Africans. Straight, very moral. It's up where the blond people are that everybody piles into the bath together.'

'Then isn't she going to have fun . . . a long courtship.'

Conversation was interrupted by Rebecca. Did she look grim?

Garoud had come visiting.

'Ask him to wait a minute, Rebecca. Is Renardo here?'

'Yes, with me.'

'Would it be too much trouble for him to sit out on the terrace?' I pointed through the shutters. 'Just in case.'

Karen looked very worried indeed. I asked her to attempt to

contact Betti. To try very hard. To tell him who had come to join us.

The chances of finding Betti were slim. Still, we were in the lunch break when all the world stood still—all, it seemed, except Garoud.

As she was retreating I asked Rebecca, 'Is he alone?'

'No, there are two men with him.'

'In uniform?'

'Yes.'

'Jesus Christ,' I muttered. 'Karen, make that call quick.'

Garoud was in the same natty mustard-coloured suit, pressed and clean. He had a gold bracelet on his wrist; it hung down while that hand clutched the handle of a flat and efficient-looking leather document case in shiny Bordeaux red. Essentially a dull-looking man with pointy features, his eyes were too small, mean—little black dots either side of his nose. His nostrils were bristling with hair.

'Mr Holt.' No smile. It would be all French from here on.

Me in pyjamas and bandage and Karen's fragrance still on my skin. I was not without a trick. Under the bedclothes, in my hot little hand, I grasped the 9mm pistol salvaged from the Entrevaux fiasco. I had kept it safe and sound in the drawer of my walnut bedside table. At bedroom range it would throw the bugger through the door and I'd languish for the rest of eternity in a French gaol.

The pistol was definitely last line of defence.

Luckily, Garoud's cronies had stayed outside. Were they sitting in their car, tapping fingers, listening to a loop tape of Princess Stephanie singing? On the way to the phone Karen had placed a chair at the foot of the bed, between me and the door.

Desdemona was growling. 'You'd better watch the dog,' I said. I smiled broadly. Garoud picked up the chair and started to bring it up to my side. Desdemona took a step forward, showing her teeth.

'Leave it where it is, that's not so far. You won't have to shout and I don't need anybody to hold my hand.'

'I hope not . . . The dog?' he asked.

'This is my house, monsieur, my rules.'

'It's my country.'

'That doesn't mean a thing. You ought to know that.'

'Ah . . . but it means everything.' He was sitting up, primly I thought.

'I've talked to the police already. Cut and dried: a man tried to kill me going into our shop; weak wrist, he couldn't fire straight. But now I know! You've come to tell me he's been caught.'

'Unfortunately not, Mr Holt.'

'Back,' I said to the Great Dane narrowing the gap between herself and our visitor.

'Pardon . . . you said?' He was opening the case, it was on his knee.

'Talking to the dog.'

His hand went in among the documents—if there were documents. I couldn't see through the lid, it opened my way. I thought he looked too purposeful.

Karen entered. Garoud snapped the case shut. She stood behind him.

'My wife.'

He screwed his head around, tried a smile. She had her back to the door.

'And?' I asked her.

'Assistant Commissioner Betti is on his way.'

'Good. Now, Monsieur Garoud—' why honour him with rank? '—I'd like to tell you something. It's for your own good, so listen carefully.'

He sat there. Desdemona was edging in again. Garoud was looking crowded though it was hard to tell why; with two men outside, theoretically he could do as he wished. And if he meant harm he would have thought it through already.

'You've come to look for Raoul Dufys?'

He seemed to like that. His face lit up as though I had given him inspiration.

'I'll tell you about them,' I continued. 'There weren't any Raoul Dufys. If there were I wouldn't touch them with a barge pole—vacuous shit.' I was hoping he was getting my meaning. My trick with French was to go straight over from one language to the other—I was often misunderstood. Maybe for 'vacuous shit' they used something like 'éclair without cream'—you never could tell. 'There weren't any drawings, I'll tell you that.'

'That is your position?' he asked.

'It's not a position, it's the truth. Nothing to be done with it; the truth, plain and simple.'

'There are other people who testify to a different truth.'

'An impasse, then?'

It was a rhetorical question. I was playing for time. But I was angry too. I didn't like the neat little figure propped straight up on the chair. The dog didn't like him either. I hated the idea of men lounging in a car outside my door. When I thought of it I didn't like the whole feeling of being a foreigner—the foreigner—the man with no rights.

'What's in the case?'

No reply, tight-lipped.

'Garoud, I don't quite know how to tell you what I have to say next.'

He remained silent.

'What's in the case?'

He just shook his head as though it was of no consequence.

'So, why open it? Why open up nothing, for Christ's sake?'

Still no reply. Had the coming of Betti rattled him?

Karen looked very nervous indeed.

'OK, Garoud, Inspector or whatever. There is a 9mm pistol pointing at your chest. From here it will blow you apart. Sit tight, listen carefully. There were guns in that house—guns isn't even Dufy backwards. A box of them is now in Switzerland,' I lied, 'with my friend. Tracing their origin. There's a dead woman back home in Australia who used to own, would you believe, a painting by Raoul Dufy. Letters were sent from Entrevaux, threatening her life. There are lots of reasons to believe that woman didn't die of natural causes . . . would you call an axe a natural cause?' Looking back I saw that I shouldn't have tried. Telling him all that made it look like I was the man they were after; I was talking Feathers off the hook. 'That's right, just sit very quiet.' I never saw Desdemona so tuned up. I continued: 'So to business. Number one: your Dufy story is weak, wouldn't hold. Two: who tried to kill me? You know the answer, don't you? Was it our Yugoslav friends, Garoud? I reckon not. I reckon it was you. Maybe not your finger—but your mind, certainly.

'I'm an all-Australian boy and I've got a chip on my shoulder because I was reared by a demented mother who mourned forever the death of my father. He was killed on Crete, went berserk under fire. They called him a hero. Half my mind says "murderer" when it sees a neat little man like you, and the other half knows that the first half is right.'

Still not a word out of the bugger.

I produced the pistol, held it in both hands and pointed it at his head.

'Very careful, put that case down beside you.' He was almost too careful. 'Good. Now push it back, gently, back as far as you can.' He bent to do as I said, his eyes fixed on my eyes. 'Back further,' I said. 'That's nice. Now, Karen, stay out of his range, go round wide, come in at the side, take the bag. Good. Now bring it here.' She'd shifted from surprise and fear to efficiency.

The gun was a hair's breadth from firing—Garoud knew it. You can't beat reality.

'Open it, Karen.' She opened it. A little tape recorder, turning, perched up on some files. Beside that a handgun.

'What's the set-up?' I asked. 'Like there's a mike, I guess.' I could see a lead to the body of the case itself. 'Got to be a microphone somewhere, Karen.' She was examining it carefully. Garoud was thinking. His body was rigid.

'Shoot the cassette out and keep it,' I instructed. 'Right. Now get a cloth—anything. Wipe down what you've touched. Close it.' She had used the edge of a sheet. She closed the case. 'Wipe the outside all over. Great.' The barrel kept on pointing at Garoud.

'What,' I asked, 'were you going to do with that?'

Before he could think of answering Rebecca opened the door letting Assistant Commissioner Betti pass in front of her into the room. The pistol was back under the sheets. Defused, Garoud stood, subordinate. Karen . . . I could hear her let out a long sigh of relief.

'Mr Holt . . . Garoud!' Betti dipped slightly at the waist, he smiled a droll smile. Even with the local strength on his side, if that was the case, Garoud was in an invidious position. He was caught between us—or were they play-acting, the two of them? It was impossible to be sure. Whatever, Garoud had gained nothing. Only a belief that he had heard what he had heard.

Part, the important part about Feathers and the box of guns, was a lie anyway. They could prove that quickly enough. Feathers had flown, Nice-Geneva. No way he could carry even a cuckoo clock without it being detected.

Mind you, sitting in bed with a 9mm pistol was not the behaviour expected of a guest of France living on the strength of a *carte de séjour*.

Garoud was standing, clutching his case too hard, his knuckles were white. 'How,' I asked, mock innocent, 'are we progressing with the inquiries? The Dufys, found?'

'Unfortunately, no.' He moved towards the door. Betti watched him, the smile still playing on his lips. I rang for Rebecca to show our unwanted guest the way.

'Thanks, Blue,' I said, taking Karen's hand. At that moment she seemed astonished by me, by everything. Finding out what she'd really married, too late.

'Essington,' she said. 'This is getting heavy. It's Gerald Sparrow, isn't it?' He got it going?'

'Karen,' I looked to Betti. She seemed to have forgotten he was there. She shook her head clear. He waited, still with a smile on his face, fixed and polite.

'I'm not going, if that's what you're thinking,' Karen said. 'This isn't the Middle Ages—knights in armour. More like little boys playing nasty games.' She was suddenly pissed off with the whole bit.

Betti shrugged. 'Then stay, Mrs Holt.' She sat on the bed. He took the chair . . . still warm . . . they used to say you could get pregnant that way. 'This affects you as much as anybody,' he added.

'Bloody oath it does.'

We sat there and talked.

Chapter 9

I was up and about by the time Dawn, overstepping the bounds
of propriety where employer–employee relationships were concerned, asked the new shop-girl to dinner at Villa du Phare.
Feathers, 'the destroyer', as Karen now called him, was back
from his trip. Where gravel rash marked his legal skin now pink
repaired tissue presented itself to the sun for the freckling
process. He was without apology, unashamed of the trouble he
had brought as a wedding gift from Australia. He had no bright
suggestions to save us from a difficult situation. As far as he
was concerned it was 'shut your eyes, country first'. I could not
comprehend what real harm a bunch of Croats could do playing
Cowboys and Indians with guns among the eucalyptuses as a
fantasy preparation for the downfall of the post-Tito government. To date the worst they had managed was to get a few
suspected war criminals among their number into official posi-
tions in branches of Australia's conservative political party.
There they proved an embarrassment, nothing more.

As far as Karen was concerned we were clearing out at the
earliest opportunity. Betti had suggested this and she had taken
up the cause. If people in the police wanted to shut me up or
wanted me out of the way for whatever reason, the trick was to
oblige, to get the hell out of it.

I could not understand why they would want to silence me
since I wasn't saying anything in the first place. The only
explanation was that, with the classic paranoia of the clandestine (that, at base, was Feathers' trouble, I guessed), people
had decided in their tiny minds that I was part of a league
against them.

Maybe, unwittingly, I was. I tried to make Feathers come
clean as we were waiting for Dawn to turn up with Farah. The
long lunch break makes for an all-over longer day in France. I
was thankful that Karen was out of it and now working on

design ideas at home. Stage two of the silk business was to find outlets elsewhere in Europe—that was to have been travel, fun.

'How does it all tie together, Feathers? I've got a crease in my head, the result of ignorance. You're to blame for that. Fill me in.'

Feathers elected to look shifty. 'Maybe I do owe you some explanation.'

'Jesus! . . . Maybe! Betti's more open than you and he's got something to lose. For God's sake, Sparrow, shake yourself up. We're only talking about friendship! What's the point of countries if there aren't friends? Friends first, nations second; that's the way I see it. A nation is just an abstraction. Think of my dad. Dead for an abstraction. On Crete of all places! Most people don't even know where it is on the map.'

'Essington, I haven't been entirely honest with you.'

'You can say that again.'

'Mind, I haven't lied. The thing I omitted was the connection. To tell you that would have been . . .'

'To let me into your secret life, your spying?'

'I wouldn't put it like that . . . if you must smear certain of my activities.'

'You mean there are others?'

'I'll ignore that. Essington, after I heard of the death of Oula Strossmayer, I sensed that there was more to it than had been stated in newspaper accounts of a small-town axe murder. When I heard of it from the legal end, something, I couldn't say what, caught my attention. On the surface it seemed straightforward enough—that she was a client because the late Richards had had Millbourne connections. We have a number like that: graziers, local business people—conservative types; like to stick with a name they know without an idea that at our end the work is shuffled about from secretary to secretary, office to office. No personal touch at all.

'No, it wasn't the Millbourne element that alerted me. Fact is I can't put my finger on quite what it was. Of course the will itself had elements of the eccentric about it. The name, Strossmayer, was hardly part of old Millbourne; there was the lack of family, not only of family cut out of the will but of family full stop. I was curious right up to when I received the challenge to the will—as I might have mentioned, a half-hearted affair, done for the form of it. But it did come from a Canberra company that certain people involved with the other part of my life . . .'

'Your James Bond side?'

'If you like, Essington, if you like. Certain people had already developed an interest in Has and Danilović . . . the Canberra firm. This because of Has and his political affiliations. Not to mention more particular allegations, unsubstantiated mind you, but serious nevertheless and a cause for disquiet among some of our nation's friends. Has is an alleged war criminal.

'The more I looked into things the more it seemed to me that Oula had been killed for political motives. Very likely for reasons out of the past. For information she possessed that could be embarrassing, even downright harmful to some group or individual. It seemed to me that robbery was not the motive—they were not after the Dufy. But they were after something. Ample signs that the house had been searched, thoroughly, professionally.

'I am, unfortunately, not free to pass on details of information that has come my way. But you may rest assured that I did not lightly cross that river, break into that house . . . risk your neck and my own.'

'Uncharacteristic, I would have thought, Feathers.'

'Uncharacteristic but necessary. Had you seen the documentation that has built up around this affair I believe you would have been inclined to do as I did.'

'Not bloody likely. So, you're sure you didn't see the Entrevaux postmarked letters?'

'No, unfortunately not. Thanks to the Millbourne police. Of course they try to deny having touched them. But they knew of Milo. And she told the Griffins. Why should they lie? Said that they were passed to the police. Why not believe that the police threw them away? The other alternative, less likely, is that they were somewhere in the house, taken from there.'

'This is no more than a rehash of what you've already told me,' I complained. 'I was expecting the big open up. You're filibustering, Feathers.'

'Essington, you must believe me. So much can not be said.

Classified material . . . classified! And the rest is speculation. Thus the continued investigation. I'm deeply sorry you got involved. I could not foresee . . .'

'I should hope not . . . Christ!'

Clever chaps, lawyers—at saying little with a lot of wind behind it.

From the terrace we saw the sun going down, smudging smoky orange across the sky. There had been a couple of minor forest fires over behind Cannes.

Karen emerged and offered the legal eagle a cold 'good evening'. It embarrassed me how strongly she had set herself against him. Bastard that he had proved to be he was still the oldest friend I had. It was necessary to stick with him if only to prove my argument about friends and nations.

Sensing Karen's hostility, Feathers descended the steps and wandered off around the garden. A crouching Desdemona watched as I reached out for Karen's hands and for reassurance that the lawyer's presence would not create a rift between us.

'Ess.'

'Karen?'

'Remember that talk about babies?'

'How they give you something to do?'

'Well, they would, wouldn't they? For life.'

'But you're a child bride.'

'I was thinking. It'd be nice, Essington, really nice.'

'Sure I'm not past it?'

'The male menopause? If we hurry we could just beat it.' She wound her arms around my neck. I felt myself responding.

'Not that quick. We've got guests for dinner. It wouldn't do to be caught rooting against the verandah post.'

'Do you think she'll wear a veil?'

'Jesus! With you around I reckon she'd need to.'

Dinner was by way of a farewell as well as hello Farah. We were getting out of the firing line, retreating.

Chapter 10

Sydney, Australia, late August. After more than a year away I couldn't believe the light, and the blackness of shadows. They said European-trained painters of the nineteenth century had trouble with the eucalyptus greens and the shape of branches in the Antipodes. Drivel! People will say anything to keep a job. (I know, I went to art school once, lasted three months.) It was the light they couldn't get right. Surfaces pushed so hard by the sun that pigment cannot render the effect; areas of shade that won't work as pretty tints.

I watched the well-known face of a government minister grimace with pain as he waddled out of the airport building—must have been his piles. He grunted as he climbed into the big black Commonwealth limousine which whisked him away to do-it-yourself-lobotomy-land.

'Who was that again?' I touched Feathers on the arm, he had caught the same flight. But Feathers isn't the kind of man who sees things. He concentrates on the condition of souls—his and the nation's.

We split up. Feathers went his way, we went to the Regent, down the end of George Street near the quays. Jet lagged, it was the only hotel name I could remember.

Assistant Commissioner Betti, the enigmatic, had accompanied us to Nice airport. He told me his name was Sammy. I said I'd send him a stuffed koala bear for his kid. I guessed I would never know about Betti. My gut feeling was that he was all right.

Desdemona was forced to remain in Renardo's and Rebecca's tender care. I figured she knew I was off. She didn't take her gaze from me right up to the moment when the Bentley passed through the grill gate. Villa du Phare was her patch. She would be happy enough. We'd be back when the dust had settled.

For Rebecca and Renardo it was holiday time—no more me, no more Karen, no more unwanted visitors. Already they would be doing wheelies in that magnificent car, throwing fire-crackers out the window. Deep down, somewhere, they must have had a wild side. Was I the only one who couldn't see it?

Karen had slept well, seat flattened right out. Me, sitting up or lying down, I was too excited. And with the head wound I hadn't been able to write myself off on champagne. Not that I had become a wine snob: give me a litre of el-cheapo rosé at eight francs forty any day. Keeps you in the race—the human race. And you get one franc twenty back on the bottle.

Thirty-seven Sunset Crescent, Catalpa, was a down-market dream with cracks. Circa 1970, spec built, garage under, early model tilt-a-door, and kikuyu grass wanting nothing quite so much as to strangle the place—nature making aesthetic judge-ments—it had even climbed up the cracked two-colour brick gatepost and was poking a green tendril out the top as though it was an explorer for a colonial power.

'Your father hit that?'

'Either he hit it or it's subsidence. All this was a swamp. They dumped garbage here then built. Development, Queens-land style.'

Late winter is the perfect time of year for Brisbane. Good for swimming too. It's the weather that makes you regret the low-grade civilization, the inappropriateness of everything. For the British Midlands Brisbane's sixties building boom would have been fine, even desirable. For a sub-tropical paradise it was bad bad bad. The early houses, wooden bungalows, have a lot of character: wooden lattice, jigsawed kangaroos and all. A zany nationalism.

'Well, here goes, Essington. Mr and Mrs Holt meet the Christophes of Sunset Crescent,' said Karen.

I could see somebody taking a peek through the curtains. We weren't going to be a surprise. Not that we hadn't rung. But give or take half an hour we could have been selling salvation or encyclopaedias or anything just as easily as we were liable to be the prodigal and spouse. It looked good Bible country. The empty suburban streets expressed the possibility of judgement and doom.

The woman who answered the door only revealed the likeness on close examination. She had painted on so much of her face you couldn't find the other one. She burst into tears then fell into her daughter's arms. Mr Christophe stood in the doorway of what I assumed to be the sitting-room. He stared at us down the corridor. He was a boozed-out looking man—small, thickset, untidy.

He wasn't going to fall about over a lost infant, not Mr Christophe.

I was standing back, leaning against the rusted railing, taking in the picture.

'Mum, this is Essington.'

The mother pulled herself together, examined me, stepped past the daughter and wrapped her arms around me. We were the unemotional Australians who don't like body contact. The Frenchman, Mr Christophe, stood in his doorway and stared. That's the worst of falling in love, you get the family thrown in.

He shuffled down the corridor: 'Karen, so you are married now.' He shook her hand. Not even cheek pecking. She stepped through the defences and rested her head against his.

I was introduced. We shook hands. He played the stern patriarch. Mrs Christophe bundled us along into the sitting-room where a multitude of cakes majestically covered a teak-veneer coffee table. We were to be feasted.

'He was always a nasty bastard. Biggest mistake she ever made, marrying him. A real *colon*, great white colonial master, thinks the sun shines out of him. Never did a tap of work, always had Kanaks do it for him. Innocent country Australian lass goes to New Caledonia and finishes up with that. Just so he can get his money out while the nickel price was falling. That's one way to ruin your life.'

'You mean there are others?'

Karen's father had made sure we didn't stay too long. Maybe he was angry at his daughter landing on her feet after fleeing the nest at sixteen. Not bad, a villa on Cap Ferrat. By French standards a finger right up his *cul*.

'Why does she put up with it?'

'I'm sure Dawn would have the answer, Bluey.'

'And such a fool. Most of what he had he's lost. Any scheme that looked like it would yield double in a few weeks he was right into. The last one was Christian pleasure cruises—instead of bingo and fucking you sailed the Pacific listening to evangelists.'

'That's the way money circulates.'

'Not in your case it wasn't.'

'Me, I've got what I've got because the gods love fools.'

'They didn't love Dad.'

I pointed the hire Ford south. We intended to bypass Surfer's Paradise to spend a few days practising reproduction techniques and swimming on the north coast of New South Wales which still looks pretty much the way it did when Gauguin visited Sydney. If he'd seen it he wouldn't have bothered to recross all that sea. That is if he hadn't been locked in a battle with French authorities over the treatment and conditions of the Polynesian people.

Karen asked, 'What did he take you outside for? The facts of life?'

'He could see I was beyond that, the head bandage ages a man.'

'Well, what?'

'He wanted to show me his car.'

'His car! I don't believe it.'

'He had a tarpaulin over it.'

'Even though it was garaged?'

'To keep the dust off.'

'What did he have that's so special?'

'Would you believe, a Holden, Australia's gift from General Motors. Could have been three years old—spotless.'

'They never go anywhere,' Karen laughed. 'She'd like to but he won't let her. What did you say when you saw it?'

'It was grey. The worst was he wanted to know what I drove. Said Peugeot were very reliable. A good car, he said. Said he had a 304 in Noumea.'

'And what did you say?' Karen couldn't stop laughing. 'Jesus! I wish I'd been there. So?'

'Well, I didn't have the heart. He was wiping the thing with a cloth when he asked me. I said I had a Renault. Only I didn't know which model because the number had fallen off before I bought it.'

'You didn't!'

'I did.'

'He probably thinks you've got a tent on the rocks . . . that we live in a canvas Villa du Phare.'

'Let him, if it makes him feel good.'

Curiosity finally took us to Millbourne. It was four hours from Sydney not counting the traffic snarl from the Regent to Liverpool. I would have liked to have seen the Dufy in Sparrow's office before we made the trip. But he was out of town and not expected to return for several days. Was he avoiding me?

Curious how you get used to things. I had been looking forward to driving again through the Australian countryside. Once it had seemed to me that those endless roads were the only thing, the strings, that tied the place together. As though before roads had been laid over the land's surface nothing had been connected. As though it was only because of asphalt that the place could be thought about at all. Suddenly I wanted to be anywhere but on those roads. Suddenly it seemed to me that the character of the country was somewhere far away from those interminable ribbons.

We sat there, belting along past animal corpses—proof, at least, of their abundance—and the treads stripped off wheels of semi-trailers. I was looking rather Continental in a beret, the replacement for my bandage. Karen was wearing a bored face. The further inland we went the colder it got. Europe had spoilt me for travel. Karen said she had never liked going places— she liked being there. After the wastes of Catalpa she yearned for city centres. She said so, emphatically.

It was not a good day to look at Australia. High cloud diffusing the sun's light threw it cold and even over everything. No shadows. The drab green of the trees, which in the sun can become a subtle and seemingly endless gradation of colour mixings, looked, under the uninviting sky, more like a stained underdeveloped print than anything else. Maybe, from jacka-roo days, I'd seen too much of it already. Or I was infected by

Karen's dislike of what slid past the Ford's windows. Whatever the reason, the worst of it was that the country deteriorated as we went along. It wasn't until we were in Millbourne pretending *bonhomie* with the locals at the bar of the Duke of Wellington—boasting motel-type rooms in a garden setting—that we learnt that they were in the grip of drought. They'd say that in the middle of a rainstorm. The man next to Karen, spurred on by the presence of a pretty lady, his face burnt by cold and heat, told us, all and sundry, how he'd cut a ewe open that morning only to find she'd been eating gum leaves.

'That's what Dad always said.' He stopped for dramatic effect and to gather in the attention of a couple of local lads still throwing darts. '"They know," he said. "That shows a big dry coming." That's what Dad said.'

'And he's right, Donny, your dad. 'Cos he knew this country like the back of his hand, your dad.'

'Got the cancer on the back of his hand, Dad did.'

'You can't wear a hat on the back of your hand, can you Donny?'

'The ants,' a small red faced man added his two bobs' worth of wisdom. 'The ants is all climbing up the stringy barks. No, the country's buggered.' To Karen: 'Excuse the language, girlie.'

Karen shrugged. She didn't think much of that kind of talk. I had to admit I'd always liked it. It was the essence of conversation. Yet sitting there with Karen, sipping beer—her bored—I suddenly felt clean out of it. It was loads of superstitious garbage.

They deserve to go broke which was what they were all loudly proclaiming they were doing. They'd been going broke since I first hit the bush in 1956, a couple of years after the biggest boom of the century. You'd wonder where they found the money to keep going broke with.

We returned to room twelve, switched on the TV, tried the two channels. We switched it off again. We had a long hot shower then sat in bed reading alternative verses out of Gideon's Bible to each other. A couple of pages had been ripped out of the Revelation of St John the Divine. Very lightweight paper. A previous visitor had been rolling joints in the room. By the stale antiseptic smell of things not all that recently.

'"And the beast which I saw—" Karen was in full clerical voice, "—was like unto a leopard and his feet were as the feet of a bear and his mouth as the mouth of a lion."'

I was acting the beast at the foot of the bed.

'"And the dragon gave him his power and his seat and great authority. And I saw one of his heads as it were wounded to death . . ."'

From outside the room the sound of a car skidding on gravel then, crash—clear in the silence of a chilly Millbourne night. Crisp cold at night, those Australian towns, just as I remembered.

'For a minute I thought it was the Lord.'

'I'll take a look.' That's what we men did, we took a look.

I wrapped myself in the pink chenille bedspread, strode, a Roman senator, to the door. I opened it and found the Ford, our hired wheels, shoved across at the back. A burly man was climbing slowly out of an old twin spinner V8 armoured at the front with a bull bar.

'Fucking mongrel,' he muttered. Then he saw me, the motel's sole guest—by a car count at least.

'That yours?' he asked.

'Yep . . . well it was.'

'Then what's it doing there?'

'It's parked. You know . . . parking.' I grinned.

He wasn't grinning. 'Well it fucking didn't ought to be. It's in the way.' He was swaying, drunk. The cliché countryman, maybe thirty. Would have been taught to drink rum by his grandaddy, for bets, in an unlined, wood slab hut.

'Well,' I replied, 'it fucking is, isn't it.'

'What is it, Ess?'

'Never mind, Karen,' I called back. 'It's a drunk. He's smashed the car.'

'We really did pass the black stump, didn't we?'

'I'm no drunk . . . you fucking mongrel.' He was stepping up to me to make a point, I suppose. 'You put your car in the fucking way . . . I could have the law on you.'

'You probably could . . . nothing would surprise me out here. Tell you what, why don't you do just that?' He was jutting out a substantial jaw, curling a cracked lip. Enough brain cells still working to screw the face into a grimace.

'Fucking might.'

'Fucking do,' I mimicked, then shut the door in his face. 'A real gentleman. Oh, hell . . .'

'Hello Australia,' Karen sighed. A crash against the door turned her serious. 'He's trying to smash it down . . . am I dreaming?'

'No, you're not, Blue . . . I know this scene, almost word perfect.'

'You might. Still, I'm ringing up.'

She lifted the phone, rang reception. They took a long time to answer. Our attacker had taken to lobbing stones on the roof.

'The manager? We've got one of your locals attacking us . . . Room? What was the room number, Ess?'

'What's he want that for? I think we're the only guests.'

'Just come and call him off, you'll find him.' She hung up. 'He didn't sound much help.'

A minute or two later, a voice: 'Barney!' Like to a dog. 'Come on, Barney, back off will you.' Then silence.

That did away with the prospect of peaceful sleep. I lay there in the dark remembering the bush that had once seemed romantic but which wasn't. Romance is in the mind. You can make romance out of a cockroach if you've got the will and the imagination. The bush is society in a state of arrested development, suspended animation. Self-selected peasants. In the dark room nasty little scenes kept flipping up like slides on a screen. Scenes from different places. From the Gulf down to Esperance. And all that time Mother hoping I'd find the pastoral heiress moping among bulrushes—or was that where babies come from?

I got up very early, at the first touch of false dawn, pulled on my beret and went strolling. Karen was sleeping like a top. Less puritan than me, any problems, she popped a tablet. I liked to suffer for my sins. That was why we must have been in Millbourne.

I smelt it the instant I stepped outside. The hint of sweetness on the air. There was a slight breeze from the east, from over where the light was breaking. I smelt it but it took a second or two to place. The abattoir's smell. It had filled in the background of a lot of my crisp bush mornings. Right out there on the stations it rose from the killing shed.

A subtly nauseating smell. It had another effect as well: rediscovery, it brought back details of the past. Like for one of the friends of the Impressionists—was it Zola who Manet painted? Proust or somebody—used to dip a cake in a cup of tea to bring back childhood. Some cake, an abattoir!

I walked out of the hotel–motel's garden setting: gravel with two dead potted miniature cypress trees—a slow and painful death, root binding. For the kiddies there was a rusted, four-gallon kerosine drum rocking-horse mounted on a car spring. It had once been painted purple. It had fallen over.

The Ford was stuffed. One of the back wheels tilted at an unholy angle. The black V8 was parked outside the back of the old hotel building, at the base of the rotting wooden fire-stairs.

The Duke of Wellington was right up one end, the eastern end, of town. I turned away from where the street dipped down among garages, grocers, stock agents, churches, to a little bridge. I headed out towards the charnel smell. I didn't have to go so far. There it was, just off the road. I hadn't noticed it driving in on account of a row of stunted golden poplars forming a memorial avenue—each tree had a little name-plate for someone who died in the First World War. The main tin shed was right at the top of the hill. I guess that was so the life of the animals could run away down the slope in all directions. Around the building grassless fenced enclosures fanned out. Beasts stood in these, silent, unmoving; breathing in the air of death, breathing out the mist of their living warmth. The only sound was a tolling—something between tolling and clanking— a loose sheet of corrugated iron hanging by a nail, flapping.

I must have stood there a full five minutes. Stood stock still in the horror of this image of my past. Cap Ferrat can surely soften you up.

A car passed. The driver regarded me with interest. I must have looked foreign in my beret.

Then a little farm bike buzzed along, its rider all rugged up. These were the workers and, maybe, the owners, going off for a day on the land. A day of rabbit digging, of crutching sheep, of splitting fence posts, of driving tractors in circles, of wrestling with gearboxes and the internal combustion engine. And, I guessed, at that time of year in a big dry, there'd be a lot of putting out of feed wheat and hay.

I was standing by the notice. It said 'Millbourne, Population 1768'. Underneath there was the afterthought stuck to the pole: 'Tidy Town 1983'.

Some bright spark had fired a bullet through the 'O' of 'Population'. Could have been celebrating a birth or a death.

Chapter 11

I turned my back on the abattoir and retreated down the main street past the Duke of Wellington. Nothing was open. A bus had dumped bundles of the morning papers outside the door of the news agency. Silence was broken by the occasional worker driving off in one direction or another and by the growing cocks' chorus. I guess it started somewhere and was then taken up all over town like a round song. That chorus lifted one corner of the blanket of gloom Millbourne had laid over me.

After an ultimate country breakfast, bacon, eggs, limp toast, I set about getting us another car. This involved conversation with mine host, a couple of phone calls to the hire company and a visit to the local police station where one Sergeant Armstrong was slow, unsure, but even-handed despite the uneven distribution of guilt.

'I wasn't in the bloody thing, Officer.'

I had a shaky assurance from the Duke of Wellington's proprietor that Barney would be led down to Armstrong to tell his side of the story.

For some reason mine host had taken a set against me. I reciprocated. Could be he had a set against the world, but not, it seemed, against Barney. Christ knew why. The proprietor wore one of those blank blond faces coloured somewhere between bronze and blood pressure. He had angry pale eyes. He was reluctant with words, with service, with everything. All across the back of his bull neck blond hair curled in tiny greasy clusters.

Not a friend to the weary traveller, mine host. Who is out there on those sun-beaten, wind-blasted, western plains?

It didn't worry me, none of it. I hadn't come to Millbourne to make friends or to get screwed up about broken cars.

We made it up to lunch-time with nothing accomplished. In search of food we wandered down to a deconsecrated and converted church which bore the name 'The Spun Fleece', a craft shop and tea-house run by some of the district's rosy-cheeked young mothers. There were toddlers falling about the place; toddlers and dogs, and a peacock. It looked a wholesome, even a friendly, alternative to the hotel–motel and to the Oxford down the other end, just before the creek. The Oxford looked like the local blood-house.

We sat primly at a gingham tablecloth in a beam of half-wiped-out sun and read the blackboard: Quiche, Vegetable Pie, Ploughman's Lunch, Nut Rissoles. That was for those who wanted something really solid. Otherwise there were sandwiches, rolls and lots of very home-made cakes, all crusty and crumby: half of them dabbed with cream where they rested happily inside their cooled glass case.

I decided to try the ploughman's lunch. Karen went for cheese sandwiches—not an ounce of the 'alternative life style' blood in her.

'Just passing through?' asked one young mother-come-waitress, bathing us in her smile.

'Trying to.' Karen's grin was not without bitterness.

'All you've got to do is go down the end there, over the creek, take the dog-leg, then off you go.' The woman crossed her arms over an ample bosom and beamed. 'That is, unless you came from that direction in which case . . .' And then she laughed, leaned her head down beside Karen and whispered. 'I found my way out once but then I got lost before I could find anywhere else to get into.' Another hearty laugh.

Karen looked puzzled.

'Only pulling your leg, love.' The woman was infectious. 'On holidays then?' Only not infecting anyone.

'Honeymoon,' I said.

'Some honeymoon,' Karen said.

'How touching, newly-weds. Shirley! We've got newly-weds.'

So Shirley came over to join in the fun.

'He's lying,' said Karen.

'I could tell,' laughed the first woman. 'You just don't look the part.' I felt offended.

As sole customers we quickly became the centre of everybody's attention. An arthritic Labrador looked like he expected me to feed him under the table. The toddlers headed our way. A kid of about ten came across and stood, staring at me. Even an aristocratic Italian greyhound with a bandaged leg decided to take a sniff at my ankles. It had mange.

'See that?' I asked, pointing at the mange.

'Oh, that's all right, only little mites.'

'Not all right for the dog, imagine if you had something like that in the small of your back.'

'I couldn't bite at it,' Shirley shrieked.

'Have you tried to fix it up?' I asked.

'Nothing works.'

'You're wrong.' They stood around me, dogs and humans, big and small, waiting for the wisdom. Karen kept on munching her cheese sandwich.

'You've tried chemicals?'

'Don't trust them, but yes. Tried everything.'

I wrote down a brand name. 'You try this, it works, it's for cattle lice.'

'Makes your hair fall out. I knew a woman once who . . .'

'Never mind the woman,' I interrupted, 'try it. I promise you. The dose, that's another thing. What was it? Ten millilitres ought to do, once a month. Burn the bedding.'

'Just a tick, I'll write that down,' said Shirley. I'd won a friend, several in fact, and the ploughman's lunch wasn't too bad as long as you weren't sitting on a tractor all day, turning the sod.

Paying, I asked about the potted jam. We bought a jar of apricot and found out where the pots were made. It was just over the bridge, then follow the Tip Road for about a quarter of a mile. I loved that in the bush—the bastards wouldn't go metric. They thought it was a fad, that it would pass.

Karen and I headed off as directed to take a look-see.

'Why are we doing this?'

'Doing what?'

'Why are we walking down the main road of this God-forsaken place to see a jam-bottler?'

'A potter,' I corrected.

'Whatever . . . you know what I mean, Essington.'

'I told you it's where the old lady was killed.'

'I don't mean that. I know that. I mean why the hell! What's in it for you?'

'Somebody took a pot-shot at me in Nice, France . . . that's why.'

'Then you're mad. You go looking for it, don't you?'

'Looking?'

'For trouble, Ess.'

'Karen, that's not true. I'm not looking for any trouble. What's more, I don't expect to find it. All I'm asking is why? Like Socrates. I'd like to find out; it's as simple as that. Is it so strange to want to know what the world that nearly put a bullet into my brain looks like?'

'It looks like this. We've seen it. Let's go.'

'Can't, Karen. The car, remember. We're here till tomorrow midday at least.'

'It simply doesn't make sense to me . . . the way you charge along without thinking.'

'What should I be thinking?'

'That's it's none of your business,' she said. 'That's what.'

'Maybe you're right. I'm a mug. Always have been. But, at my age, it's too late to change.'

'If they'd killed you? Where would that leave me, Ess?'

'Rich and eligible, my love.'

But by then we were almost there, dispute unresolved.

A notice 'WOOLABAR' hung askew from the once-grand entrance—once a hell of a long time ago. The gates of white wooden pickets were tilted back and jammed in dried-out weeds. A car had been using the drive regularly. Must have been the jam man, Winikie—that's what Shirley had said his name was—Jim Winikie. His wife was Rita. They had a son the same age as the kid who'd watched me eat. They were in the same class at school. Only the boy from the Spun Fleece was taking a day off, pretending he was sick.

There was enough room between scraggy bushes for a car to make its way up the drive. We were not so far above the level of the creek which was still flowing despite the 'dry'. The creek explained the tip. They always liked to place a tip so that seepage went into the creek—would have been un-Australian to do otherwise, even sissy. The garden must have got its roots into the water-table. It was a jungle; almost impenetrable.

'Feels like a house of the dead,' Karen observed. Then she shuddered.

'That's the trouble with gardens. You plant them in your prime, keep them in order in your maturity, then they turn on you in old age: take their revenge.'

Rabbits had moved in. Even then, in the middle of the day, they were hopping about. Maybe because in that place there was a perpetual feeling of dusk.

A long walk in. Finally we rounded a bend and there it was— a nineteenth-century building with full-length shutters hanging open at a variety of angles, revealing the four symmetrically-placed tall windows it had once been their job to shield. Smack in the middle there was a door complete with fanlight. The door was open. Steps led from what would have been a smart gravel drive up to a verandah which ran the entire width of the house and returned on both sides. Above the rolled iron of the verandah roof there was a pediment with flaking paint obscuring rusted roofing iron.

Whoever used the drive followed it around and past the house to where it penetrated further into the jungle.

We stepped gingerly over the verandah's boards and entered. Inside was a total wreck—destroyed by the local lads was my first thought. Even a lot of the plaster had fallen away from the laths and in every room floorboards had been lifted. Considering the time the house had been unoccupied the destruction was excessive. It was more like the work of years. I reckoned that the locals must have had the demolition gene mutating something dreadful. Here and there genitals had been scrawled on surfaces still substantial enough to support the image.

'Gets worse and worse, Millbourne,' Karen was eyeing dried and all too obviously human faeces in a corner.

'You're not wrong, this is the pits,' I said. 'Somebody's been through this place . . . looks like with a purpose. See, they went under the floor in every room.' There had been a system in the lifting of the boards. Could be they, whoever 'they' were, had been searching out a disused cellar.

'Creepy . . . I'm going outside.'

'Fine, just give us a few minutes to look around, poke about a bit, Blue.'

'I don't know what's got into you, Ess,' Karen threw over

her shoulder as she picked her way over the floor. 'Still, it's your life.'

There was a cellar—empty as far as I could make out from the top of the steps, empty except for a foot or so of water. Must have sprung a leak or the water level lifted with all the tree clearing in the region.

Everything I saw in that house confirmed my idea that it had been subjected to a thorough going over by people with a purpose. Then there had been a veneer of graffiti laid over the top. There was every sign that the place had become the local Saturday-night bouncy-bouncy barn. And even a couple of syringes littering the floor—sign that Millbourne was not going to be left behind, not for anything.

When I emerged into the chill of the afternoon, the sun by then too far behind cloud to save the situation, Karen was chatting up a desiccated young-old woman dressed in calf-length, hand-stitched sheepskin boots, jeans and layers of knitted things out of the sweat shops of Bolivia. She sported a balaclava which I wouldn't have thought could have been anything other than a creation of her own genius. It was maroon. Her skin was the colour of weather-aged butcher's paper and the blue eyes seemed pale, washed out, even a fraction glazed.

'Essington, this is Rita.'

'Pleased to meet you, Rita.'

'Rita wants to know if we'd like a cup of tea.' Karen was not without compassion or she wouldn't have passed on the invitation. She would have refused point-blank. You would have to be a locked-up bastard for Rita not to strike some chord in you. She just looked so sad.

'We'd love a cup of tea. You sure it's no trouble, Rita?'

'No trouble.'

'And, you live here?' I asked.

'She lives further along, down the back of the block.'

'Do you, Rita? It's a nice place,' I lied.

'Used to be,' she replied. 'When the old lady lived here.'

'Old lady?' There was no reason why I should know anything. 'We chanced on it. Must have been a grand house once. Quite a garden too. We just happened along, didn't we, Karen?'

'That's what I was telling Rita. How the car got hit and we've got all this time to kill.'

'There isn't so much you can do around here, Rita,' I added. 'Not if you're a day-tripper.'

'Not too much really.' Rita looked apologetic, as though it was her fault that Millbourne was such a dump.

Karen adopted a midly sarcastic tone: 'But in the country you make your own fun, don't you, Essington.'

Rita beamed at me awaiting confirmation of that dubious truth. Like it had to be true.

'She hates the bush,' I explained. 'Yet it's true, isn't it; you make your own fun. You wouldn't understand, Blue.'

'Blue?' Rita pricked her ears.

'It's a—how should I say—a nick name.'

Her face set serious: 'Mine's Mixi.'

'That's nice, Mixi . . . why's that?' I asked.

'Calls me that because I'm always sick. It's after the rabbit disease . . . what's it called again?'

I couldn't bring myself to say it. So I said: 'I think they get enteritis. Doesn't sound like that though does it?'

The old shearers' quarters weren't too bad really—little brick huts without eaves. There were four set as a group leaving a square between them in the middle. It looked a very early set-up going back to when the water-table would have been quite a bit lower. Each hut had a door and two windows—they hadn't intended on spoiling the working class. The Winikies were spread out between the four, living in two, a pottery in one and the jam-bottling going on in the other. There was a bush pole and iron lean-to outhouse walled with a half-hearted attempt at concrete block work—the ablution centre. A rugged existence for the late twentieth century I would have thought, though there were a hell of a lot of human beings doing worse.

The jam tins were stacked a little way off. A pile of them, just as Feathers had said—the big tins they use for hospitals and for the army. They were rusting down pretty quickly. Must have made a terrific multi-storey block for rats and snakes.

Mr Winikie wasn't home. Nor was the car.

We were led into a kitchen which Rita kept spick and span despite the odds. She poked the wood fire in the stove then popped out to fill the kettle from somewhere. Maybe Mill-bourne had town water. Often places do.

There were candles and lamps scattered around; no telly—one of the advantages of the hard life: there was no electricity hook-up.

'Make youselves comfortable, why don't you?'

We did. There were lots of old pieces of furniture. Some quite good. Surprising really in such a depressed environ-ment—had they been bounty from the house? Still, someone should have been proud of Rita, it took a kind of courage to go out and live like that. For women particularly. They bore the children, did the work, worried while the men played at life.

'Your friend? Does he work in town?'

'Just outside.'

'Doing what then?' I asked.

'At the abattoir.'

'So you do the pottery?' Karen was turning a clumsy piece, dripping honey-brown glaze, between her fingers.

'No, that's Jim. He does that too. Learnt it at Tech, took classes. He's a slaughterman by trade.'

'Handy, the abattoir, then.'

'It was. Then they closed it down. The Council's just reopened it. Take milk, do you? It's powdered.'

I asked for black.

'Me too,' said Karen, looking with apprehension at the stained cups.

'Not that he likes it . . . hates it in fact. I hate him having to do it. Puts him in such a mood. Like, tantrums too. Me, I'm vegetarian.'

'A great way to be,' said Karen without enthusiasm. I guess she was just filling in; my attention had been attracted by a row of drawings pinned to the wall. Different studies of a woman—she could almost have been Indian—reclining against cushions and an ornate cloth. She was holding a fan. She wore a necklace of big beads and a pair of slippers. There were just little changes from drawing to drawing.

'They reckon it's going to close down again,' Rita said.

'The abattoir?' I asked.

'Now you see it, now you don't.'

'Tough on you,' said Karen, trying to look sympathetic.

'I guess you could say that. But it depresses him . . . the blood and all.'

'You do drawing?' Essington sounding as casual as possible.

'Me? No. Oh, those . . .' she giggled.

'They're of you then, I'll bet.'

'Not of me, they're not. I don't look like that.' She laughed high and shrill in the way I sometimes think only a truly Australian woman can. Her pale cheeks flushed red.

We just sort of sat there, sipping. There were no biscuits. 'He'll be back in a jiffy, Jim will. It's a quota system. He'd be through by now. Fast, Jim is.'

I took another cup of tea. Karen didn't. Rita leapt up; there were biscuits, after all. I accepted a limp one—an Anzac cookie—out of a tin with the paint worn off: a picture of a Highlander in full regalia. We chatted about the weather, about the bush, about the vegetable patch, how to make compost. Rita used to be a psychiatric nurse. She talked a lot about the kid; he was called Nathaniel. He found it lonely out there; there weren't any other kids to play with.

'He could walk in, it's not so far to town,' Karen observed.

Rita shook her head: 'I wouldn't like that, not wandering about on his own, there's some bad types around the district. No, I wouldn't like that.'

A car pulled up. In came Jim. Little and wiry, his face prematurely creased up with the tensions of life. Jim wasn't getting a hell of a lot of spiritual nutrition out of the natural world. Who would, working in a killing house?

At the start he just muttered, not able to bring himself to meet our eyes. Maybe he was ashamed. No need. Before I went to France I'd lived in a lot less than the Winikie set-up, only I'd had electricity.

Once served his cup of tea he turned and asked, almost aggressively: 'So, what's up then?' He stirred in four spoons of sugar.

'They just happened to be looking down at Woolabar.'

'Nice house once,' I said.

'Yep.' That was all he said, just 'yep'.

'Nice joint you've got here.'

'Suits us.' Taciturn.

'I was just saying to Rita here . . . somebody drove into our car. So, we're stuck here, see.'

'It was you, was it?' he asked.

Rita, all anxious: 'How'd you know, Jimmy?'

'Barney . . . pissed, I'll bet. Jesus!' he said to me. 'He's dark on you, but.'

'His fault. I was in bed.'

'Small difference to Barney.'

'Anyway,' I said, 'gives us a chance to look about. Good for my business.'

'What would that be, then?'

'Oh, not so much. I buy a bit of stuff. You know, maybe an old fireplace or a jug or something. Then I sell them, if I find a buyer.'

'Antiques,' Rita prompted.

'Sort of antiques, or a bit of art and things.'

'So, how about these?' Jim asked. And he was pointing at the drawings of the reclining woman. I'd hooked him. 'Only they'd cost you.'

Rita said, 'He was just looking at them, Jim.'

'I was,' I said.

Karen sighed: 'I feel like a cigarette.'

'But you don't smoke anymore.'

'Yes, I do . . . from now on.'

'I've got a rollie, but we're out of paper.' Jim laughed. He thought it was funny being out of papers. Must have been rolling joints; they used them up, joints.

'Doesn't matter,' Karen said.

I got back to the pictures. 'I like them; they look good to me. Who did them?'

'Some geezer.' Jim walked up to take a close look. 'Dufy . . . D—U—F—Y, it is.' He threw his arms out like he was in a bazaar. 'Wouldn't know.'

'Where did you get them?'

'He . . .' Rita started. But Jim beat her to it.

'Just sort of came by them.' He ruled the roost, Jim did.

'They'd cost you,' he reiterated.

'How much do you reckon?' I asked.

'Have to be a hundred apiece. Real art. Don't look much

. . . just lines and that, only Dufy's a big name; really big in the US.'

'Never heard of him, Duffy!' I turned to Karen.

'Nup,' she said. 'It's not Duffy, he said Dufy. And it's not Dali. There's Dali . . . you don't mean Dali.'

'Duffy, this is Duffy,' Rita dared to stick her oar in again.

'Dufy,' said Jim.

'There aren't even frames,' I objected. 'Tell you what, I'll take your word on Dufy, on him being big. How about three hundred the lot.'

Rita's eyes dilated.

'Five hundred,' he said. 'A hundred each.' Jim had his tough streak. He liked the world to know it.

'What do you think, Blue? Karen's the brains,' I explained.

'We've only got four hundred, Essington. And the car's bust.'

'OK. Make it the four hundred,' Jim said. 'On account of no frames.'

'Agreed . . . you strike a tough deal, Jim.'

Rita dropped a plate.

Chapter 12

It was an even greyer late afternoon. The two of us were cold as we crossed the bridge—me with the drawings rolled under my arm.

'Not a word to Gerald Sparrow,' Karen thought out loud.

'Not a word,' I said. 'This evens things up a bit. Jim, he must have pinched them. The old lady would have chatted on about her art—them being sensitives, potting jam and all—and after they found her dead, he nicked them.'

'Didn't know what to do next. Essington, they went for the money!'

I needed a drink to warm my bones. The bullet scarred head was up to it; I figured if it could take twenty-seven hours in a plane, it could take anything.

Back at the Duke of Wellington I ordered a brandy. Karen ordered soda water.

'Why'd you suddenly want a cigarette?'

'Can't say. When I first left home, went to Sydney, I rented the worst little room you ever saw. In Darlinghurst. I think everybody else in the block was on smack or a pro or both. Always pimps and hoods hanging about. After a while I wouldn't go out. Just sat on my bed, smoked. It was something to do, to smoke. A way of joining in the dying game everybody out there seemed to be playing. Rita made me feel the same. Her stuck in those sheds. Looking at her my brain suddenly filled with cigarettes: I wanted to smell the smoke.'

Barney came through the door. He went to the bar. The proprietor nodded in my direction, drew him a beer then came round the bar to me for a chat.

'Evening, Squire.' He had 'Squired' me when I ordered the brandy too. 'I took the lad down to the shop, like I said, had a chat with the police. All straightened out. All smooth.'

'Thanks a lot,' I said. Karen was holding the drawings.

'Artist, are you love?'

'Picasso,' she replied, scowling.

Barney drank four more beers quick. It crossed my mind he was priming himself. We got up to leave. The proprietor signalled to Barney with his eyes—they might have been in love, only it wasn't love eye-talk. Barney swung around.

'It's the bastard who can't park a car.'

It was early yet. Not many people in the narrow bar. It would fill up later on. I ignored Barney. We headed straight out. At least we tried to. He grabbed me by the shoulder at the door.

'Not so fast. I've got something to say to you about parking.'

I let him hold me. 'Ring the police, Karen.'

She fronted the bar, tongue-lashed the proprietor till he picked up the phone. But reluctant. That's how it seemed to me.

Barney was giving me hell. Holding my shirt collar together a little too tight so he cut off most of my air intake. I was on the receiving end of a cross between a talking-to and a philosophic lecture on the nature of existence if you happen to be called Barney. It could have been the beret he hated most. I should have taken it off, showed him the bullet wound. They respected bullet wounds out in the bush. Should have told him I was a digger just returned from some war—they worship war, Australians; say Gallipoli and they go dreamy-eyed.

I calculated that their Sergeant Armstrong would take as long as possible to get up to the pub. Your country cop, he likes to get there after the action's over. Karen was looking like she wasn't certain what to do next but she was going to do something. I looked Barney straight in the eye and was going to say I had a brain tumour to scare him off—they don't like bad health, they think it's catching—only just then he jerked his fist, the one holding my shirt. The blow caught me on the tip of the chin, knocking my teeth together. Abandoning avoidance I drove a fist into his stomach, followed with a left to the side of the head, then kneed him in the gonads. As he doubled over howling like a bear caught in a trap, I kicked him in the face. Very clean. He just hit the floor and lay out flat.

I turned on the proprietor, snarling: 'You always encourage people to beat up customers?'

'It's all right, Mac.' Placating me. 'Calm down . . . I didn't do nothing, say nothing . . .'

'Oh yes you did,' said Karen.

'By the time I've finished with you, you won't have a fucking licence,' I said. 'And I'm not even agitated.'

Good timing: in came Sergeant Armstrong. With us watching, the proprietor told it just the way it was. Then the sergeant tried to do something about Barney.

Big-hearted me said I wouldn't press charges against the slaughterman. All I wanted was to avoid him till I could get out of town, till I could get a replacement for the car that had been put off the road.

Armstrong said he would lock Barney up. Seemed as though it was a regular event.

It was the publican Karen wanted to get.

'Forget him, Blue. I guess Millbourne just isn't our town.' I had no intention of going back there even though, as fate and my own madness had it, I did. But not till a lot of water had passed under the bridge. Even under the Millbourne bridge. It rained for a month after we left. We were the rain gods come out of the east, come to wash their sins away. Could that be done?

One thing about the visit, we were in front money-wise. In front by miles. The Dufy drawings, if my memory served me right, dated around 1928–29—the period of his paintings, *The Hindu Model in the Studio at Le Havre*. It was not long after that the quality really started to fall off. A funny thing, getting to know an artist's work—any detailed study of the whole *œuvre* makes the viewer much more appreciative. The five drawings were superb. So good I started to wonder anew how Oula Strossmayer came by the Dufys. Let alone Jim and Rita.

When we got to talking about the house, Rita, lamenting the destruction, had told about how these men had come and gone over the place. How they'd seemed ready to take it pieces. Jimmy had been out. (He was giving Rita hard looks while she told her story—most likely trying to get her to shut up.) She'd watched from the cover of the overgrown garden, frightened they'd start in on the shearers' quarters next. 'Seemed like they'd been looking for something; desperate they were,' she said.

'What would that have been?' Karen asked.

Jim rushed in at that point with a whole mouthful of words—words about other things, changing the subject.

Luckily the car came at nine am. By fifteen minutes after that it was goodbye Millbourne—the blood and bone capital of itself. How it ever won 'Tidy Town', or wanted to for that matter, I'd never know. It must have been before the tin rocking-horse fell over or before iron sheeting started to fall off the abattoir.

As we sped along Karen said, 'You really can do that stuff, can't you, Essington. You're good at it.'

I was thinking of my Dufy drawings. 'Good at what?'

'With Barney.'

'Got to be good at something, I suppose.'

'I always hated violence. Dad, he was violent. Kept Mum and me terrorized.'

'Sorry . . . I tried to do nothing. You saw, I just hung there at the end of his arm.'

'Don't be sorry, Ess. He was an arsehole . . . the whole lot of them . . . playing get-the-odd-man-out.'

'A national game.'

'No, Essington, that was clean; one minute he was up, then he was down—like magic.'

'Magic?'

'Somewhere between magic and surgery.'

Then the first drops of drought-breaking rain hit the windscreen.

In Sydney we moved out of the Regent and back into my old stamping ground, Chippendale. Into Friars' Mews which looked out over heavy traffic to the park beside Sydney University. A new building in a style best described as red-brick-post-modern, serviced apartments intended for short-term visitors. We set up temporary house. I guess, with my means, it was a strange choice of accommodation; but one way or another I felt inhibited about living in that city I knew too well in a fashion that was dramatically different from that of the old poor Essington. Seriously, I couldn't shift into Bellevue Hill or Vaucluse. Maybe I could ease myself across town a little bit at a time. But to make it in one leap . . . you would have to be some kind of retard to let yourself get away with it.

The apartments were all right. There were fruit bats, thousands of them, in the Moreton Bay figs over the road. It was comforting for me to hear them scream at dusk. Next to man there was a theory that they were Australia's most evolved creatures—thus the scream.

We arranged for Karen's mother to come down the following week and stay in the apartment next door. If she could shake off her worst half. And I went into Richards and Partners to take a look at the Dufy hanging there, confounding Feathers' judgement that the artist's work was trite. Karen wouldn't come.

'The head, Essington . . . how is it?'

I still featured the beret. I was hoping I didn't become attached to it. Clothes are a habit—I was starting to notice when it wasn't on. I don't like berets. They seem to shorten the top half of your head.

'Just a scar, doesn't look too good.'

'Terrible, simply terrible.'

'We know who we can blame for it.'

It was a new office. Celebration of Feathers' elevation to senior partner.

'Isn't it a splendid view?' Rubbing his hands, smug. 'Who needs art when you have Sydney?'

He was high up. I didn't count the floors, concentrating instead on my stomach as I shot up the gleaming glass-and-aluminium tower. Fast track—give it thirty years and they'd knock it down again with an explosives charge. Down below, under our noses, the wave forms of the Opera House and beyond, the wealthy unemployed boating on blue water right out to the Heads. And you could see the smog, a smear of red-grey hanging over everything—over the 'coat-hanger', the Harbour Bridge.

'Watch out it doesn't get to you. Think you're an angel, try to fly.'

'Never an angel, Essington.'

'A sparrow then?'

A phone rang somewhere among the papers strewn across his desk. He found it, answered, then gestured for me to look at the painting. Time up there in the sky was money—two hundred and fifty dollars an hour.

The Dufy was a complex picture. There had been drawings, right up to 1914, demonstrating the wrestle between natural inclination and the artist's desire to show himself to be made of the stern stuff of the true avant-garde. Dufy's thought process was clearer, much more evident on the canvas than in the photos of the painting Feathers had shown me in France. Images constructed over images—the low ridges of lost edges showing through overpainting, telling the story of the building of the picture and of the way he'd slip into decoration and then pull back, stridently drawing a hard angle over the top. It was as much a document as a painting. An important statement in the history of twentieth-century art. As a picture, Dufy had resolved it. It hung together despite the battle, maybe because of it. Like Picasso's *Demoiselles d'Avignon* of five years earlier.

'Well?'

'Terrific.'

'Essington, that's what I think. It's grown on me. Quite a surprise, really.

'Mind if I take it down, examine it?'

'Dr Holt . . . feel free. Only thing is, I've got to leave you. Sorry, old son. No way out of it.' He was gathering things together, papers, manila folders. 'How about dinner? Tell you what, ring me.'

I sensed, behind his Sparrow exterior, he felt guilty, even embarrassed. Could be that was why he had pissed off to Geneva. Was there sensitivity underneath the legal skin? I had a memory of him sheepish at my hospital bed, behind Karen. Since then he'd avoided contact. Maybe fallen into the trap of divided loyalties.

So I said, 'An ASIO meeting? In a cellar? False noses?'

Which gave him the opportunity to put on a stiff face. He marched to the door with a 'Miss Bassano will look after you if you need anything.'

'Need anything! I'm a grown man.' But I said that to the door's stained wooden panels.

I was working on the back of the picture, had it face down. There was plywood screwed across the frame. Sometimes they put it there as protection. That ply had been in place a long time. Nothing was written on it anywhere; I hadn't expected anything in particular. Not if the displaced-person theory worked: Oula Strossmayer carting the canvas about under her arm, probably rolled, or inside a roll of newspaper so nobody would suspect an art treasure. Would Dufy have been considered a treasure in those days? Maybe yes—Derain was certainly famous and rich and mad on his motor cars. A Dufy would have been useful currency.

I ventured out for a chat with Miss Bassano.

Richards and Partners were pretty smart in their high-rise gleaming in the Sydney sun, computers humming, storing, thinking, but could they lay hands on a medium-sized screwdriver or a tack hammer—any hammer?

Miss Bassano's appearance emphasized efficiency. So, she was really put out to find that she couldn't provide the goods. Miss Bassano called a Mr Zabo who wore a dust coat. She thought a dust coat meant tools? But Mr Zabo fiddled about with photostat machines and things and certainly didn't have a screwdriver for me to use as a lever or to hit with a hammer. Mr Zabo had a disapproving mouth. He looked like he listened in the evenings to the sound of one synthesizer clapping.

The cleaning staff might have helped only there wasn't a cleaning staff—they worked on contract, came in at night. I'd done that sort of work myself, used a false name; saved on tax and you could nick stuff as long as you were careful—not too much at a time. The driven, up in their city towers, were wasteful of shareholders' funds, didn't mind losing things. It was a new charity system.

Miss Fong, who was so beautiful I think even Miss Bassano noticed, was summoned from the next floor where, I guess, she must have been part of a pool of people who did whatever typing is called now microchips have rearranged the world.

Where, Miss Bassano asked, would Miss Fong find a hammer and a screwdriver? Well, offered this glimpse of an older reality, Miss Fong positively went up on the balls of her feet with invention. She asked Mr Spangler who was an associate or something—he had parking rights—and who, she assured me, was a very nice man, which probably meant that Mr Spangler lay awake at nights slowly removing articles of Miss Fong's clothing in his mind. He replied, over the telephone, that if she just popped up to his office he would give her the keys to his car which Miss Fong assured me was an old Jaguar—it was his hobby, she said.

About half an hour later a triumphant Miss Fong brought the tools to where I sat in Sparrow's office watching miniaturized boats move a million metres below.

She had a mechanical bent. I had Miss Fong all to myself. She actually knelt beside me holding the painting while we tapped and twisted, removing the backing board oh so gently.

There were screws to shift and panel pins—quite a number. Between us we extracted them all. She must have done a carpentry elective at school—she led, I followed. It was nice kneeling, sometimes touching heads. My beret fell off and she became motherly in response to the wound. But we left it at that. I figured Mr Spangler and her keyboard were as much as Miss Fong could handle and I got a fringe feeling that she had me calculated as a beat-up old bum: not associate material.

When we got off the backing board, what we found was an oil-cloth bundle stitched up and wound over with surgical sticking tape. We also discovered the dust of the ages and lots of examples of the substandard living conditions of our minute and distant cousins in the insect world.

Eureka! I had something. The next thing was to offload the beautiful Miss Fong. She was keen to hang around as long as possible—crawling around the floor was a lot more interesting than whatever it was they had her doing down below. It breaks my heart to think of the millions of our species' flowers who tap at keys all day so that information can disappear into the black hole of computer storage.

I said I felt like a cup of coffee but unfortunately Miss Fong was back, styrene cup in each hand, before I could get the ply into position pretending I'd replaced the parcel, let alone shove it into hiding down my shirt front.

We drank our coffees while I planned a go at the open

method of deceit. I put the package to one side, asked Miss Fong if there was something to wrap it up in, and then, happy together, we replaced the backing so that it looked like it had never been removed.

'Thank you Miss Fong,' I said. And thanks to Miss Bassano too—even Mr Zabo . . . Mr Spangler *in absentia*. Bowing, scraping, smiling, package in hand, I plummeted to earth in the lift.

Back in Chippendale I opened the packet at a photocopy place on Broadway, took a print of the contents—there was a lot of stuff—bundled it up again and headed for my favourite café, Chez Catz.

'*Alors*, Charles Aznavour itself!' Peter recognized me straight off.

'Jesus, Ess . . . what's with the beret? Don't tell me they graft them on after you've been there a year?' Patrick and Peter had escaped from 'the media' when it got too anti-thought. Chez Catz was supposed to be for the upwardly mobile but, creatures of a semi-extinct Left, they kept on doling out free meals and that brought the tone down. The New People of the age believed poverty and failure to be like VD—catching. They gave Chez Catz a wide berth.

In fairness to those who withheld patronage there were a lot of marginal types at Peter and Patrick's. Square old Essington had had to bite back hard on a few occasions.

On that sunny day, however, there were only the owners and a grey-faced young couple who looked like they might have treated themselves to the odd hit of smack—they had that skinny God-fuck-it look. Truth be known it was probably the Mr Spanglers and the Sparrows of this world who wrote the contract for the importers.

Peter clasped his hands together: 'It's *escargots*!'

'And you haven't got them?'

'How'd you guess?'

'Steak and eggs.'

'Not that either,' laughed Patrick. 'We're in the middle—Dantons, if you like.'

'What's a Danton?' I asked.

'More like an omelette.'

'It's in the middle—Danton in the French Revolution . . . piss weak,' Peter explained.

'Like the filling of an omelette,' said Patrick.

'An omelette's the last thing I ate here . . . remember? You didn't charge.'

'The only customer to chalk up a meal and make good, Essington.'

'*Malheureusement*,' added Peter.

'What's a *malheureusement*?'

'Don't come that with us, Ess. We've heard. You're word perfect. Next step, the Comédie-Française.'

'Sparrow would say that's a contradiction in terms,' I said.

'We haven't seen so much of Feathers since his elevation in the world.' Peter still did a bit of free-lance; he kept up with things. Patrick was right out of it. Lived for his low state-of-the-art cooking.

'Omelette coming up.'

The grey couple stared at one another like Cézanne's card players. Only she had a half-grown-out mohawk, the crest of which was collapsing as though she was a chook with Marek's disease. No gel. I gave her a big smile. She glared back with something like contempt for anyone who made it through to my age. Made me feel like a coward.

'Peter . . . tell me about Father Down.' I thought I might as well go hard at it. Karen was off to Canberra the next morning to see a man who was a trade intermediary for the China silk printing. Funny coincidence, the designs she was taking along were all based on those made by Dufy for Bianchini-Ferier between 1912 and 1930—the great years of Modernism, before the cards all fell over. We had done a lot of work with them, Karen concentrating on colour, me trying out any drawing required. Most of it was based on paper cut-out, colour blobs, cutting abstract designs up and sticking them down again. Playschool.

'Who doesn't know Father Down? For Christ's sake, Ess, you're only taking the neighbourhood saint's name in vain.'

'You heard of Father Down?' I asked the girl with the falling crest.

She snarled. If it made her happy, why not? Maybe she

aimed to become the saint of snarling. You used to get canonized just for sitting on top of a post all your life, taking in the view. So why not snarling? That took real talent.

'He comes in here?'

'*De temps en temps*.' Patrick had heaps of French.

'Why, Ess? Thinking of taking vows?'

'Nup. Just heard his name. Figured he had to be really doing something.'

'Like I said . . . we're talking about a saint.'

Back in Friars' Mews to examine the documents: the secrets of Oula Strossmayer's life, some of them at least. There was a bundle of what looked like family photographs which came out in the photostats as grey smudges. I spread the originals around the room, propped against the furniture, so I could absorb anything they had to say. Karen would have understood more about the images than I could. She had lived her life between two cultures, her ideas were less set.

In one photo a little girl stood dressed in a pale double-breasted button-up overcoat. She was holding the hand of a man wearing a Homburg hat. Behind them was a large sporting car, hood down. Something out of the 1920s—endless bonnet, a long line of cylinders underneath.

The same girl, only bigger, clasped flowers to her breast. She had short cut hair. Her dress was what you might wear to a first dance. She was smiling. She was dark, big dark eyes, a strong nose: dark and beautiful. But for the white skin she could, at a stretch of the imagination, have been Dufy's Hindu model.

In another photo the same girl was standing beneath one of the statues on the Pont Alexandre III that crosses the Seine from des Invalides to the Grand and the Petit Palais. There were two baby photos. One old, in sepia—a mother holding a child all wrapped up in its best blankets. The other, a lot later by the look of it, just a baby in a cot. That one had been taken from above.

There were a number of other photos of men in Homburg hats; men in heavy top-coats; men holding silver-topped canes at an oblique angle across their bodies. I thought that they could all be of the same man. One in a military uniform had to be the same man who had posed with the girl in front of the car. The same man but older.

I went through the photos again putting them into a sort of chronological order. My fantasies were interrupted by the phone.

'Essington.'

'Gerald.' I couldn't call a voice as stiff as that 'Feathers'.

'You betrayed my trust.'

'Betrayed your . . . what was that?'

'No games, Essington. We have known each other too long. I have Miss Bassano and Miss Fong in my office.'

'Lucky you.'

'They say you took the back off the picture . . . removed property.'

I thought for a moment. 'Feathers, I did. I cannot tell a lie. I took the padding out. It could have rotted the canvas.'

'Padding! Miss Fong said it was a parcel.'

'It was. A parcel of padding. God knows why . . . I've never seen anything like it before.'

'You opened the parcel?'

'No need to. Wadding. I could feel it. You take a look at the canvas . . . it's a fraction loose now. See.'

He asked me to hold on. He was no fool and didn't want to be. It was me, I was the fool. Always had been. That was the relationship.

'Yes, I see the slack.'

'OK take the back off. Miss Fong's good at it. See for yourself. There are no wedges; it's a fixed stretcher. So, I guess they stuffed some—maybe it's cotton waste or something—in the back to hold the canvas tight.'

'Miss Fong says it was like a parcel.'

'Is this some fucking round song? Tell you what, you can come over and see for yourself. I brought it with me. Thought I could find out who framed the thing . . . something about its history. I haven't taken a look yet; no time.'

'How can you be so sure?' I hadn't convinced him, he still sounded testy.

'Sure of what?'

'Wadding.'

'The feel, Feathers, from the feel. Tell you what, I'll open it right away. I find something, I'll let you know. Ring you right back.'

'Most irregular. I do wish you hadn't done that.'

'Don't start telling me what you wish I hadn't done. Last time you did something I nearly got killed.' Go up his nose, that's what I thought. Put him off the scent. 'And you would have been . . . killed, that is. Are you listening, Feathers? If it wasn't for yours truly. Now they're trying to kill me . . . confused identity.'

'Keep your shirt on. All right, Essington, you'll ring back. Let me know either way.'

'Either way,' I confirmed.

I'd got that far. Still it meant I'd need a lot of old cotton waste quick smart. Feathers liked to keep things neat and tidy—he was an ASIO man, looking after us all.

On the backs of some of the photos there were words scrawled in pencil, and there was a pencil list of names among the documents. All the pencil was worn thin, just legible. The list of names hadn't come out as a photostat. The stuff on the backs of the photos was either just scribbles without meaning or it was . . . it was hard to say.

Arranged in order I guess I could have been looking at a baby photo of Oula. Then she's standing with the man—with her father? There wasn't that kind of grinning playful affection you would expect if he had been a family friend or an uncle. The man in the photos was there as an act of duty. Where they were in front of the car there was a scribble on the back. If you wished hard enough you could believe the first letter to be an 's' . . . Strossmayer? Or maybe a 'p' for Papa. Papa was a lot shorter. The word read somewhere between the two, if it was a word. Papa is pretty universal—not like Dad.

The man had a big moustache drooping down over the corners of his mouth. He was young, the moustache was black. He could have been the villain of a silent movie.

I tried to make the sepia baby become the girl with the man, who was without doubt also the girl on the Paris bridge. Gradually, one of the other men became more and more positively the man with the girl, only older. There was a scribble on the back of that one too. Several words. If they were words. One had an 's' or a 'p' at the start. Maybe the rest of the scribble looked the same as that on the other photo.

I put these two images together with the man in uniform. Definitely the same. The moustache grey-white by now. The uniform Germanic I would have thought. What uniforms weren't . . . from that era anyway?

Among the papers, apart from the list, there were a lot of documents, some newspaper cuttings and a couple of bundles of letters. None of these made any sense to me. They must have been in Yugoslav . . . if that was a language. I checked these papers against the photostats . . . pretty good, all readable with the exception of the pencil list, the original of which seemed to be in some other language, more like Russian.

Then I set to work on the reconstruction of the package. Only I'd need some plausible stuffing, a needle, thread.

Where to find?

Chapter 13

I wondered: Was the baby in the cot a son? The son who was claiming against the will? Maybe I should have been going to Canberra with Karen—talking to the Yugoslav lawyers; to Has and Danilović.

I rang Gerald Sparrow.

'Cotton waste, I was right.'

'Humph.'

'But in the middle, letters and things . . . sorry about that.'

'It pays to leave well alone. That's property of the estate of Oula Strossmayer.'

So were the five drawings and they were staying with me. Bugger Feathers' law. Five drawings for my trouble, for the creased skull.

'I'll hold them,' I said.

'I'll send a cab.'

'As you like, Feathers.' I gave him the address. 'It's taxpayer's money, ASIO.' No bite. 'Do you want the cotton waste?'

'No, Essington, you can keep that.'

'Posthumous gift. One thing, Feathers . . . and I really am sorry I took that stuff . . . I'd never have thought.'

'She must have wanted them hidden. Might contain valuable information.' Little boy's spy games.

'Feathers . . . what was the address of that couple?'

'Couple?'

'The ones who had the picture, remember? They were interested in Oula Strossmayer . . . in her story.'

'Them! Doubt they'd know anything.'

'Have you got it?'

He gave it to me, reluctantly. And a phone number.

'I forgot how beautiful it is, Essington; how exciting. It's reality. The people are real.' Karen slumped down on the wool tweed sofa. The whole apartment was a tribute to the sheep's fleece and the colour brown. There in all their variety.

'Christ! Ess, when I think of that Riviera afternoon parade . . . the fur coats . . . those terrible stockings that make women look like they have spiders walking up their legs. Here in Sydney I always thought, as a woman, I got a bad deal. It's probably true. But don't let anyone kid you we're better off in France. To be out of fashion . . . even the way you look, like your genes . . . you'd be better dead.

'How's that for an ideological tirade?'

'Not bad, but you're not the ideological type. Aren't you going to ask what I did today?'

'Did you ask about me?'

'No need,' I said. 'I know. You did potted sociology.'

'And the rest.'

Karen had been to Dawn's old co-operative, checking out their silk printing. 'It was good, surprising. Fifteen dollars a metre. A lot against the Chinese but we could give it a go. More say about the finished article and they prefer short runs. We can experiment.

'So, what did you do that's so important, Superman?'

'I crawled about the floor with a beautiful woman.'

'Shame. Who was she?'

'Miss Fong.'

'Velly nice . . . it go crosswise?'

'Karen!'

'You'd better get used to crawling about the floor anyway. I saw the doctor. You're going to be a dad.'

'Me! I don't believe it. My sperm still swim?'

'Some did.'

'Wowee!'

'And Miss Fong?'

'No . . . I don't think she's going to have a baby.'

'That would be too much. Mr Fertility 1987.'

I walked over, knelt before her. We kissed.

'This carpet crawling . . . a new thing with you, Ess?'

'Used to do it when I was little.'

'You saw Miss Fong and it all came back?'

'Miss who?'

*

123

When I'd finished describing my day Karen said: 'Brick.' Only it was spelt BRKIC. 'That's who you want. He was really sweet to me when I first hit Sydney. A Serbian.'

'I thought you said you lived in a den of hookers.'

'Brkic owned the den. He came round one day—owner's inspection. It was in the hands of an agent; that's how I got the room. So, he saw me. Must have known the set-up with the prostitution. Asked what I was doing there. This old man, like a bear he was . . . wearing a beret just like yours, Essington. Only more chic.'

'Me?'

'Brkic. I hardly answered, too shy. I was confused by the big city. Anyway, he let me a room in another house he had over in Paddington. A balcony, I could see the water. Brkic let me have it for the same money. Then he lined me up a job—washing-up in a Serbian club in the city. Really nice it was. Paid cash—no tax—and a good meal every night, more than I could eat. Just little old me and a lot of men playing chess or cards.

'He put me on my feet, Brkic. Said I was a second daughter. He'd go all solemn when he said that. I never dared to ask what happened to the first.'

'So, where is he?'

'In the phone book, I expect. Here, give me a look.'

'Careful . . . the baby.'

'Come on, Ess, it'd be the size of a broad bean by now.'

We found Brkic. He was in Surry Hills where Karen said he'd always lived. We would meet at the Serbian Club, at six-thirty.

While on a good thing I rang the Griffins, the couple who had picture-sat the Dufy. No answer from Tom and Jane. Tom and Jane Griffin—with names like that they should have been compèring *Kindergarten of the Air*. Maybe they were out chasing money for some film project or other. That's what film-makers mostly do—hunt money. Suffer from grant addiction.

I drank the firewater, it tasted like jet fuel. Rajko Brkic smoked cigarettes and carefully read through the photostats, one after the other.

I'd kept the pencilled list with the photostats. That was for myself, when I split the material to send to Feathers.

Occasionally the old Serbian would shake his head, make a little noise at the back of his throat like the last gasp of a dying chainsaw. Cigarette-butts built a mountain in the ash-tray.

There were mirrors around the room except on the side where the shop window was hung with unmatching green floral curtains. The tables were covered with plasticized floral cloth. Geometric-patterned worn lino covered the floor: black, white and pink. A couple of grand old gents looked down upon us from where they were framed behind soot-stained glass. I guessed they were some of the great Serbians out of the past. We were ignored by the groups of men seated at the tables— talking or playing parlour games with a curious intensity. The radio transmitted rock music, softly, incongruously.

Karen stared at Brkic. She must have needed a father when she came down to Sydney. Fleeing the boring little bastard with the clean car up at Catalpa.

A waiter brought coffee and cakes, dumped them on the table. Brkic grunted then read on.

'So,' he said at last and a gnarled hand dropped widespread fingers over the pile of photostats. 'So, you come to see Pappa Brkic, Karen?'

He had seen a lot of Anthony Quinn movies—could be too many. Or he was a natural. 'She was a child . . . a little child when I found her.' He beamed, touched her on the shoulder. 'And look, she's like the sun.' He took her face between his hands, kissed her on the forehead; paternal. 'You have children?'

'Not yet,' I answered.

'We've been in France,' Karen said.

'Ahh! *La Belle France*. No matter what they believe, always on the winning side.'

'Why do you say that?' I asked.

'I say it because it is the truth. Very clever people who cut off a thousand royal heads to crown a king.' He refilled the glasses, skolled—I sipped. 'So,' he said again, then frowned. 'This is a bad story. These things, where did you get them?'

'Essington got them.'

I sort of filled him in. Told him about Oula dying in Millbourne, about guns in Entrevaux.

'A bad story.' He shook his head. 'These things are better left to lie like a sick dog. But they will not stay buried. We say the past is stones in a ploughed field.'

He sorted one of the press cuttings out of the stack, read it through again. 'You know something of these things?'

'Well,' I said, 'I know what everybody knows, I guess. The Ustase, they get a lot of press still—Croats training down on the state border, down near Victoria. A bunch of them were brought to trial I seem to remember, a few years back.'

Brkic nodded. 'This is all in the war, these things. None of it . . . I've never heard of it before. There are lots of stories, each one the same. It concerns a man. There are letters from him to his daughter. He was killed by partisans at the end of the war. It seems so. He was an officer of high rank. Many people were put to death. Always the same story. And then he is killed. He was denounced in the newspapers—the Communists' newspapers. No doubt they'd tell the truth.

'Tito became like a king, himself. The French Revolution again. Always the same story. The Serbians, we are a poor people. We are the losers.

'This man, Strossmayer, it is a name associated with the Croats. Once a progressive name . . . a bishop of that name worked for the federation of our states. But that was a long time ago.'

Brkic called for more firewater.

'Strossmayer, this one here,' tapping the papers with his fingers, 'he made peace with Mihailović. That is a story too.' He looked to Karen for forgiveness.

'Go on,' she urged.

'I make this short. Mihailović, Colonel Mihailović, retreated to southern Serbia, to where I come from, the source of the River Morava. The Germans are advancing. He fought them from this stronghold. His soldiers, they were called Chetniks I think by the British; you have heard of Chetniks? By Winston Churchill . . . he called them that.'

I shook my head—Chetniks were news to me.

'Winston Churchill wanted them to fight more. The Colonel, he had so little to fight with. He could not fight. A brave man,

126

but a brave man has need of his sword. And there was conflict within. Mihailović was a true patriot, he was a great Serbian patriot. He knew it was Croats that had destroyed the Yugoslav army. They made the advance too easy for the Germans. Also, Mahailović hated and feared the Communists—the Partisans. Hated the Communists more than the Germans. He feared them worse.

'He made some peace with the Germans, with the Italians who had made a separate Croatia, a strong Ustase—an organization the same as the Mussolini Fascista. The British became tired of the treachery, of the betrayal. Churchill gave his support to the Partisans. Maybe he regret it later but he supports Tito.'

Indicating the documents: 'This man, Strossmayer, has been a Fascist, a big man in the Ustase. He has co-operated with Mihailović because he has had in his family this Bishop Strossmayer who once respected the Serbian cause. Mihailović has respected Strossmayer, no problem.

'He has been a rich man, very rich, Strossmayer. A good family you understand, proper, respectable. In the Ustase he is very powerful. These letters tell this story . . . part of this story. There are so many stories, still.

'He has written not so many letters to a daughter in Paris. She went there young . . . young like when I found you, Karen.' He turned to me. 'She was living with prostitutes, my friend. This young girl, she didn't know where she was.

'But this daughter does not reply to the letters. He asks each time: "Why do you not reply?" There is no answer to this question. The letters of a father to a daughter he does not know. They have no quality. They say nothing.

'And then these,' he pulled out some of the sheets written in a different hand. 'These are letters telling the girl that Strossmayer is dead. He has been killed. They are from a relative, an aunt. These are written to Paris. They are dated 1945.'

I had noticed that.

'They describe the problems: death, conflict, vengeance. It is a very hard time because if you have an enemy, or your family has enemies—maybe for one hundred years—you say that they have worked with the Nazis, with the Ustase. Then they are killed. Everybody says everybody worked with the Nazis. Who has not enemies? Only the clever people they escape. Some go with the Germans, some to Austria and there they bargain. Because now the world has done with the Nazis, now they fight Communists.'

'Are there answers,' I asked, 'to the aunt's letters?'

'There are no answers. It is one way. You see, there is always somebody to fight. But me, Brkic, I am Serbian. Now I believe in nothing, only in God. That is all, God. He brought Karen back again to an old man.'

'What's this then,' I asked, fingering the pencil list that was now hardly legible. Everything else had been written using the Latin alphabet. That list, in its faded pencil, neatly printed, appeared to be in another letter form, possibly Cyrillic—the written language, of the Serbians, I was told.

Brkic had no problems with either letter set. He had explained to me that both were used in the official language, Serbo-Croat. He scowled at my list, creasing its edges between his fingers. He said it was a bad list. To be forgotten.

He stood, walked to the back of the room and there, to my horror, he set the list alight. The aged paper flared an instant, then was gone. By the time I reached him it was floating ashes.

'It is best,' he said simply. He knocked back another drink. 'The innocent seek justice. There are no innocent. There is no justice. Those were names of war criminals. Had history been written different . . . heroes. Today they are only old men.'

I was outraged: 'War criminals!'

'The worst.'

'Then why?' I asked.

'Because I told you. The past must settle like the dust after a traveller passes. Nothing, not even justice, is worth the disturbance of its surface.'

The coffee had gone cold. I helped myself to one of a pile of cakes. Karen just sat, staring at him with something like love.

The cakes had been for starters. We ate together, a huge meal. Karen picking to be polite, feeling a little off her food. If somebody entered the room our host ordered him over to be introduced. 'This is my daughter, Karen. Back from France. This is her husband.' He wasn't able to keep my name in his head. Nothing even vaguely Yugoslav about Essington, not enough 'j's and 'k's and 'z's—none in fact.

*

We didn't get back to the apartment till after nine. It was a bit of a let-down, just as soulless as a hotel—maybe more so. Our only poetry was the screaming of the fruit bats swarming over the road, and the sense of ourselves; knowledge of the child.

It's a bugger, how to live; the worst solution is the sterile temporary lodging. I did a bit of pacing about, picking things up, putting them down. We were going to be around Sydney for quite a while. More or less till I felt confident I was safe on the Côte d'Azure. There were a lot of other places we could go. Aunt had an apartment in Paris, in the sixteenth arrondissement, where the people speak proper. That could be nice. But so was Sydney sunshine.

'Karen, it'd mean a lot of rearrangement.'

'Rearrangement! You've never really bothered to work out what it is you've got. It's all in other people's hands. Money rolls in, sure, but would you know, would you really know, if somebody was taking you to the cleaners?'

The Australian side of my affairs was handled by Richards and Partners.

'Feathers! You suspect Sparrow would do that? You've got a right to dislike the guy. So have I. But one thing he's not is a crook.'

'Devious, all the same. Just because you went to school together. I wouldn't know anyone I went to school with if I fell over them. We weren't so special at Catalpa High. Not like we thought we were God's chosen.'

'All right, agreed. I try to get on top of it. I take your point. Is this what parenthood means . . . I sit around adding up all day?'

'Somebody's got to. You can bet they'll skim off what they can if you let them. It's the world, Ess. It's the modern world. If not Feathers then somebody else. They lend it to their friends at a discount rate. It happens all over. In my opinion, if they've been to a good school, it makes them more suspect, not less— scratching each other's backs.'

'Not Feathers, Karen. The oldest friend I've got.'

'Lucky he doesn't hate you then. I mean, he's not much of a friend really. Not after what he dragged you into.'

A little further down the track I agreed to look into buying something—a house. Soft in the head! As Karen pointed out,

'Just a city place, somewhere to call our own.' The five Dufys would just about cover it.

'Houses are cheap, Ess, says so in the papers.'

'Fine, Karen.'

'Like right now the stock market's through the roof. Everything's going bad and the stock market's booming. Things like that, Ess. Think about it. Maybe you should sell something. I don't know. But I do know you ought to think about it.'

You can't dodge that side of life; you can have a bloody good try though.

The phone rang: 'Essington! that's important material. I've got it in front of me now.'

'Do you know what it means, Feathers?'

Karen hurled a *House and Garden* across the apartment. 'Fuck him.' she said.

'What was that?'

'Nothing, Feathers, Karen telling me something.'

'How is she? Do give her my love.'

'I will.'

'No, very significant, Essington—should clear up a lot of this Oula Strossmayer business.'

'Is that a fact? Couldn't make head or tail of it myself.'

'Of course, I'll have to get it translated.'

'Will it say why I got shot?'

'Perhaps not that. But significant, Essington.'

He didn't have the photographs.

They hadn't meant much to Rajko Brkic either. Except that he recognized the uniform straight off. Anyone who'd worn that uniform then should know the man—it was a high rank, lots of braid and stripes and stars and crosses and stuff. The metaphysical symbolism of war—five stars in a row mean . . . well, something . . . they'd have to mean something.

We played name games in bed. Reluctantly, Karen decided against Rajko. It wouldn't suit a girl—we were both sure it would be a girl; I was the type to have slow-swimming male sperm. We could have got a photo taken, they can do that with alpha waves or something. And there was a test . . . maybe it was the test? They know what it's going to be. Takes the surprise out of it though. We went to sleep . . . 'H is for Harriet.'

Karen took the plane to Canberra. She was picked up in a cab at seven-thirty leaving me a long two days to fill. The advice was—spend it looking for houses.

First thought I had, I thought I'd like a dog. Missing Desdemona. I rang Friars' Mews reception and asked if I could bring a little canine pal into the place. They said no. Not like France—they like dogs in France.

I took a walk around Chippendale. Patted a Blue Heeler. Noticed what I hadn't noticed before—a lot of the houses were up for sale. You only see things when you look.

It was frightening. I'd envisaged more obstacles. All I needed to do was dial one of about four phone numbers and they'd fit me out in bricks and mortar in the wink of an eye.

Back in the brown-toned room I spread out the Dufy drawings comparing them with the photos of the girl. There could have been a likeness. Yet Dufy's faces looked more like one another than like Oula. Matisse was the same—no interest in the face as mirror of the soul. Simply a pattern of dots that say 'nose', 'mouth', 'eyes'; yet catching something, more than a generalization.

I rang the Griffins. I convinced myself they would not answer. When a voice said hello their name disappeared from my mind. I asked: 'Do you know Oula Strossmayer?'

A woman demanded to know who was speaking—very defensive. Then I heard her say, as an aside, 'Tom.' And it came to me.

'Tom Griffin,' I said.

'Just a mo, I'll get him.'

'Hello . . . who is this?' Pretending to be commanding.

'My name is Holt, Essington Holt.'

'Mr Holt?' Not quite so uptight.

'I was given your name by a Mr Gerald Sparrow, Richards and Partners. In connection with the estate of Oula Strossmayer.'

I could feel him unwind further. 'Yes.'

'I'd like to talk to you about it.'

He paused, then asked: 'You're not connected to Has and Danilović?'

'Mr Griffin, I couldn't even pronounce them. I have trouble with Strossmayer.'

'It's just that we've got rather a lot of calls lately.'

'Not to worry.' Me sounding jaunty. 'I'm interested in the Dufy. That's where I come in, the painting. I was hoping we could have a talk. Mr Sparrow thought you might know about its history.'

'He's still got it?' Anxious.

'Well, yes. Yesterday at least. It's nice.'

'Tomorrow's out. It would have to be today, I'm afraid. You see, we're . . .'

'Suits me,' I said. 'How about now?'

He said something to Mrs Griffin, then, 'Fine. Where are you?'

So I told him and we agreed to meet at the Regent in an hour. That was the only place we both seemed capable of bringing to mind.

Chapter 14

It's quite nice down by the Regent. They have horse and carts to take you for a ride if you like. The horses are a bit lean on it—quite a haul for them up the hill breathing carbon fumes. Still, pollution makes for lovely light. Looking straight up the sky was yellow-pink. That's what Monet celebrated in his city paintings—smog. Curious the way people wet themselves over it, over smog. Of course, in Monet's day, it was from wood and coal fires. What we need is a new race of artists who can rediscover the beauty of filthy air.

It wasn't yet ten o'clock. It seemed to have become fashionable to go out for breakfast in Sydney. Brunch was big too. I noticed that when we first booked into the Regent. They're very fast, the people of Sydney, catch on quick.

I had tried to describe me. They had described them. Jane was going to have long red hair and I wouldn't miss her because she't tie a green scarf around it. I saw the scarf and opposite it an earnest young man with the spiky crew cut of a model in man's *Vogue*, Milano style. He had one of those blue-white faces that keep themselves out of the sun. His jaws were very tight together so all that part of his face looked locked up. I guess you would have to say Tom was locked up. He wore black.

'Hi,' I said. 'I'm Essington.'

His jaw relaxed a fraction. I recalled tenseness on the phone an hour before.

They both stood. We shook all round. We sat down.

'Tom says the Regent's ninth in the world.' Jane explained.

He expanded: 'That's out of *Courvoisier's Best*. Read it in the *International Herald Tribune*.'

'Wow! The *Herald Tribune*,' I said.

I ordered a coffee, just to have the cup, something to do with my hands. There was still a lot of Serbian cuisine surging through my tubes and a firewater ache in the old Essington brain.

Whatever they'd been expecting I wasn't it. Not that I seemed to scare them, even with Tom being half my size.

'Nice painting.' I tried out a foolish smile.

'Isn't it beautiful . . . really important too.' Jane made it sound like a universal truth.

'Why's that exactly?' I asked.

But she could only supply reasons like the ones I knew already—when it was done, where it fitted into art history, Dufy history. Him coming out of his Cézanne phase, making a gesture towards his mature style.

'Gerald Sparrow said you were interested in the lady's life.'

'It was an epic.' Tom had been looking forward to this. 'I'd been working on a script. We already had interest.'

'Why past tense?' I asked.

'After the murder it was too horrible.' Jane swept her thick red hair from a lightly freckled skin.

'Jane does scripts,' Tom explained.

'Does it change it, Oula Strossmayer being dead? I would have thought it gave you the standard big-sell freeze frame.'

'It wasn't to be like that . . . the soul of that woman . . . she'd come a long way.' Jane wasn't talking about Eastern Europe. I could tell that—it was cosmic talk: like a long way spiritually. 'A fantastic history. And then she found a link, a sympathy with this landscape, with the plight of its original people. Gemini . . . she was born under Gemini.'

Gemini! What next? I thought. 'Then she gets cut up. It fits; more like life.'

Tom explained: 'We don't want to associate with anything . . . no negative thoughts, if you get what I'm trying to say. Jane and I, we embrace life.'

'No cynicism,' Jane expanded.

Tom stared at me, considering. 'You're a Libra.'

'Virgo on the cusp,' I said. I didn't know what it meant—cusp sounded like tropical fruit. I settled in to wait for the Tarot pack. My aunt, Mrs Fabre, she used to buy and sell on the way the cards turned out. 'Must be a little hard, to think positive, if you'll excuse me. There's a lot you'd just have to cut out. Like putting blinkers on a horse so it only sees straight in front. Nature took millions of years getting horses to see out the sides a bit.'

Tom had to be a product of the Christian Brothers broken free. He had the sing-song voice, the affected vowels. He was still chasing something like God: 'The world has turned its face downwards under the weight of all the anti-thought, people aren't able to carry that weight any more.'

Jane regarded him as though he had just walked out of the desert.

'You drop it then!' Those two were getting on my nerves. 'You're crazy. I don't even know the story. But you're insane to drop it simply because it grew a nasty tail. What doesn't? Why don't you tell it like you were going to . . . hey, Jane,' I suggested, slapping her lightly on the arm. 'All you've got to do is write up on the screen: on the such and such of whatever she got chopped up. I've seen that done. It's a technique they use.'

I was hamming it up. I knew those positives could clam up if I let on what I was thinking. I was thinking that breakfast at the Regent wasn't a scene I needed. I was thinking Tom and Jane should pull their fingers out. 'You know, white letters on black.' Sorry, that was negative too.

'It's just . . .' Jane felt about in the air, taking handfuls of it then squeezing them against her temples beneath long elegant hands. She had the look of someone who'd dropped straight out of the womb onto her feet—little golden slippers. Could Tom have been a touch of reality?

I scratched under my beret. Everything up there felt funny since the wounding—scar, hair, skin, beret, had all got into my act.

Tom noted the action. He glanced at Jane—sympathetic?

So I said; 'Brain tumour. Had it removed . . . big ball of negative tissue.' I grinned. 'Never say die. Ha, ha.'

'But that's what we're talking about,' Tom said. 'Only making it really positive. More than a thought, an idea . . . making it a belief.'

'And diet,' Jane added. 'Have you thought about that.'

We were getting on better. I kept my face at a distance, trying to breathe to the side. I didn't want them catching the

Serbian spirits on my breath. If you'd put a wick in my mouth I would have worked as a cigarette-lighter.

To keep the tumour story alive the beret had to stay in place. Nothing positive about gunshot wounds.

Oula's story had begun to flow. It was on tape. Oral history it was called—straight from the horse's mouth. After being brought up by my mother I would have thought oral history the least reliable. All it could supply was a picture of people's self-deceptions, their fantasies. Tom and Jane thought it got you closer to truth. They might have been right—it rested a question for philosophers.

I didn't show them the photographs, nor the photostats. I decided they might talk about them to anyone who came along. People had come along already—Yugoslavs—the origin of the idea that I might have been from Has and Danilović, from the Canberra lawyers who challenged the will. For all I knew the challenge was still alive and well, Feathers keeping mum about most things.

Finally we all promised to meet again. Karen, I lied, wouldn't be able to wait.

'Yes,' I said as we slid out the automatic doors into the roar of traffic and not a little dust caught on a light wind. 'Yes, and we'd love to hear the tapes . . . the authenticity of the voice.' That 'we' included Karen, my positive thinking spouse.

I grabbed a cab that decided to take me home the wrong way, via the Eastern Suburbs. The beret must have tempted him to try his luck. I told him: 'Switch the fucking meter off till we're back on the track.' Then I named all the hotels from the rocks up George Street to Broadway and the University. They came to me like poetry, like verses of *The Rime of the Ancient Mariner*.

When I was let down at Friars' Mews he said he was sorry—tried to let me off the fare.

'There's no redemption, sonny,' I said. 'But then, there isn't any hell either.' I paid up, told him to be nice to strangers—a year away makes you sensitive about things.

Upstairs I laid the photos out again and began to relate the story to myself.

No mother—died not long after Oula was born. She'd been

brought up in a Zagreb household. The family had come from the middle Adriatic coast. Jane Griffin gave the town a name— I forgot it. An artisan family, lowly, but the grandfather, marrying above his station, got his teeth into a bit of money and a lot of property. Being clever, like Karen wanted me to be, he became a banker on the side. That was when he moved up to Zagreb, where the world was more Austro-Hungarian, more genteel. There he raised up an only son as a little gentleman—the same old story. In Australia they started out as shopkeepers, selling things to the adventurers who made history. The adventurers got forgotten but the shopkeepers became the backbone of the clubs. Lesson one, sell things. Lesson two, start a bank.

It was a conservative household, fixed on the ideas of what had been its social superiors. Control of the bank passed from the grandfather to Oula's father not long after he was widowed—around 1910. Oula had been vague about birth dates . . . vanity?

She became interested in ideas that were afoot further to the west. Ideas of a more liberal world. Where she got these ideas Tom and Jane didn't seem to know—they hadn't asked.

Perhaps she had tutors, French tutors. Because she nicked off to Paris when she was seventeen. Ran away—I wouldn't have been surprised if she'd carried a fistful of family jewels with her. She must have had something to survive on, to make the trip.

She got a job looking after the children of a respectable family but found herself trapped in an environment which was a replica of the one she'd fled.

Holidays were taken at Le Havre. There, through the family that employed her, she met Raoul Dufy. Date—1928. The meeting was the beginning of Oula's new life. Dufy was a cultured man. Keen on music, a painter, book illustrator, he also designed cloth for high fashion. The complete working artist. It could be that he felt a sympathy for the foreign girl. (He'd had difficulties wrestling his own way up, one of nine children, even though his parents had been tolerant and musical.) It could be as simple as that he thought she looked good.

The bourgeois family returned to Paris *sans* childminder. She stayed back there by the sea, posing for Dufy, living in his household as general factotum. They oscillated between Paris and Le Havre, occasionally travelling further afield.

Through the Dufy household Oula met a variety of people; she established friendships. The most notable being with a young cellist with whom, in 1931, she set up house in Montparnasse, just off the rue Vaugirard—a tiny, two-roomed apartment with a studio for practice which was in fact an unused maid's room stuck in the roof.

The world economy had gone bust. Life was getting tough.

In 1935, for reasons which are hard to understand, Oula returned to Yugoslavia to see her father. She stayed there with her aunt, her mother's sister, a woman of liberal opinions. The banker, Strossmayer, had become a staunch believer in salvation through Hitler and was a money-bags for Yugoslavia's clandestine far right.

Oula's friend, the cellist, had not escaped the period's political intensities, going to Spain in 1936 as a member of the International Brigade. So, when Oula returned from her visit to Zagreb thoroughly radicalized in reaction to her father, she returned to a departing lover. She stayed on in Paris. She had a small circle of friends. She was by no means alone or at a loose end.

Through this period she remained in contact with Dufy and visited him from time to time. In 1937, when he was commissioned to paint the gigantic mural for the Paris International Exhibition, he employed her to help with the work. The painting, sixty metres by ten metres, was for the Pavilion of Electricity, it told electricity's story. It was an over-ambitious undertaking totally unsuited to a painter known for delicate arabesques and an intimate touch. But Dufy was already past his prime.

It must have been a comfort to Oula to be working with an old friend. She claimed to have laid down some of the vast areas of background colour. While she was performing this bland task she was passionately fighting to hold back the rising Fascist tide.

Once returned from Spain her cellist abandoned music altogether in favour of political action. They struggled through together right up to the time of France's surrender. At that moment he went underground. Oula, who had never regularized her status, once more returned to Yugoslavia. This return arranged through the influence of her father—a man now coming into his own on the floodwaters of history.

Her war in Yugoslavia must have been a horror. She was stuck in the midst of a group whose ideology she hated, a group who she had vowed to defeat. She was living under the uninterested domination of a father who had never displayed affection and who only boasted of atrocity and revenge.

In that Croatian-dominated town her only support was the sympathetic aunt. But that was not enough to assuage the guilt she felt for living in relatively comfortable circumstances while the man she loved was participating in the struggle of the French Resistance—as a part of a largely Jewish and foreign resistance cell, mostly Poles and Hungarians. Born in France he was of Hungarian parentage.

Through the war Dufy moved to lower Normandy and then, in 1942, when the Germans spread and tightened their control he moved south, mainly because he was suffering from arthritis. Not so bad in such a vast sea of suffering but a problem none the less. He was sixty years old when Oula undertook what was for those times a dangerous epic voyage.

She made her way to Venice and from there across Italy coast to coast. Then by boat to Corsica. From Corsica, after a stay of several months, she procured a passage on a steamer which took her to Toulon. When she disembarked she could not have known that her old friend, Dufy, was only a few miles to the east. She travelled to Paris with papers that she bought along the sea front of Toulon, arriving the month that the whole of the cell that her lover had joined was betrayed to the Nazis—rumour had it by the French Communist Party, under orders from Stalin; an anti-terrorist move designed to win the hearts and minds of the people.

Oula was alone. Former friends avoided her like the plague. Her cellist had been tortured along with his colleagues and then killed. Stood against a wall and shot. She herself was in danger from the French and from the Germans whose goals seemed to have become indistinguishable. People were starting to go headhunting to prove loyalty to the Reich.

Oula was a foreigner; the natural target for suspicion.

Dufy was in Perpignan, under treatment at the clinic of one Dr Nicolau. Then, after the allied invasion, he retreated to Vence in the hills behind Nice. His health demanded warmth and dry weather.

A woman of apparently endless resource, Oula again made her way south. She found Dufy. Well, that was her story. It is just as likely that she stole the painting and the drawings— there was no mention of the drawings from anybody; from Tom, Jane or myself. Oula could have stolen them in 1937 while employed as an assistant. Dufy worked fast, his studio would have been cluttered with works. She claimed he gave her the Mozart bust painting as currency, to start a new life. That was to be the way they'd tell it in the film. If they could get over the axing.

Only, I wondered . . . surely the drawings . . . it would have been more natural if he had given them to her right back in 1928 when they were done. He would have produced a lot at a session, given them as a gesture. But why would he give a picture that he had hung on to since 1912? Such a significant picture?

Oula made her way to Australia with the picture and drawings. It must have been the aunt who collected the material on her father unless Oula had been crazy enough to wander about with that kind of documentation on her person. In late 1944 such letters and photos would have provided sufficient evidence to get her shot by any of Europe's abundant self-appointed vigilantes of the new peace.

None of which explained Oula's aunt's 1945 letters to Paris. Had they been posted at all? A puzzle.

Chapter 15

Karen rang around four. The designs would go off to China for a firm-price calculation of set-up costs and guarantees of colour match. On the face of it it looked cheaper than the local alternative. She elected to keep three designs for the Sydney workshop as a trial.

'There's a lot in this, Essington, Dawn really worked.'

'Let's hope she does still.'

'Mind, if the Aussie dollar goes any lower we won't be able to afford China. So it's best to stay in with the Sydney crowd.'

Karen had a capacity for that kind of thought—residual from secretarial days. That's where we met, either end of a telephone.

'Ess, did you find a house?'

'Nup, but I thought I'd like a dog.'

'You're impossible.'

'I'm looking . . . sure I'm looking, I promise. Today I had a lovely time with a couple I just know you'll hate.'

'Half your luck.'

Next day at ten am I was to be shown a two-storey place around the corner—courtesy of Estate Equity Limited on City Road, Newtown. It was to be a Mr Dilas.

When we met outside 40 Rose Street I was reminded of my encounter at Entrevaux: Dilas had a broad head and swept-back grey hair. He was keen about the eyes. I received his card—Dilas was D-J-I-L-A-S.

'Yugoslav?'

'Australian, Mr Holt.' He had an accent.

Djilas knocked, we waited. 'I rang the owner at work but it's as well to make sure. Don't want to barge in on anyone.'

We stood there long enough for the completion of most

human activities; except, maybe, dying. 'Quite a Yugoslav community here in Sydney.' I was leading him.

'You'd know, Mr Holt. Holt,' he repeated thoughtfully, 'would that be Bosnian?' He laughed. 'I reckon there's about a thousand Yugoslav communities in Sydney if you really want to know. Me, I don't want nothing to do with any of them. I'm Australian, like my children. If I want to be Yugoslavian I'd go live in Yugoslavia. Probably not such a bad life. Get away from all these cars.'

He opened the door. The smell nearly knocked me over. 'Take me no further.'

'Why, what's the matter?'

'Cat's piss . . . you can't smell it?' Mr Djilas began a mime of sniffing.

'It's cat's piss,' I assured him. 'Know it by heart. I lived among it for years. Piss and gas. So, what have you got odour free, cheap and vast.'

'Nothing. But if you're after a nice chunk of paradise I have something just listed in the next street.'

We strolled around to take a look. 'I'll come clean with you, Mr Djilas. Right now I've got myself into a funny situation on the Yugoslav front.'

'Not interested in a house? I've got better things to do. You're wasting my time.'

'I didn't say that. Jesus! You can do two things at once, can't you? Someone talked about walking and chewing gum.'

We were there already. He had the key in the lock. 'Different price bracket,' he said.

'Show on. Getting back to Yugoslavia.'

'I sell houses.'

'If you want a chance of selling this listen for a moment. I need help.'

'And I need to get home to Mrs Djilas, Mr Holt.'

'At ten am?'

'A very possessive woman.' He pulled out a small cigar, lit it.

'Such passion, it's touching.'

We'd gone through a stained wooden door set in a green wall.

'You rang these people too? Then you sprayed one house with cat's piss and here we are.'

'Where'd you learn your love of humanity, Mr Holt?'

'Would you believe, Mr Djilas, from three of your country-men up in the French Alps.' I whipped off the beret. 'Take a look at this.' It was getting less dramatic by the day—hair regrowth.

I had lifted my headgear to a wonder of architectural recreation. We were in a large interior, glass all along one wall. Then a verandah. There was a bar kitchen on the far side. It was really something. I was glad Karen wasn't there to see it. But he was looking at my head. 'So?' he asked.

'That ridge,' I ran a finger along it, 'that was a bullet. The Yugoslav connection.'

Suddenly he was impressed. 'Are you an agent or something?'

'Mr Djilas. I'm an innocent. Till I found Yugoslavia on the map. Now I am in Sydney trying to buy a house. Desperate stuff.'

'Rubbish,' he said. 'People do it every day.'

'I'm not people. I'm me. A one-off. Sensitive. One life . . . and that only by the skin of my teeth.'

'Then, what do you want to know? Tell me so you'll understand I can't help you. I'm Australian, like I said. The Eels lose, I weep. It was not easy . . . I had to work on it. Do you know I can even bowl an in-swinger.'

We had walked down a wooden stairway to a lower level. The place had been gutted then rebuilt. The front bit was what remained of a tiny two-up, two-down, with the windows bricked in. Everything else had been put between it and a two-storey brick stable-loft that went with the L-shaped block. There was a courtyard with pool. In the diffused light I could see the red bodies of carp lazily hunting between the water-lilies.

'I want a lecture on the Ustase in Australia, that's what I want.'

'Go and see Alexander Has then.'

'Of Has and Danilović?'

'I don't know what he's of,' Djilas said. You could see it was a subject that did not appeal. 'But the papers say he's a Nazi war criminal. The papers say! They also reckon Terry Jones has had it.'

'Who in Christ's name is Terry Jones?'

'Quarter-back for the Eels. Don't you know nothing?'

'Where to find Mr Has?' I had a pretty good idea but I wanted to keep the conversation rolling.

'Wouldn't know. Try someone in the New Right. They were trying to offload him not so long ago. After the accusations started. He's in Canberra someplace. That's where the politicians are.'

I gave the house a good looking over and liked it. 'How much?'

'A hundred and eighty.'

'I've only been here a few weeks, fresh off the plane.'

'You sound it,' he laughed. 'Make an offer, why don't you?'

We arranged to meet outside, same time next day. Me with Mrs Holt.

'I don't know where I'd find the money.'

'Banks, Mr Holt. Try banks. They give it to you. All you've got to do is ask. Now, can I go home?'

'Unless you want a drink.'

'OK, a drink then.'

'Mrs Djilas won't fret?'

I didn't learn anything more about the activities of Yugoslav extremists over a couple of beers at the Pride of Erin on the corner of Cleveland Street, a run-down pub trying to go up-market. But I ate a lot of nuts and got to like Djilas.

His name was Fred. He must have constructed that over whatever scramble of letters his mother and father had bestowed upon him.

Fred was having trouble right then because some old scrooge had departed this vale of tears leaving half a street of houses to Mother Church who, being all heart, whacked them straight onto the market aiming at a buyer big enough to rip them down and build a nice block of inner city apartments. It was in Redfern where there was a substantial Aboriginal population. You couldn't miss the hint that Fred wasn't a fan of Aboriginal people. I wouldn't have thought that they'd have much time for landlord's agents either.

The bit of the story that interested me concerned the priest who'd arranged for the occupation of the houses to keep his church out. When it came to a priest Djilas was not so quick to condemn, even where he disapproved.

I got the name of the street and left ideological argument to more worthy, more dedicated minds.

We ambled back to Fred's Honda Prelude, shook hands. It was 'till tomorrow' all around.

Tomorrow is a day that never comes—especially if you keep your eyes shut it doesn't.

As I walked up the steps of Friars' Mews I glimpsed a character jogging along the far side of the street. In transitional inner city areas joggers are no strangers. But this fellow, replete with bright green track suit, was not looking right. His heart wasn't in it. It seemed to be in me rather than in the jogging.

At reception I asked if there had been any phone calls. None—never were if you asked. I took the lift up, walked to the end of the corridor then waited in a blind turn that led to the service-room—where the maids kept their cleaning gear.

I gave him lots of time to find the door, heard the knock, then walked briskly down the passage. The tactic caught him off guard. I guess he was preparing some door-opening spiel and suddenly there I was, looking down. He was no longer just in the natty green number with zips and yellow piping—Australian international sporting colours. A sharp, deep blue, nylon jacket was pulled over the top. He looked like Alain Delon relaxing; if that was possible.

A hand slipped inside the jacket. I nudged him and grabbed the arm. His fingers were locked around a spray can. I cracked the hand against the wall. He let out a squeal and dropped it. It was easy.

'Frightened I'd rape you?' I asked.

He didn't try and run away or anything. He'd just gone blank. I opened the door, ushered him in. The photos and stuff were where I'd left them, strewn about the place. He saw them, no problem. I kicked the can in with us like a soccer ball.

'Sit down.'

He sat.

'Why the mace? That's what it is, right?'

He regained composure. You could tell he was no heavy. A nasty thought entered my mind: Sent by Feathers. Sent to check up on what I had, what I knew. That was real Australian mateship.

So, I asked him.

He blinked. 'Rings no bells.' Curiously, he didn't seem upset at being caught out, and he was not at all afraid. Must have been a fanatic—ASIO fanatic. Just graduated to mace at the university of . . . it wouldn't have been life, would it?

I was leaning against the door, watching. I threw the beret, frisbee fashion, across the room onto a chair. Half of me was throbbing with anger, the other half—could have been the non-reptilian bit—was gradually realizing that I had caught an officer of the Commonwealth's spy network. No prizes for that.

No word was said. I was watched. He didn't look like he was thinking, not from the expression.

'There's the phone,' I said. 'Ring him. Or else we're stuck here for the rest of our lives.' There's people like that in mythology, they freeze waiting for a kiss or a phone conversation.

That got him thinking.

'The number's in that little book, see, beside it. Try under 'R' . . . Richards and Partners. All you've got to do is dial then ask for Gerald Sparrow. Say you're calling for me. You and I don't need introduction. If you didn't know who I was you wouldn't be here.' I winked. 'That's philosophy. And here's some more. Things only exist once you know their name, and I don't want to know yours. Get it?'

He was still nursing the hand that had hit the jerry-built fabric of Friars' Mews. Transcending pain he used it to pick up the book, found the page, dialled. I had guessed right. He knew what he was doing.

I crossed the room, picked up the canister of mace from where it had rolled. I sprayed a drop into the air. Very nasty, it smelt. I was surprised it hadn't been adopted by the rurals for gassing rabbits.

He went through the switch at the law firm, then I guess to Miss Bassano—eventually the man himself, Gerald Patriot. One of the sort of chaps who would have sent their neighbours off in cattle trucks for some higher national cause.

'Got him?' I asked. 'Clever . . . a very busy man.' My guest was trying to speak and to hear so I kept on, loud. 'Tell him to come to dinner. I've got some photos for him too . . . Chez Catz.'

'What's that?' he asked.

'Never you mind. It's KGB code.' Keep the bastard rattled.

He hung up the phone. 'A thing you've got wrong. Nobody sent me here. Gerald Sparrow explained what had been going on. On my own initiative I decided to take a look. I needed to find out what you know. All that paper . . . I was right, wasn't I? Not to mention the photos.'

'Shove it,' I said. He was a prissy man, prissy voice, fussy articulation. 'Couldn't have been at all busy, unusual for Feathers.'

'Feathers?'

'Sparrow, the man you didn't know at first.' He elected to look vacant. 'Ah, well,' I said, 'it's off we go then. By the way, don't forget this.' I reached out with mace, gave him a quick blast, just for fun, right in the face.

'You bastard!' He clasped his hands to his eyes. 'Oh shit!'

I grabbed him, steered him to the bathroom. 'Take a shower—with luck it washes off.' Then I shut the door. Feathers could wait—do him good.

I put all the photostats in an inside pocket and two photos under the mattress—the baby in the cot, and the older Oula on Pont Alexandre III. The rest I shoved in my jacket. Best to be seen to come clean.

The mace went into a drawer with my socks—keep the moths away.

At least he was looking sheepish—that was something. Not enough. He had a way of walking, Feathers, feet turned slightly in at the toes, emphasizing the whole idea of legs and knees and ankles. Along with the head, the feet put the impeccable clothes a fraction off key. They simply didn't work, even after years of sartorial labour.

He had come by cab. The Porsche was kept airtight in a garage, reserved, like Karen's dad's Holden, for special occasions, like a couple of times when he'd done good turns for me nobody in their right mind would have done. Funny thing, friendship. . . unpredictable.

Peter and Patrick looked surprised. Me with a red-eyed strange man whose hair was wet. Perhaps they thought I'd turned. Peter exclaimed: 'Look who we've got. And the legal mind . . . just like old times. Do tell . . . but who's the new boy?'

Feathers was trying for a natural, for a relaxed look, but was having trouble sustaining it.

I stayed standing, like I was ready to run. The grin on my face felt as stiff as a butterfly collar. We three were the only customers. Peter had no need to feel inhibited in offering a bottle of wine despite his lack of a licence to do so. The unnamed man in the track suit asked for water.

'Top man?' I asked, facetious.

Feathers rolled his eyes.

'"Give unto Caesar those things . . ."' I quoted. 'So, where does God fit in? Or is he ASIO?'

'All right, Essington, you've made your point. I'm sorry. Now stop.' That went back a long way, as long as the friendship. Always it had been me who, once I'd got hold of the bone, couldn't leave off shaking it. My obsessive side. A form of tunnel vision. I had seldom shown an instinct to view the wider picture. Once I'd decided to win I kept on going in my own laborious way. With Feathers, then, I knew I had the upper hand. What he'd always been known for was the Sparrow moral dilemma.

'I made my point. But did you take it?'

'This isn't the time or place to talk about it,' he replied. But I could see uncertainty in his eyes. I took the photos from my side pocket. 'You were after these?'

He accepted them, flipped through the images, passed them to the man in the tracksuit.

Patrick had come across for the order. 'Family?' he asked of the photos.

'Almost,' I said, then ordered the fettucini with ham and cream.

Feathers and Track Suit followed the leader. Was it my day? 'Salad?'

'Yes thanks, Patrick,' I responded. A nod from Feathers, a

nod from Track Suit. 'Patrick, I hear your Father Down is running a big squat up towards Eveleigh Street.'

'I'm not so sure he organized it, Ess. It's a together community around there now. He's living in, anyway.'

'Most of the time?'

'I hear so. It's where his flock is, at any rate.'

'Good for him.'

Patrick padded off in his happy-shoes bearing the orders to Peter. Feathers said, better late than never, 'Randall Gregor,' indicating the track suit. 'Essington Holt.' It sounded like the *Boy's Own* League.

'Feathers, that's your Father Down . . . the Strossmayer beneficiary.'

'Hardly mine, Essington, hardly mine.'

'Have you talked to him, sounded him out? Couldn't she have told him about the threats?'

Randall was flicking through the pictures—just rolling a few of the images of the moustached man over and over again. He seemed to like Oula's proud father.

'These in the painting too?' he asked.

'No,' I lied. 'I found them in Millbourne. You guys, you just don't know how to concentrate.'

Feathers answered my question about Father Down: 'Not a forthcoming man that priest. Too wrapped up in his cause to confront reality.' What a fatuous thing to say that was.

Randall said: 'I went through that house with a fine-tooth comb.' I could tell it was too late for Randall and me.

'Your comb missed.' I gave him the broad grin. 'The photos . . . do you know who it is, Feathers?' He shook his head.

Randall was just staring at the snaps. Was he working out what they were, or where they'd been in the house at Millbourne?

I put my finger on the moustached man. 'Papa Strossmayer,' I said. 'So there, I've given you that. You didn't need to come in like a guerilla army, you only had to ask.' To Feathers in a theatrical whisper: 'Where to you recruit dummies like that?'

Of course he ignored the question; tugged at his cuffs. Randall went sullen.

'A trade,' I suggested, 'for friendship's sake. I told you about

Papa; what did the translations say?' I brought out the photocopies. Brkic had only provided the vaguest indications of their
content—frustrating.

'You copied them?' Feathers, alarmed.

'In honour of Entrevaux, thought they might tell me why.
Randall, did they explain to you about Entrevaux?'

Patrick brought the salad—little chunks of avocado nestling
in amongst the lettuce.

Under Feathers' disapproving look I told Randall about our
French escapade.

'Hyperbole, Essington!'

'Hyper-bowl—crap!' I retorted. 'Now maybe you can see
you were lucky, Randy, I didn't throw you out the window. I
tell you it was all I could do to keep from shoving the mace can
up your arse.' He didn't like that, not the man for crude talk.
'Tell me,' I added, 'what do you do when you're not chasing
shadows?'

'He's with the organization, Essington.'

'You're professional! Jesus Christ! The amateurs must be
really something.'

Feathers was sorting the photocopies. He came to a press
cutting. I'd ignored the press cuttings even though Brkic had
given one a close second look—had the old man thought of
saying something, then pulled back?

'There is a name in this,' Feathers began, 'a name which
might be a key. Both from the point of view of the will and of
the gunrunning, though there's nothing here to use against him.
I had them translated; unfortunately I don't have the drafts
with me.' He passed me the cutting. After a long pause he
added: 'All right Essington, I'll send you translations.'

'Gee, thanks.' I was examining the typeset lines thrown into
contrasting relief by the copy machine—full black on stark
white. It stood out. It was all I could see. Twice, once in the
second paragraph and once in the last—H-A-S. I said it out
loud: 'Your Canberra colleague!'

'A disappointment, Essington . . . that it's Has. He's been a
whipping-post for years. Accusations raised against him time
and again. Mind you, he's got a thick skin. Could even enjoy
the game. Each time it gives him yet another chance to deliver
a warning against Communism, to condemn the excesses of

Tito, to decry the moral decadence of the Western powers. He's not that wide of the mark.'

'We suspect he manufactures the accusations.' Randall took up the tale. 'It's always good for a TV interview—free airtime.'

'I don't see anything particular in that.' I said.

'Not really, Essington, no.' Randall getting familiar. 'There're connections between Strossmayer and Has. However, to be connected is nothing in itself.'

'And Strossmayer, the father, is long dead,' said Feathers. 'There's no mileage in a dead war criminal. Even if their ghosts inspire, they don't actually run the guns to support Croatian aspirations. Ghosts don't train terrorists.'

'None of which explains chopping up an old woman.' I looked from face to face in the hope that they would protest, that I'd missed the point. 'And in the translations . . . any mention of a child? Of Oula's child?' If Brkic had elected to omit Has, maybe he'd left the child out as well. It would fit with his 'let sleeping dogs lie' philosophy.

'Nothing.'

Nothing, yet a lot of huffing and puffing.

'One more question, Feathers, then we can kick up our heels, have fun.' They didn't look like takers. 'Are Has and Dogsbody still challenging the will?'

'Danilović.' Feathers liked to get things right. 'Your answer is "yes" . . . or I think so. Still without enthusiasm.'

'Then they'd be interested in Oula being dead if they thought they'd benefit. More than anybody else anyway, I guess.'

I was thinking out loud. 'Never mind.' I picked up my glass. 'Skol,' I said. Like with Brkic, only we'd run out of wine.

Feathers rushed off to get another bottle. Eager to be nice or to be seen to be nice. He would have given them buggery at the bottle shop. He could really go on about the grape.

Chapter 16

The FM radio was soft in the background. Monteverdi, they said; not exactly my scene, yet soothing enough. It was too late for me and music—jazz was what I enjoyed: people like Mingus, Parker, Coltrane and the occasional club song like 'Autumn in New York'. I was on my back. The light was out, eliminating the room's browns.

The wheels of the Essington Holt brain were turning.

It had to be the cash. Cash, pure and simple. That was the way I saw it. The only explanation. Those guys could have been screwing the old lady, or trying to, so they could get the house and painting as contributions towards the saving of *La Patrie*. But Oula was not having any. The Homeland was not her scene. She liked Father Down—good works.

That left the son, Milo. Was he real? Was he the baby in the cot?

Did he write threats? If so, why? Why not confront her, the long lost son? Better than threats. As for the painting, it seemed to have been what worried her most. She'd got it off her hands as soon as the nasty letters had begun to come in. Was it the painting she'd got off her hands or the documents? Or both? Then there was the whole question of how such a significant Dufy got into her possession in the first place. A painting by an essentially minor painter who must have had hoards of less important works to give away.

Who would have known she had the Dufy? How would they have known?

And more questions tumbling about after that lot, none turning up with answers.

It was frustrating that nobody had seen the threatening letters; thanks, it seemed, to the good graces of Sergeant Armstrong or whoever. It could have been that the threats were of a different kind . . . nothing to do with inheritance.

Everything to do with the documents. That bundle of papers might well have been dynamite for someone. Even now, so long after the events. Particularly now. But why?

I guess I wasn't going to find out the answer to that one.

Paranoia. Was Feathers being straight? With his secret other life, his James Bond games, maybe he wasn't letting on about the letters for reasons of his own. After all, something had put him on to the guns.

I had another go at the Griffins. It was late but they were up. Film buffs never sleep, not with late-night revivals on the telly.

I asked Tom to search in his mind for anything more that Oula might have said about the threats. He asked me to hang on while he turned off the background noise, and when he came back to the phone I repeated the request. 'Surely, if the lady goes to the trouble to entrust you with her most valued possession she's going to try to explain why.'

'She was close, didn't want to talk about it.'

'Said: "Here's the picture, see you later"?'

'More or less,' he replied.

'And you didn't get to read the threats? Didn't see what was being threatened?'

'She took them to the police.'

'Who ignored them?'

'That's the way it turned out.'

'Funny really, the police, to ignore them. Don't you think so, Tom?'

'They couldn't give a stuff.' And then he threw a bit of light on the matter: 'Maybe they weren't in English,' he suggested. 'That would have thrown them.'

'Certainly would,' I said. 'Well, thanks anyway, sorry to interrupt.' I hung up.

I rang Feathers. He would have had enough of me for the day. That's partly why I rang. I wanted to see if I could trip him up, get him to make a mistake, admit where he'd heard about the guns.

'There's nothing to say, Essington. We've been through everything already.'

'I was just checking.'

'I'd like you to know that I resent you mistrusting me like this.'

I don't know where he got the gall.

'Leave it alone,' he advised. 'It's our problem, not yours. Take my advice: a Mogadon, then sleep.'

'I wish it was that easy. They tried to kill me, Feathers. I just can't forget that. I don't have the legal training, the objectivity. It keeps on running through my mind. One thing then another. And me trying to make sense of it all . . . getting bugger all help from anyone. I can't get hold of anything. I keep on thinking that if I could read what they'd written to the old lady, know why she suddenly decided to offload that painting, maybe that would be step one in the direction of making sense of the whole thing. I could even come to understand your crazy nationalism at the same time.'

'I do wish you'd take my advice and go to sleep.' He said that as though it was of such value I'd get a bill for it in the morning's mail.

Except I would have been asleep when the postman arrived. I didn't manage to close my eyes until day broke and the fruit bats prepared to settle down from their nocturnal revels.

Parts of Redfern have become semi-closed-off Aboriginal territory. A ghetto in the making, or made. At the gate of the squat I was greeted by a tall, elegantly dressed man in gold-rimmed half-glasses. The effect of a severe pin-striped suit was rendered incongruous by his knitted tam-o'shanter hat featuring the colours of the Aboriginal flag—black, gold and red. He had been chatting to a small fat man wearing a grease-smeared boiler suit.

A hand was placed on my chest. 'Friend, what can I do for you?' Presentation of self in everyday life, not too unlike a first-wave black cop in a US telly series. Only he wasn't so black.

'Firstly,' I said, 'you can take your hand off my chest.'

The guy in the boiler suit was holding a screwdriver—not threatening, just holding. The hand stayed in place.

'Charlie?' The little man asked, eyeing me.

Charlie laughed out loud, dropped the hand. I asked my question and was directed up along the dilapidated street, five doors.

I didn't realize it then, but I was going to see quite a bit more of Charlie Lawrence.

A couple of women were sitting in an improvised office. Posters added a random and bedraggled gaiety to cracked walls. I asked for Father Down and was pointed out the back. In a rank garden, shaded by a jacaranda, a group of men stood chewing the fat.

'Father Down?' I asked of inquiring faces.

A wiry man in black with a boozer's nose and bright blue eyes responded. Had to, he was in the collar.

While intoducing myself I suddenly realized that with my bulk I must have looked like a developer's heavy. But if so, why were these people being so open, so off guard? Then I remembered the beret—the dotty touch. Could I have looked the perennial cause supporter? Trying to find happiness by picking up on other people's misery?

'What can we do for you, Mr Holt?'

'Nothing to do with the squat,' I said. 'To do with a woman who died a while back, out at Millbourne.'

'Ah, Oula Strossmayer! I have to warn you, I have virtually nothing to say on that score.'

'You knew her, you were her friend. Didn't she leave everything to your cause?' Father Down folded his strangely white and manicured hands over his stomach. Not the hands of a worker priest.

'To me, personally, I believe. Right now I'm working out how to divest myself of the encumbrance. What use have I for property?' Radical his opinions might have been but he couldn't throw off a touch of ecclesiastical pomposity in the voice.

'As I understand it, Father,' I said, 'not yet yours to get rid of. There's a challenge.' The group which I had joined broke up like an amoeba—split in two then drifted apart. Me and Down, one part; them the other.

'Be that as it may, I'm informed that, in due course, it will pass into my hands.'

'And you're the executor, right?'

'Correct—it is clear that the money is intended for my work.'

'You must have known Oula Strossmayer pretty well.'

'Why do you ask? Perhaps you should declare your interest.'

Declare my interest—yes, well what was it? A gunshot in Nice? Beating Feathers to the hare?

'The painting,' I explained. 'The Dufy.'

'Ah . . . beyond my expertise. I am no aesthetician.'

'But worth a quid.'

'So I am informed.'

'What I want to find out, Father, is how she came by it. The history of the picture.'

The other men had by then moved inside. Down gazed with longing in the same direction—to where the cause was so strong you could feel it. Not a cause against my own inclinations either. But Essington Holt was an ideologically shaky monster who liked to feel his heart was in the right place without putting much mouth or body there.

'Legitimately, Mr Holt. Legitimately, I believe.'

'Beyond doubt.'

He didn't trust me, Father Down. Didn't like my questions. I came clean, even removed the on-off beret. And let him have all that I knew of the ASIO interest both sides of the big wide seas. He tilted his head back, face to the sky, to God's sky, like he was a tracking communications dish. His eyes were closed in thought. Dandruff drifted as manna upon his black-clad shoulders. He might have been the unconventional priest—trying to break the ties with mammon—but he chose to dress the traditional part. His trousers were drifting to the green side of black, like broken liquorice; for the feet, black sandshoes. Soft cloth uppers to comfort an old man's toes. The white collar of his office was begrimed.

He had impact, just the sight of him. Father Down didn't look as though he would have any problems stepping through the eye of a needle.

I said, by way of further explanation—the man's simplicity turning me into machine-mouth, 'It's of no interest to me at all, except this.' I pointed to the ridge of scar tissue that wouldn't grow hair. 'But I've picked it up, can't seem to let it go. My personality, Father.' I was telling the whole truth.

Down examined me, then glanced at the building's rear door to which he threw a charmingly crooked smile. The man in the pin-striped suit, Charlie, was standing there now. Was he making sure no harm came to the priest?

'Oula Strossmayer,' I coaxed.

'We've got work to do here, Mr Holt. Yes . . . work to do. And, if it doesn't sound too pompous, it's God's work.'

'Not so much of that around, these days.'

'It's around, but undone. Oula Strossmayer . . . an unhappy but generous woman who met an unfortunate end. I was her confessor, you must understand that. There is nothing I can add.'

That left a trip to Canberra; left a go at Has.

'Thank you,' I said. 'For nothing.' But I grinned. It was a phrase people used, no meaning. He returned the smile, shook his head.

'Perhaps—' here the smile had turned mischievous—'you would like to assist us here, our cause. Take your mind off unnecessary problems.'

'Not my style, Father. Me, I'm the spoilt rich boy and still learning the part. I've got a long way to go before I start fretting over my immortal soul. You want to try the heroin bankers who run this place, they've got a lot to buy their way out of.'

'We don't work here for salvation, Mr Holt. Nobody does— I hope not anyway. This is simply a job to be done, like the planting of staple crops.'

'The woman, Strossmayer . . . was she buying salvation?'

'Good try, Mr Holt.' Father Down placed a hand on my shoulder, he had to reach up to do it. I was guided through the house and out into the street. Behind me I could catch the echo of laughter, conviviality, purpose.

'Anyway, think about it.'

'Think about what?' I asked.

'Our cause.' He held out a hand, we shook.

I felt like saying I was on their side but how could I? Too easy, too shallow. If I was, I would have been in there with them.

'See this sleeve—' I pointed to the blue-and-white stripe of the seersucker jacket I was sporting—'nothing on it, no hearts.'

'Pin one on. Even a hypocrite . . . at least a hypocrite expresses a higher calling with part of his being.'

I headed back towards Chippendale. Walked along the stained streets, past the broken-down fronts of terrace houses where weeds pushed up through concrete, bitumen and stone. A group of kids tried to block my way, they stood shoulder to shoulder between a slumped, half-stripped Toyota and a tilting corrugated-iron fence.

The oddball in the striped jacket with the European piss-pot on his head was brought to a stop. They grinned with contempt—insolent contempt. Why shouldn't they, for Christ's sake? Pushed to the bottom of the sparkling city, the jewel of the South Pacific? For them, no way in—just walls and grills.

The skinniest of a skinny lot pulled a knife. Broad daylight and they wanted my wallet!

'*Pardon, je ne comprends rien.*' I held out open hands in Gallic despair.

He made a couple of tentative thrusts in the direction of the Holt solar plexus. I spewed out a more exuberant stream of French, advanced, walked through, was untouched. I didn't turn around, kept on straight ahead, all too conscious of the fillable void between my shoulder-blades.

'Grow up! This is a pad. You'd call this a pad. This isn't a house . . . a home. It's a weirdo's dream. And Chippendale! Oh, Ess, you're just a great big kid, that's what you are. Chippendale, much as you might love it, it's not the place to bring up a family.'

'Karen, we'd only be here sometimes. Don't forget the villa . . . would that pass as the domestic dream?'

'I don't. That's what makes it even worse, Ess. I mean you can't live there half the year and spend the rest of your time between the breweries and Parramatta Road.'

'It's Broadway here, not Parramatta Road.'

'The same bloody road, whatever you like to call it. It's cars, and filth. City Road the same, Ess. Oh, Ess . . . it's just not the place. It won't do. And it's not as though we have to buy it . . . don't have the choice. We can buy anything. Any-bloody-thing. So why not get something nice. Someplace children can play without old men offering them lollies and junkies sticking them with needles and developers fighting it out with the blacks.'

'That rules out Sydney then.'

'Nobody lives this side if they can afford better, Ess.'

We'd been shown through the place by Mr Djilas. Karen had not said a word, not one word. A tight, constant smile and her eyes glaring at every detail, every selling point. Under the cloud of her gaze even I started to perceive the house's weak points—that it was all applied chic, sort of stuck on, right down to the fish-pond. A tarted-up, grotty hole, pretty trellising, folksy mezzanines. The truth was I did not care enough. Never in my life had I chosen a place in which to live. They'd always sort of turned up. My aunt, Mrs Fabre, she had selected the villa and the Paris flat. Before that, most times, I had moved in with friends—a bit of a sponge really. And, earlier still, just quartered out on cattle stations—nothing all that *House and Garden*.

Karen and I were sitting in our soulless room, the house pages of the previous Saturday's *Sydney Morning Herald* littering the floor. A street and suburb guide was open on the table. We were going into it properly—Karen's words. Prospective parenthood was transforming an already effective mind into a veritable office computer.

We had drawn half-circles radiating from the town hall. We were looking to the inner east. It was not easy . . . so much of the best of the city had been taken over by drug dealers, street-walkers and pimps that you began to see why the respectability set chose the harbour's North Shore—up where Karen used to live on Pacific Highway. Only they kept back a street or two.

Preferred locations were found, underlined, listed in order of preference along with the sellers' telephone numbers. During the process my input became reduced to short grunts indicating yes or no. Useless grunts since they were ignored.

Yet I felt that we had had a first battle of wills. That the female of the species, the mother-to-be seeking a nest was, as she must always be in the whole world of living creatures, the eventual victor.

And the mother of the mother-to-be was due on the following day. Between them they would have no trouble at all offloading half a million dollars—not so much money really, as Karen pointed out, not with the dollar down by half. They could do the damage, I was off to Canberra to have a chat to Has.

No problem making an appointment, he would be pleased and interested to meet me. I pulled no punches about my interest. Had he thought I was another journalist? A chance of more publicity for the cause? Whatever the cause was.

They are sad, tragic wind-up people, those who catch the morning and evening business flights between Australia's capitals. Altogether different from the long-haul passengers who come psychologically prepared for a twelve- or twenty-four-hour sit-up. The short-hop executive types sent for a day in Canberra by indulgent bosses—they were doing nothing that could not be achieved just as easily by phone, express freight or Fax machine—are very bright eyed and bushy tailed. Cartier lighters clicking; natty, hand-stitched leather satchels at the ready. They are the players in the TV world of the mind. Lacking only what they dream of: germ-free women with golden legs reaching right up to their armpits.

Busy stewards rammed packaged breakfasts down our gullets to distract attention from popping rivets along the wings. A burnt landscape of umber, terre-verte and bone slid past, mysteriously, underneath our feet. And then, just as the last plastic coffee-cup was gathered in, we began the descent.

Chapter 17

We came down softly.

The taxi driver delighted in low-level tyre squeal as we Fangio-ed our way into the centre—into Civic—cubes of building sparkling in clear sunlight under the blue sky. Not much atmospheric pollution in Canberra, it's all done with words and political thoughts.

Has and Danilović had offices in one of the blocks of steel and concrete. Brown was the theme inside, beyond the named double-glass doors. Brown wood panels, sandy brown carpet, a big brown semi-abstract painting of desert country—the kind of thing Aussie artists turn to when all else fails. Even the receptionist, perhaps from the Philippines, was brown. She regarded me through her violet-tinted contact lenses.

'Mr Has?'

'Your name please.'

We knew our parts. She ran a finger down the appointment book, found Holt. Even looked up at the clock to check a time we both knew: Miss Efficiency.

She spoke into the phone as softly as possible, asked if I would mind waiting. Mr Has would be with me soon.

Life games. All that stuff that kept me out for years—kept me at arm's length. Finding myself independent, with money in my pocket, I didn't need to take the professional's manipulative arrogance any more.

'I'm on time, Miss . . . ?' She didn't assist me with her name. 'If Mr Has isn't, stiff cheese.' I strutted to the glass doors, was half-way through when she called out.

I kept going. She caught me just as the lift doors were opening to reveal brown carpet climbing up the wall. The arrow was pointing down.

'Mr Holt!'

I dazzled her with a gentle: 'Can I help you?' The lift closed, me not in it.

'Mr Has will see you now.'

'Mr Has should learn punctuality.' My smile broadened. 'The question is, will I see Mr Has now? There is a time, Miss . . . I didn't catch your name.'

'Marmol, Maria Marmol.' She told me that as though I was a cop at her car window on a highway.

'Well, Miss Marmol, what we should try to learn is that you can bedazzle only most of the people most of the time. Tell that to Mr Has with my compliments . . . if he's got the time to listen.'

In my mind I could see the other side—men standing round squats in Redfern. More welcoming, more gracious by far. A thought entered my mind. I filed it. Not so often that the Holt mind opens its arms to a thought.

'Sorry to keep you.' He would be. Has was small, thickset with a long narrow head dominated by a broken nose. His chin was cleft, so cleft that stubble filled the indent. Age had tinted his skin grey—age or a faulty liver, or both. Wispy white hair was swept back on either side of a balding dome. His dress, fastidious, with a continental accent in the double-breasted suit, plaited shoes—in everything.

'Mr Has, I'm unkeepable, I promise.' Of course I would have stayed, it had only been a game. I'd paid the air fare.

He shrugged, grinned, guided me through a brown door to a brown chair. He took up combat position behind the desk. We were on.

I reiterated what I'd told him already on the phone. Filling him in on the background story. He doodled . . . drew Viking ships with rows of galley slaves straining, a big sea tossing the boat. By the time I got to the photos and the documents he was putting in a wind—puffy-cheeked as on an ancient map. Quite an artist. I threw my bundle of evidence onto the desk.

'Where can I help you, Mr Holt?'

'Perfectly obvious. I just told you everything. Now I would like answers. Most important, I want to find the man who fired the shot—my would-be killer.'

'It might not be advisable to find such a man. A dangerous

162

man. Perhaps he would try again. Second time lucky, isn't that the saying?' He didn't smile, but I could see he was pleased with himself as he turned the gold shaft of a ballpoint pen around with his fingertips.

'The saying . . . yes. Mr Has, do I have to drag it out of you? Does that look like the way it's got to be? Perhaps I could test you with some questions?'

'Test ahead, Mr Holt. But first, coffee?'

By the time Miss Marmol brought in the tray I was asking about the claim against the will.

His hands were in the air, palms out warding me off. 'Confidential! It is between myself and my client.'

'Oula Strossmayer's killer.'

'How could he be? He was not in the country. That can be proved, Mr Holt.'

'Naughty people do that sort of thing for money, Mr Has.'

'Not with axes.'

'What about Trotsky?'

'Ah, but now we talk of Bolsheviks, ordinary standards do not apply.'

'The coincidence,' I protested. 'All the action at once: threats, death, the claimant. There has to be a connection.'

'Bad science, Mr Holt. Very bad science indeed. There is never a case where there must be a connection. One might seem likely, even probable . . . that it must exist, never. Things happen everywhere. Sometimes actions coincide.'

'And I get shot.'

'And you get shot.'

Has offered me a second cup of coffee and another go at the plateful of incongruous teddy-bear biscuits. I had bolted my first cup—too keen, too anxious, despite my pretence of being cool, I bit off a bear's head. The legal hands were playing with the two photos, putting them this way, then that. He would purse his lips from time to time. Thinking? Remembering?

'And you, Mr Has, that's your name there I see.' I put my finger on paragraph two of the relevant cutting. 'You've got a reputation, even now. Certain well-advertised sympathies.' Suddenly the face broke into a broad grin which failed to inhabit the eyes.

'What sympathies do you have, Mr Holt?'

'None with people who try to kill me.'

'Self-interest?'

'You could call it that.'

'Like the world—the entire world. Greedy little people. You know, Mr Holt, you Australians are a simple, innocent people. You worship war because you know nothing about it. For you war has been to take a holiday in another country . . . a dangerous holiday. Just as the people of the New Guinea Highlands used to worship aeroplanes that dropped good things from the sky—the "cargo cult" they called it—so you worship the magic of war . . . you worship because you do not understand it. You do not understand that there is no magic.

'I am an Australian, but by adoption, out of necessity. In my heart, a Yugoslav. First and foremost that is what I am. It would be dishonest to claim anything else for myself. In Australia I have done well. I love this country. Yet it is a fantasy. Always my thoughts go back to my home, to the reality of my youth, to those days. To those heroic confused days of despair. Do I bore you?'

'Not at all, I'm not all that nationalistic. Australia, I can take it or leave it, it's a trading post. Unless you're Aboriginal. I semi-understand your position, Mr Has.'

'Just a ceremony, Mr Holt, a shabby ceremony and I became what I am not. I became a citizen of your sunny land. My children, they are Australian. And they have developed the habit of innocence. I admire it, I envy it. Yet I fear it as well. People here are unprepared. You Australians play games. On the television, over and over again, actors play at being your blue-eyed boys charging a Turkish hill. It is stupidity. They knew nothing. This country worships stupidity.'

'Stupidity,' I echoed. He was getting going. No marks for interrupting the flow. Has gathered his fingertips together, tapped them up and down on the image of the wind blowing the ship which the slaves rowed.

'I will tell you the story of Oula Strossmayer.' Was I going to get yet another version? Has continued: 'I cannot guarantee that knowing it will solve your problem. First, a thing or two about myself. I read in the papers, it arises from time to time, that I am some kind of war criminal. This I tell you is untrue, totally untrue. There are claims that cannot be supported that

I am responsible for atrocities. I'll tell you this . . .' He rose, walked to the window, a ramrod of a man, hands clasped behind his back. He turned to face me. 'In France the Gestapo was forced to abandon reports of anti-German activity. In one case it is believed forty thousand inhabitants of a city of twice that number had been reported to the SS. That, Mr Holt, is war. And that is human nature also. Let me tell you one more thing before you hear the story of Oula Strossmayer who came to such a regrettable, though not, we would all have to admit, such an untimely end. This is the trick to my story, Mr Holt. Though, if you tell it, if you repeat it, I will deny everything that I have said. Of that I assure you. I keep it a secret because I enjoy the game, even the notoriety—I get some power from that.

'You see, Mr Holt, I am Jewish. My mother was Jewish. For me the Germans were a greater threat, the greatest threat. And I had shouted "Better war than pact—Better grave than slave" in the streets of Belgrade as a very young man, as a student. That was our cry. Two weeks later the city was rubble and dust. Twenty thousand people were killed. Yugoslavia was invaded.

'I fancied myself a young national, a young hero. I fled to the south, joined up with Mihailović. But then we fought amongst ourselves: Communists on the one hand, Mihailović on the other. I was never a Communist, Mr Holt, take my word on that. The allies betrayed us, we were discredited by propagandists. In the end we holed up in the south. By the time our leader, Mihailović, was tried and shot in 1946, I was in New Zealand. Then I came to Australia. He had been a great man. At his trial—who could call it a trial?—he said: "I wanted much, I began much, but the gale of the world swept away me and my work".'

Has turned away again. He surveyed the panorama of new buildings. 'That is why I am hated, why my name is smeared. In that Stalinist period under Tito, directly after the war, it was not the heroes who seized power, but the ideologues. Many were turncoats. It is a profession, being an ideologue. Which ideas? It matters not at all.'

I reached forward, picked up another biscuit, bit it in half at the waist. 'Good therapy,' I said. 'Biting replicas of little animals. Sort of preparation for life's swings and slides.'

He watched me, cold eyes working me out—watching for reaction.

I was impressed. I guess I looked it. It sounded all right, the story. They usually do; it's later you find out what was true, what wasn't. If you ever find that out. I didn't really have much idea about Yugoslavia. England, yes—from Ethelred the Unready right up to VE day. I had been fed that over and over again. Yugoslavia had always been beyond the pale.

The phone rang; Has picked it up, requested no interruptions over the next hour. I got a hard, world-weary grin. Was the ice melting? Then he was off again.

'You must remember in this story we are not talking about innocent people. This does not concern the black and the white. We are talking of the real world, of a lot of shades of grey. Of compromise, the desperate need for constant forgiveness.'

I'd bet . . . he didn't look like he would forgive a baby.

'I fled south with Mihailović, Chetniks, as we had been called. My sister, she was my older sister, the winds blew her in a different direction. A woman, her choices were different. She remained in German Belgrade. Her Jewishness was easily obscured since our family was well connected and we came from Zagreb, the centre of Croatia. We were not pro-German Croats, we were Yugoslavs, my family thought of itself like that.

'In Zagreb we had known the Strossmayers. All the world knew that family, descendants of a great patriot.' I felt I was going round and round, the same names, the same facts, coming up again and again. Always it was the emphasis that changed.

Has ground on: 'We have limits, there is not enough time here for historical byways. Suffice it to say that Oula Strossmayer was an internationalist, a radical. As much Parisian as Yugoslav. In her heart what did she care for our country, for its fate? . . . She cared nothing at all.

'She bore a child in Zagreb, in early 1941. Then, a year later, she fled. She attempted a return to France. It is believed that she died in that attempt. A ship in which she was travelling was sunk off Ajaccio on the Corsican coast. We know the ship was sunk in 1942. Oula Strossmayer was said to be on board.

'To survive in Belgrade, my sister, to my shame, became the companion of certain officers of the occupation forces. She was a whore, Mr Holt. Could I put it more simply? But it is all terminology . . . what does it mean, whore?

'With the Russian invasion I was forced to retreat in front of it, making my way through our country, moving by night. The Russians crossed the Danube into Serbia in September. By that time I was in Belgrade and Tito's army was twenty miles away. Then, with my sister, I went to Zagreb. We made use of the favour she had found with the Germans. In Zagreb, by extraorinary coincidence, it became possible for my sister to take precautions to protect herself from recrimination, punishment, even death—the stories of Partisan justice were travelling as quickly as armies, more quickly. By the most remarkable good fortune my sister was able to become . . .'

I said it for him: 'Oula Strossmayer?' Christ! Eastern European convolutions.

'She purchased the identity, paid for it with everything we owned. That was the deal demanded by the dead woman's aunt, who was also caring for a child, Milo, an infant. All this, Mr Holt—can you believe it?—accomplished in one afternoon. In one afternoon! It was chaos in those times. The woman's brother-in-law, Oula's true father, had been dead a year already. His family fled. This aunt, with the tiny child, was clinging there. Perhaps she felt she had nothing to fear. She was of a certain age, a spinster, neutral in every way—safe as few people were safe from the anarchy.

'Yet for my sister the coincidence was fantastic. My sister had known this woman. Had taken piano lessons from her as a child. There was some bond there. Fate, its mysterious hand, had steered us to the one place where we might find a vacuum— how should I say?—with a name . . . it was like a being waiting for substance.

'A new identity, that was at a premium on the market. People wanted gold, wanted diamonds, but papers were the rarest prize of all. Which identity? That was always the question. For whom? Russians? Americans? Germans? Tito? It was a lottery. My sister won the lottery.

'By new year we were in Trieste. For baggage, the painting, drawings, some letters, photographs . . . proof of my sister's identity. She must be the anti-Fascist hero. Oula's credentials were impeccable. The aunt obliged with writing letters, recent ones. Also she supplied papers pointing to certain people.'

I interrupted the flow. 'But those papers incriminated you. That Mr Has, is why I'm here. It's a nice story you're telling me. Good for putting little children to sleep. Only problem is, it's crap.'

'The press cutting! Oh yes, of course. I forgot.'

'You forgot! Come off it, Mr Has.'

'I am afraid that you will have to believe me. It is true that there is the name, Has, printed in this ancient piece of paper. I emphasize the word, ancient. What you have shoved under my nose today is a scrap of paper printed I don't know when. In it there is the name, Has. It is my name but I do not have exclusive rights. Let me put it this way, perhaps then you will understand. I have often found it difficult to get you Australians to understand . . . you who have what to your credit? The invention of a rotary clothes-line and a rotary mower, I believe. And now you have a man working on some new kind of rotating engine. You see, after two hundred years you always like to go around in circles. But listen to this: the name, Has, belongs to more than one person.' He raised the flat of one hand, smiled. 'I surprise you, I will allow you time to absorb this fact.'

He was playing with me now, having fun.,

'Your name is Holt, correct? When you see this name written down do you think always that it is you who is being referred to? When I read that an Australian Prime Minister named Holt goes swimming and drowns am I supposed to think that everyone named Holt has drowned? Of course not, my friend. And neither is it the case that where you see "Has" written in a newspaper that it refers to me. With reasoning like that, would I or would I not like to have you on a jury? It might depend on what I was attempting to prove.'

He rose to show me out. The interview had come to an end. I protested: 'All right, it seems unlikely but I'll buy it if you insist.' I was struggling not to appear the total fool.

Has stopped, almost at the door. He turned, regarded me

for a long moment. He dropped his forehead into one hand, I saw the big diamond flash on a finger. 'My sister became the dead woman,' he told me then. 'She was taken over by Oula Strossmayer, became convinced by the rightness of the things for which that person had stood. She became weak in the head. That is since we, the two of us, arrived in New Zealand . . . that was where we could obtain a permit to go, to the other side of the world. It had been New Zealand soldiers who held off Tito at Trieste in 1945. But as soon as we arrived, my sister and me, in that new world . . . since then we have made no contact.'

He had opened the door, was waiting for me to exit. 'No contact at all. My sister, you see, suffered great mortification. To escape herself she chose to become this other person. She established links with people who had been associates of the lost woman. Long after it was no longer necessary to do so she clung to these things of the past.' He pointed to the bundle of photographs and documents I held in my hand. 'I came to Australia, she followed. Nothing changed here. She continued to disown me, to live her strange, her remote counterfeit life.'

We were standing at the lifts. Has had pressed the button, was waiting to eject me from his floor.

'OK,' I said, 'let's pretend I believe all that. What about the aunt? What about the kid? Did she get to believe that she'd given birth to little Milo was well?'

The lift arrived, the door opened, closed. I stayed.

He told me that the child had been reared for a decade in Yugoslavia. Then, under a scheme for the reuniting of families, he had been claimed by people in Canada. That had been a more liberal time by then, it was after Tito's break with the Soviet Union.

As I moved into the lift, Has keeping a hand on the door to hold it open, I asked, as a parting gesture: 'You'd think she would have got together with the boy, wouldn't you? She takes over everything but leaves out the kid. Why was that?'

'It was the other way about, Mr Holt. Milo grew up to become a patriot. He is today a staunch believer in a free Croatia . . .'

Well, I guess that was how what he was saying finished up. The doors cut me off from the last word or two.

Chapter 18

Mrs Christophe was a better woman away from her husband. She was almost fun. I couldn't rid myself of a fantasy of him doing nasty, intimate things to the car while alone and free: creeping into the garage, whisking off the cloth cover to reveal its naked shining beauty in the gloom.

The search for a house had progressed. It was dangerously close to a conclusion.

The choice was between a huge ex-boarding house with three grimy floors of rooms divided into smaller rooms, most with a spectacular view of the water and its yachts—that was Mrs Christophe's preference. She had already advanced to planning the restoration in shag-pile carpet and buff suede-covered furniture—things she'd drooled over in the homemaker glossies. Me, I thought the whole thing looked like one hell of a headache and, rich as I might have been, I didn't look forward to the stream of tradesmen taking me for all they could. I just did not think I could stand the strain.

Option number two was a top-floor apartment at Darling Point—you could see the Heads in one direction and in the other you looked over Garden Island onto the sweeping concrete sails of the Opera House. A fussy person might have felt the need to clean one of the windows where dust had marked out a pattern of raindrops. Otherwise, trouble free. As Karen pointed out, the price of apartments was doing worse than houses. Whichever way you looked at it an eyeful of water never came cheap.

I voted for the apartment. That made one voice each way with Karen holding the decider. After some umming and ahing she came my way and put her mother into a huff for a full ten minutes: Mrs Christophe was a hard woman to keep down once let loose. Chatting and laughing she was rediscovering a daughter she had lost six years before—lost because of Catalpa and her arsehole husband. She was doubly pleased when Karen, in a moment of weakness, announced the developing baby. From then on it was like playing a bit part in a TV soapie, watching them clucking and cackling and planning. Me, even the old Essington, I was entering into the spirit of the thing. Infected by Karen, I couldn't help it. I had not seen her like that before, the almost dutiful daughter.

It was instant possession—nobody to move out, just us to fill the fashionable void created by the block's developers. Two days before the big move we got a letter from Dawn. She and Farah were making money hand over fist. News that turned Karen triumphant and heralded an attack on the nice-but-useless-things boutiques that gradually displace all else in the inner cities of the world.

I blew the whistle when we acquired a blackamoor that was too obviously fake. 'That,' I said, 'goes back.' Karen flicked me a mischievous grin, Mrs Christophe's face fell—it had been her choice. 'A fucking monument to slavery.' That really upset the apple-cart. A rich man, but foul-mouthed.

'Essington, the Dufys . . . surely we should frame them up.'

I shook my head. I had decided they belonged with the will—at least if it went to Father Down. Otherwise we would see.

After two extensions Karen's mum headed back north. I had grown quite attached to her. She was so normal, so much a human being. In the mother department I'd been sold a little short. Mine had been so demented I had come to mistrust the whole sub-species. With Karen heading in the motherhood direction it could have been argued that mother-conditioning would be a necessity for the provider; for the boy from the bush.

I avoided Feathers but I kept an eye out for his ineffectual mate, the ASIO mace king. Funny thing was Feathers kept clear of me as well. Maybe he reasoned he'd trod on my toes too hard too often. He was giving them time to mend.

The next report from the silk trade contained news of an arrangement being made between the Rue de France shop and a place on the Île St Louis in Paris. That was the way it went, money piling up on money. Dawn included a press cutting—

the report of an explosion in a car thought to be on its way to plant a bomb. The police were investigating. It gets lively on the streets of Nice. Three of the four people killed were believed to be Croatian separatists. One was named Milo Strossmayer. There was a photo of him; a face I knew. A pleasant enough open face, only the photo was of a younger man than the Matt Smith who had, for reasons of his own, started my involvement in the whole damn business. The man who, outside Entrevaux, had shown us the house where Feathers had found the guns.

It gave me no pleasure then to believe him dead. I had a lot to get back at him for and yet I couldn't relive that breaking into the house without experiencing a terrible sense of foolish unworldliness, without shuddering at the memory. There had been times when I'd wished I could find a way to hand them Feathers on a plate, if revenge was what they'd wanted. Of course it wasn't, not the way it turned out. They were too sophisticated for that. Just as Milo was too sophisticated to blow himself up, never the fool like that.

I sent a photostat of the cutting to Gerald Sparrow and one to Has, anonymous. I was being even-handed and figuring that it should clear up problems with the will. I expected Feathers would let me know if and when the Milo claim was dropped or defeated.

Still I kept an eye out for Randall, and for substitute Randalls, as well, confident of my ability to pick them. The look, it was in my head. The opaque stare peering back inside itself at nothing—once seen never forgotten.

Milo Strossmayer, if Has was to be believed (why should he be believed?), had been turned into a fanatic by circumstance. Less dramatic circumstance had exposed Gerald Sparrow to the same infection. The effect was pretty much the same. Fate had brought them face to face at Entrevaux—opposed but on the same psychological side, blind to the needs of us poor mortals. Believing in it, then, I concluded that there had been justice in the method of Milo's reported death—blown sky-high by his own addiction to a cause. Maybe the cause had broadened, got more generalized. Had that bomb gone off for the Croats or for the more general cause, separatism and tribal sovereignty? That's what those racial obsessions boiled down to. The big question was: Would such a man have bothered to cut up an old woman in the open spaces of New South Wales? Axe a member of his own tribe? Answer: Yes, and quick-smart too if she was seen to be a turncoat.

Milo had grudges, perhaps psychological reasons to perpetuate the violence of an older generation. And Oula Strossmayer *manquée* had stolen from him, usurped the identity of a mother he could hardly have known. Instead of a dead mother he had finished up with a fake one living the life of a hermit in the Australian bush. All that understood, I still didn't reckon he'd hacked the old biddy up.

Unless there was something missing.

Nothing about the documents supported the idea that they were really important. None of them except perhaps the list of names destroyed by Brkic. Funny, you forget a piece of paper like that at your peril. The rest didn't finger anyone particular. The Has cutting—well, maybe. I didn't forget the value of the painting. Milo had been denied his inheritance, but would he kill for it? Milo, the hardened soldier for Croatia? For that matter would he buy a killer? In the end he hadn't finished up with the painting. There'd been no attempt to snatch it, or to lay claim to it before the death. If there had been threats they were more like a kind of warning to the old lady. Has went to some trouble to take the threats out of the hands of the police who'd thrown them away out there in Millbourne, and to relocate them within the fog of Oula's imagination. They were, he suggested, the product of a confused conscience.

Why, I'd asked, would her imagination have them come from Entrevaux? He didn't answer that one. I didn't inquire into why they'd had substance enough to get her to entrust the Dufy to semi-strangers.

Had the drawings been passed to the jam-bottlers to keep them safe as well?

I'd worked out answers to a lot of the questions. The trouble was I kept on changing the answers around.

We settled into Sydney. Days then weeks ambled by. Good days, good weeks; a domestic time. It was relaxing living without the discipline imposed by the always helpful presence of Rebecca and Renardo. The rest was Millbourne's problem or ASIO's, or a headache for Assistant Commissioner Betti. Out there in the bush some myth would be built . . . the closing line: 'Cut up by an axe she was, a foreigner.'

It occurred to Karen that the baby should be born in France. It would re-establish the family connection, provide future French nationality possibilities. The baby was a plus—our big plus.

So, no sooner had we settled into the comfortable life of the South Pacific than we were planning to be off again. First a farewell trip to Catalpa for Karen. I was excused. It must have been anticipation of the empty time ahead that made me think again of Millbourne. Then I kept on thinking of it. That had to be where the solution lay. Just like Has said: 'There's never a case where there must be a connection.'

There was no connection, that was the solution. Or there was no solution.

Something else prompted me to want to go. If there was no solution why was it reported on page four of that Wednesday's *Sydney Morning Herald* that a seventy-year-old woman had been found chopped up with an axe at Smales. Smales was where you got to if you drove on through Millbourne, on over the bridge. It wouldn't have taken much for Smales to be called Millbourne West.

It was meddlesome of me to go. More like Feathers really. None of my business. I wanted to know, nothing more. Information is the cure for curiosity. It crossed my mind to rent a big macho pick-up with bullbar and everything, so I could bash into cars all over town—the trick was to fit in. And no beret this time, no eccentric presence. With luck it would be all peace and sunshine and stories at the bar by the convivial light of an open fire.

'I wish you wouldn't, Ess, I really do.'

'No harm; keep me out of trouble, Karen. More danger all by my lonesome in Sydney. Sin city, remember?'

'Be serious. Millbourne, it's creepy . . . What's to gain? It's over now, all over.'

'Interest, Bluey. I . . . well, I don't know. Small towns are small. If you manage to hang around you find out everything in

174

a couple of hours. The axe man has to be around there someplace.'

'Not necessarily.'

'Likely.'

She shrugged. 'You're crazy. Essington, I want you in one piece when I get back. Would you believe it, I love you. We can't have an orphan, can we?'

'I was . . . didn't have a father at any rate.'

'Half your luck.'

'All the more reason then.'

'Not you, Ess, you're not as horrible as you make out. Full of nice surprises.'

She caught a taxi early in the morning. I hung around waiting for the peak hour to pass, for traffic to thin out. Midday I rang for a car. It was delivered half an hour later. Checking myself in the mirror, getting the effect right for Millbourne, I registered 'ECAM' out of the corner of my eye—the reflection of Randall's mace canister. I was clutching it as I stepped into the lift.

I'd gone for the rural look to put the natives at their ease—blue shirt, bone trousers, tweed jacket. Oh for a plaited kangaroo-hide belt. Improperly, my head was naked, only trimmed hair for cover. And that a touch grey at the sides.

I hadn't gone for the pick-up but a Holden—the national wheels—a straight six. The quick tin box. I pushed it along once I made it over the mountains. Pushed it as though I was trying to catch the moon that hung low in the west. A bad-looking moon with the crescent's horns pointing down on the flat blackness where Millbourne lay. Where its people were no doubt setting out for another night on the town, axes in hand.

I would have needed a bulldozer to attack the cars outside the motel rooms at the Duke of Wellington. I was glad I'd rung a booking through before setting off. And there was Barney's black Ford right over the far side. I'd almost forgotten about Barney. Could I be so lucky that he'd forgotten about me? The manager had. I approached him in the bar, asked for the key. He was reaching for it when the aggro slaughterman leapt to his side, whispered in his ear. The hand drew back from the keyboard.

'Full up, sorry,' the manager said. Too stupid to even look embarrassed. 'A beer?' he asked, figuring on blandness as the way out.

'A room,' I insisted. 'It was booked.'

'Sorry, like I said, full up.' He stood before me, were his eyes trying to bore holes?

'You took the booking, I rang.' The bar fell silent. At one table a bunch of big men, fat men whose buttocks were trying to make it right up to the shoulders: cops I would have thought. Then I remembered the axing. The brains had come down from the smoke to help sniff out the old-lady killer. They just sat there, sort of motionless, faces between bears' and pigs'. Had mothers loved them? It occurred to me that they were why Barney wasn't smashing glasses, pushing them into the features I'd inherited from Mr Holt senior.

'If I don't have a room there isn't one.'

'Fine, you don't have a room.' I leant forward and whispered: 'Try the beer as an enema.' Then a smart exit. I figured the trick was to get going before Barney.

That left the Oxford down the other end, just before the bridge. The 'B' had gone off the front window leaving an 'AR' through which shone an unwelcoming dull glow. I backed to the kerb to angle park then entered. Behind me I heard the skid of a braking car.

Mine host was full as a tick, obviously so, but in control. That was the way they get. He was big, the Millbourne Goliath, with a bemused face that looked semi-accidentally formed. His top lip hung out creating a shelter for the lower one and for the extinguished cigarette that hung there.

Three other drinkers were sharing the lack of warmth. Two, pensioners they would have been, were playing cards. The other was Winikie. I would have sworn it was him, the jam-bottler, only gone downhill a thousand feet or so. He looked as drunk as the barman. Except he wasn't carrying the booze with the same style.

'You wouldn't have a room?' I asked.

The eyebrows went up.

Barney entered at my back. I didn't look around, I could see him in the mirror behind the bottles.

'A room?' The drunk was giving himself time to think. Then

176

he focused, glared. 'Get out of here . . . you're barred. You know that, barred!'

'But . . .'

'Not you, mate . . . hang on, I'll see what we can look up.'

Barney was talking fast at Winikie. He'd draped an arm around the little chap's shoulders.

The barman kept at him: 'Get out, you mongrel bastard or do I have to come round and throw you out.'

'She's right, Hughie. She's right, I was just . . .'

'You was just fucking nothing. You was just getting out of here.' And he was coming round past the card players who acted like they hadn't heard a thing, raising each other with matchsticks.

He might have been sixty or more, but he scared Barney. Scared every ounce of Barney's fourteen plus stone. Every inch of his six feet. He was off, out the door. Jim Winikie remained—grime turned to scale within the stubble of his beard, blood marks creeping across the whites of his eyes. He looked sheepish and he was in for a dressing-down.

'You there, Jimmy Winikie, you ought to know better.' Laying down the law. I could wait till the dust settled. 'You've been sitting here since twelve noon. It's gone nine o'clock and you never move. What do you think you're doing, Jimmy? Trying to kill yourself or something? How about the wife, the little fella? Christ! Your dad, if your dad could see you . . . you know as well as me he'd belt the shit out of you. Letting things go like this. What do you want with Barney Sedges, Jimmy? He's dirt, do you hear me? And trouble. Take my advice, son, steer clear.'

I was watching, Winikie watched me watch. From his eyes it looked like he hadn't heard a word.

'You cheating bastard.' To me, that was. That was all he said. His moral guide returned behind the bar, pulled a couple of beers, slid over. 'You want a room? Well, I dare say we could fix you up. Take half an hour, mind. It's not so often we get a visitor. Here it's regulars.' He gestured to the card players. 'Live in, board and lodging . . . more like family.'

Winikie said: 'Throw the bastard out, Hughie.'

'He don't like you, he don't. Seems to have come over him all of an instant.'

'Of course he doesn't, he's drunk as a fish.'

I was ignored, he was pressing home for salvation: 'Why don't you go home to Rita now, Jimmy?'

'Can't.'

'What do you mean, "can't"?'

'She's not there no more, is she?'

'The little fella?'

'Gone too . . . pissed off yesterday. I never told anyone. You're the first I told, Hughie.'

'Why? What'd you do? Must have done something.'

'Done nothing. She just pissed off like. Couldn't take it any more. The abattoir closed, didn't it? Well, what is there?'

'How about the pottery you learnt, thought that was doing all right.'

'You thought wrong, didn't you? You got it wrong. It's not like we're swarming with tourists, is it?'

'Wouldn't know . . . you're telling me, Jimmy.'

'And that bastard . . .' Jimmy pointed his glass at me.

'You know him?'

'Never clapped eyes on him before,' I said.

'Liar! Fucking liar!'

'Another beer, mister?' To me, like an apology.

'Yeah. And could you tell your little mate not to call me a liar. "Fucking" I'm not against; but nobody calls me a liar.'

'Nobody lays down rules here, mister. Nobody but me, that is. Me, and I guess, God.' A Christian no less! He gave me a grin; half humouring, half a warning. Wouldn't have surprised me if he had a shotgun under the counter. He looked that confident.

The card players played on. The one with his back to me had a great pile of matches. He also had a pair of threes. He was raising his pal.

I lay on the bed shifting out of the way of randomly aggressive springs while listening to possums or rats scuttling about in the ceiling. Bits of nest, straw and twigs, had slipped down the crack where the cornice had split from the wall. Outside my window, one floor down at the foot of the back steps, a compressor motor worked intermittently, waiting each time for the moment when I might be dropping off. My stomach rumbled, I was hungry. Hughie had said there was nothing to eat in the pub—lazy bastard hadn't wanted to cook. The Spun Fleece shut its doors each day at four o'clock.

At eight o'clock sharp Hughie cooked bacon and eggs. I had been warned.

I was up at six, a couple of hours to kill. I thought I'd take the Holden for a little tour. I headed up the street to the Avenue of Remembrance that pointed the way to Sydney past the hill-perched killing-sheds. The sheet of iron still flapped but there were no animals awaiting death. Where the last tree marked yet another victim of WWI I did a U-turn, headed back through town, over the bridge, swung off on the Tip Road till I came to what had been Oula Strossmayer's drive. I took it slowly up the rutted track, branches scraping the hired sheen off the car.

Suddenly a roar, then crunch—I was rammed. I saw him in the rear vision. Barney rammed again. Vicious bastard. He must have been waiting, watching. There were two of them, I could see: Barney and another, Barney and Winikie. The black Ford V8 reversed then came at me a third time. I shot forward with the impact. No fun in that.

He hit me three more times. Not only was the car getting a thumping, I was getting whiplash. I'd been rammed to a spot where there was a gap in the bushes. Barney was reversing for another go. No problem for him, the bull bar was built to push houses around. I flung open the door, dived for it, bunching into a forward roll. The instant before ejection I locked my fingers around the mace can that had shot out of the map rack onto the seat.

I made it to my feet then dodged down in the direction of the creek. The idea being to get to the bridge and from there to head back up into town where the gaggle of fat cops might afford protection. But easier said than done. While dodging through undergrowth down the slope I heard a shotgun blast— a random shot? It pulled me up. I propped like a stag. I listened.

Silence. Was there a faint rustle to my left . . . a little distance off? Could I hear the quick in and out of breath above the sound of my own heart pounding? Nature itself had gone silent. Birds, everything, waited in the air of the morning.

A branch cracked—somewhere below me a heavy foot. I took off along the contour, electing to head away from the bridge. I was running I guessed in the direction of the Winikies' house. That way I had to be in front of them, even if deeper into a trap. Again I propped. I could hear two bodies crashing through the scrub at my back. They had heard me in flight; no longer any need for stalking. They were madmen both, but intent on what? Not just a bashing, the gun indicated more than that.

No time to think. I took off again, ploughed my way through an overgrown hedge of privet and out into the open. I belted across the clearing and into one of the four shearers' buildings. Luck or misfortune had made it the kiln-room. There was only one door. The way in was also the way out.

I could hear their voices: 'Where's he gone? . . . Told you to get in front.' A controlled whisper.

'I seen him, Barney. Sure I did.' Barney was the leader . . . the leader in what? 'Went that way, to my place.'

Though he kept his voice down, Barney sounded like he was struggling to control rage: 'I fucking told you, Jesus Christ! You stupid cunt . . . Why the fuck didn't you do like I said?'

Whining: 'But I did, Barney, only he was fast. He was too fast. Anyways, we got him now . . . up the house. Has to be holed up there, doesn't he, but.' He sounded like he was pleading for his life, not mine. Begging, asking for mercy. I wasn't going to beg.

I pressed against the wall behind the door—between the kiln and the door. I waited. They were going so quiet I couldn't locate them any longer. I could see nothing, only the strip of light between the door and its frame where it hung open.

A tread . . . I thought. I kept my eye on the strip of light. Something broke it, was passing inside, into where I stood. The twin barrels of the gun appeared level with the handle. They stopped.

I flung the door shut, hurling my body to go with the swinging wood. I was part of the impact. The gun dropped, the door jammed on its breach and on an arm. I leapt forward, hauling the door open again, treading on the gun in the same action. I was waving the mace, indiscriminately spraying as I attacked. Barney, rising to his knees got a full blast in his face—enough to clear a warren. He went down, hands over his eyes. He was roaring like a de-horned bull—scrambled rage and pain.

One gone, the dangerous one at that. And I had a shotgun with a cartridge in one barrel, with any luck. There wasn't time to break it and check. Winikie was out there someplace. He'd have to have heard Barney but he wasn't saying anything. He wasn't even moving. I dragged Barney all the way inside. What to do with a mad dog? He was on all fours, still roaring. I got into him with the shotgun butt. Not an easy beast to stop, your slaughterman. Eventually I must have hit the spot. He went limp like a rabbit with a wrung neck. A final groan, then silence.

Silence continued outside as well. How many guns did they have, the two of them? In the distance I heard a motor, the V8, distinctive: the black twin spinner. Then a car smashing through trees.

I ran back towards the house where Has's sister had played her life's masquerade. I ran on down the drive, rounded a bend and there it was—the Holden and beyond, the V8, half-turned and stuck. Behind it Winikie was hacking away at the vegetation with an axe. Wild-eyed and crazy.

As I saw him he saw me. He was a medieval marauder caught in the act. Slowly I edged forward, the shotgun level, pointing at his chest, at a spot just above the horizontal axe handle.

'Shoot, you bastard!' He screamed. 'Shoot then . . . why the fuck don't you?'

I pulled back the hammer.

Strangely controlled, low level, he said, 'You tricked me on those pictures, didn't you? They was worth a fortune, wasn't they?' Like he was schizoid.

'Throw the axe down, Winikie.'

He tightened his grip. His eyes grew big and round, and then slowly, a leaking balloon, he let all that anger, that adrenaline, that craziness, go out. The axe fell. His arms hung loose.

'Winikie!' I shouted too loud—much too loud. 'Step clear.' He walked towards me three or four paces. 'Down, Winikie, on your face. Keep your arms and legs spread wide.'

He did as he was told. I broke the gun. It was empty, Barney had loaded only one shot.

The captive was babbling by the time the police car came up the track. They'd been called by neighbours over the creek. Most of that end of town must have heard the commotion—the impact of car on car, the shouting, the shot. The cops all had issue revolvers drawn like they'd been taught in college. It took them a long time to work out who was who. It took them even longer to realize that the reason for their visit to Millbourne, well, half of it, lay at their feet. The other half was up in the kiln-room just ticking over.

Nutters, the pair of them; that's what they were, crazies. The slaughtermen taking it out on their own species, on lonely old women who they reckoned the world could do without. Justification—we all need one of those don't we—robbery. That's what Winikie actually claimed, when he was being lucid: his need against their need. I never heard anyone claim that and not finish up backing themselves. But the pickings had been poor and in each of the two cases it was obvious that the killing had been committed more like some art form, like some hyped-up cathartic ritual.

You can't tell any more—crazies everywhere, sniffing and shooting up and peering into the future and justifying . . . justifying everything.

Crazies, like in the hire videos. Barney and Winikie had made their own do-it-yourself horror films in their brains. They were something to keep, to play over in the slammer—forever I hoped.

There was a message at the Oxford sent down too late from the Duke of Wellington. It had come when I should have been in my booked bed the previous night.

At the post office I put through the call. Mrs Christophe answered, she sounded tired. Then, after a long time, Karen, very thick. 'Oh, Essington. Thank God . . .' she was sobbing.

I went numb.

'Ess . . . Oh Ess.' A long pause. 'I lost it. The baby.'

'Hang on,' I said, 'I'm coming.'

Mrs Christophe: 'She's very tired, Essington. She just wants you. Be quick, please.'

There was an airport an hour and a half away. I took the

Millbourne cab. We sailed out of town before anyone could think.

I just stared at all that brown land, didn't say a word. Just prayed to be out of there and far, far away.

The connecting flight to Sydney was gone. But a private charter operator leapt at the chance. Couldn't believe his luck.

Up there in the clouds two images jostled with one another in my mind: Karen's face in anguish and the deadpan look of the licensee of the Duke of Wellington—the man who had left her thus all the long night. He had hours of human pain to answer for. I was going to return, I swore it to myself, and get the bastard.

Chapter 19

Total psychological change: Karen was turned in on herself. She sat, staring, sucking a finger, in what had been her room in the Christophe Catalpa house. She said she wanted to be alone. Her mother fussed. Mr Christophe shrugged his shoulders, made a mouth, walked a well-beaten track between house and garage to make sure no one had nicked his spotless if undistinguished car.

I tried to just be there, nothing more, to ignore the sense of being an intruder. But there didn't seem to be anywhere for me. If I retreated into the sitting-room to sample information from the house's only books, a dated set of encyclopaedias, either Mr or Mrs would hunt me down. They didn't say anything, they would simply hang about the room, fiddling, until I removed myself. If I went into the garden the mower started up.

What could I do? Karen had a right to grief, to her own specific grief, and she could exorcize it and attendant demons any way she thought fit—fine by me. I tried talking. She'd watch me almost with pity, a smile playing on her lips, the flesh swollen around her eyes. 'Oh, Essington, words . . . it was our baby. Words can't do anything about that.'

It was a total personality change and had me floored. Wholly unexpected—Karen just didn't seem the type: she had her feet on the ground, a droll sense of what was and what wasn't. With the miscarriage she'd blown a fuse. Could I ever discover what it was—the faith—she'd put into the child? Or why?

Part of the problem was that something else had gone wrong inside. There were doubts about her having a child now. Whatever the reasons, there was no getting away from it, I had been placed on the back burner . . . maybe forever. Perhaps something in my being expressed things I wasn't saying. My mother had gone into herself in her own special way. I'd seen a lot of her withdrawal and of her irrationality; so I allowed for those things in life. And nobody who handles horses could afford to turn their back on the evidence for languageless communication—if it existed between species, why not within them?

I figured she was right, it was words. They just will not match emotional reality. Yet without words it's difficult to understand what's happening inside, particularly if you believe that they're the only means you've got. Karen had always been great at talking things out.

My thinking things like that didn't do anything real about the problem.

Karen never said it, yet the question hovered in the air: What would it have been like if the events of the previous six months had never occurred? If there had been no Feathers stirring, no gunshots, no visits to Millbourne? I could tell that she believed that she knew the answer—baby doing well. She might have been right.

No, she never said it but, to an extent at least, I was the culprit. Me and my bull psychology.

She was having tests. If she was being less than scientific about the miscarriage I was the same way about predicted problems we may have conceiving children. For me the trick was no more doctors. Instead, a lot of lying about in some sunny pleasant corner of the world giving it a go, slow and gentle. There is quite a possibility that the harder you try to have babies the less chance you've got.

'I think I'll stay here, pull myself together, Essington. Then maybe get right away, head back to France, keep clear of the associations. Maybe take Mum and even Dad. I need time, Ess.'

'It's all right, Blue.' You could see I'd said the right thing. First time in a while. I suggested that I push off, stop putting them all on edge. Departure seemed the best insurance for getting Karen back in one piece.

I went south, aimless. It rained all the way.

A couple of days later I was heading towards the place in Redfern, in search of the good Father Down. It felt even more foreign, Redfern, with me resident in the harbour-view apartment over on the correct side of town.

I inquired at the improvised office. There was only one person there, a man, maybe about my height but not as burly—light-boned, elegant; he wore gold-rimmed half-glasses propped half-way down his nose. He was as dark as, say, Sylvester Stallone, but there was an intelligent gleam in his eye. I'd seen him before, on my last visit. Charlie, that was his name.

'Yep?' Conceivably, I was recognized.

'I was looking for Father Down.'

'Hey,' he laughed. 'Father Down—' an ecclesiastical imitation. 'What do you think this is, the Vatican?'

'There's nobody outside selling light-up electric Madonnas that fell off the back of a truck.'

'That how you tell, is it?' He raised an ironical eyebrow.

We watched one another. He was cool, collected. No need to say anything. I had some ice too, I could switch it on. Biding my time I examined the crudely printed posters done in the colours of the Aboriginal flag. There were photos of culture heroes, all related to the original human settlers of Terra Australis. I recognized some—poets and painters mostly.

I had never managed to share in the white Australian fear and loathing of the Aboriginal people. Up north they had often seemed to me the only civilized beings around those God-forsaken cattle stations, stuffed full of every form of white misfit ever devised or dreamed of by psychologists—right through from owners to the fresh-faced jackaroos just out of boarding-school.

After working up there I didn't think of them as all that different either. Other countries, like France, kept on pointing the finger at Australia for its treatment of the remaining Aboriginal people. They had a point: a lot of babies died; they made up a big proportion of the gaol population. OK, they drank and fought a lot like the poor in Hogarth's London who, translocated, bred up to be Australia's clubmen.

It was a problem. I didn't have a solution. 'I don't want to bugger about. I want to talk to the good Father.'

'And I'm not a cop on point duty, Whitey. I don't sit here waiting to give casual passers-by directions.'

'Let me put it another way, then,' I suggested. 'If I want to do business with Father Down how would I go about it?'

He laughed. 'You know what this reminds me of? One of those problems they used to put on matchboxes . . . if this, if that, what colour is the driver's hair?'

'Having fun?' I paused. 'When I find him who can I tell him was so helpful?'

'Charlie.'

'And I'm Essington. I think you tried to go up my nose once before, Charlie. And I guess you reckon you've got a million reasons. But I've got only so many minutes in a day and you're burning them up. Would you believe I am the bearer of good tidings for Father Down?' Charlie looked like he wouldn't believe anything unless it suited him. While I was talking he was reading through some letter, or pretending to. 'Good tidings for the lot of you, money news. Fistfuls of the green stuff.'

The word 'money' didn't bring him to his feet. Not that he looked like he needed any—hand-stitched lapels, discreet silk tie. (Had it fallen off the back of a truck with the Madonnas outside the Vatican?)

'Sit down, Essington. Don't excite yourself. Tell me what you've got.'

'I'll tell it to Father Down.'

'Because I'm Aboriginal?'

'That's paranoia, you should get it looked at. This is legal, lost wills, you know.'

'You've got the right man,' said Charlie. 'I do the legal work.'

I wasn't there to pass on the news of a bomb exploding over in Nice. I reckoned lawyers would have worked that out already or could do so in their own good time. Me, I was passing over the Dufy drawings—all but the one I'd decided to keep as a reminder, and as payment for services unintentionally rendered. It was the one I liked best. The one in which the curiously blank yet erotic stare of the semi-naked woman seemed most compelling. Looking at it you were looking back in time into the eyes of the woman who was called in paintings of that period 'the Hindu Model'.

*

Life can move slow when you're depressed. I was depressed but I was determined to keep it moving. Days were flying past; I rang Catalpa every one of them. Karen seemed to make a point of sounding pleased enough for the intrusion but she'd made up her mind. Stay away Essington.

Charlie—Charlie Lawrence it was—had arranged for me to see Down. And I had filled him in some more on what was happening. He didn't seem the least surprised to learn that Richards and Partners had failed to be in contact about the death of the party claiming against Oula Strossmayer's estate— either he left a lot up to God or he'd grown used to the ways of the world.

For all I knew Feathers might have whisked himself off to an amateur secret-service training camp up in the Blue Mountains just in there behind Sydney. Maybe that was why he hadn't reacted to news of Milo's death. I could picture him, burnt cork smeared on his face, stalking straw-stuffed scarecrows togged up as foreign nationals. Clients could go to hell.

We were at a dingy pub that smelt of sick and urine, where there were a lot of people gone a bit starey-eyed with the booze—a lot of port and sweet sherry was being served; quicker and cheaper than beer. The drinkers weren't the types that had got a stranglehold on the financial game.

I was tossing down rum and cokes—that was Charlie's drink and I am suggestible. The little priest stuck to beer pepped up with a whisky chaser. He kept pretty much in his own world which was, at that moment at any rate, defined by the sports pages of the morning paper. Dogs were racing not too far away at Harold Park and the good Father had put a few dollars each way here and there. We could watch what was happening through the blessing of a television mounted above the bar.

Charlie was more interested in my story—me, a bit like the Ancient Mariner, holding his attention while outlining the cursed history of my recent life.

'Millbourne,' he spat. 'Don't talk to me about Millbourne. What's the cop down there . . . the bastard's name?'

'I guess there's a few. Me, I exchanged words with a Sergeant Armstrong.'

'Armstrong!' he exploded. 'That's the man. A total redneck. Used to be up here at Redfern till a kid—he was sixteen about—was found in the cells, dead. An inquiry, the usual whitewash. Always the same story. Then they sent the bastard to Millbourne. Sort of place you send people like that. Deserve one another—Armstrong, Millbourne. I was born not so far from that dump. I know the kind they go for out there.' He drained his glass. 'Morons,' he said.

'You can say that again.'

If Charlie was getting aggressive it didn't show. 'Wouldn't mind seeing Armstrong, sort of evening things up.' He said that with the calm of a man advising on a corporate takeover. 'I was involved with the case. A bastard, he was.' Peering through the gold rims he looked the man of peace, the negotiator. Charlie Lawrence couldn't have been more than thirty years old. But in those years he'd learnt control. I looked at the hands beyond the regulation length of white shirt cuff. They were chunky hands, they'd done work—maybe even worked out. I knew exactly what he was saying when he said he'd like to see Armstrong.

In Millbourne I had a score to settle as well.

'Bugger it,' said Father Down. I figure that was the fourth or fifth race in a row where his selection was unplaced. 'Proof,' he said, 'of the existence of God.'

We went to Millbourne, Charlie and I, we left our mark. It was a kind of blind revenge. On my part for what Karen had been through—or that's what I told myself, anyway. Charlie went along in the hope of levelling the score with Sergeant Armstrong. No such luck, the bastard had the night off and missed the action. It was child's play but, in the end, no good for the soul. We both should have known better, but then so should the publican, and maybe he would in future.

Back in Sydney all I could think about was that maybe Dawn was right, maybe there was something terribly wrong inside the male of the species. Karen had been through the centre of hell and all I could do was rush around the countryside trying to knock people's blocks off. The reward was self-loathing.

Charlie was off overseas, heading for France, having conned the government into paying to send him to a conference of lawyers representing Aboriginal people who'd found themselves losing out in their own land. It had been given a fancy name that sounded like the invention of a Paris philosopher. Because of what had happened in Millbourne we reckoned that the quicker we both vacated the country the better, Charlie staying with me until conference time. It wouldn't take too long before somebody thought about assault charges.

That evening we boarded a flight for London, the quick, safe and uncomplicated way out.

'Karen?'

'Essington.' She sounded more perky. 'Where are you?'

'You're not going to believe this, Paddington Station.'

'Paddington doesn't have a station.'

'In London it does.'

We'd talked already about heading back for France. Karen thought she'd get a kick out of reintroducing her father to his mother-country. How you could get a kick out of doing anything for a bastard like that I'd never know. So the whole gang of us were heading for Cap Ferrat. Happy surprise for Desdemona. I was the advance guard, only more in advance than expected. Pissing off like that I hadn't even allowed myself the luxury of ringing. It could be that shame had something to do with it as well.

'Only, Essington . . . would you mind if we still take it slowly?'

Take it slowly! I was footing the bill. And I was starting to feel excluded. Emotionally manipulated. That's the trouble with your older man, he's a bit of an old rag really. I made up my mind to make a stand, somewhere, sometime . . .

The tube in my luggage contained the Dufy drawing I had salvaged. The painting had got itself an estimate of three hundred and seventy-five thousand dollars from a man who had just kind of snatched that figure out of the air. You get a lot of them among the hangers-on of art—dapper little chaps with style, and custard between the ears. The house at Millbourne, I wouldn't have thought it could bring more than fifty thousand. There was a total rebuild required. And that, no job for the faint-hearted. Father Down and his friends were likely to finish up with around four hundred and fifty to five hundred thousand if the drawings sold all right. The sort of money that keeps a small government department going for half an hour.

*

With a foot still in Australia, just as we had been passing a final barrage of duty-free garbage—not the booze of course—I caught sight of a stuffed koala bear. I remembered Betti, the promise I'd made to bring one for his son. I got the biggest I could find. It sported a little tag which read 'Made in Taiwan'. With the transaction came the reminder that I could well be on somebody's wanted list over there in France. The way I was going I'd become the man without a country—there's been a book called that by Jane Austen or Ken Follett or somebody.

I couldn't know what lay in store for me when I delivered the koala bear. But then nor did I realize that the drawing of the Hindu Model I carried had not yet finished telling its tale. Her eyes, like those of a lover, would not or could not reveal their innermost secrets.

I tried to explain to Renardo that the Bentley was mine, my property. If I wanted to take it I could. He chose to look offended. If he was actually sulking it would have been hard to tell, he was never all that expressive even at the best of times. I gave in. More in honour of the memory of my aunt than anything else. It had been in the will—be kind to servants. I had good reason to follow the direction, they had been more than kind to me.

And they looked after Desdemona. When we headed up the road to Entrevaux, Charlie and I, we left the Great Dane more confused than ever. She was a one-man dog but the man was never there.

Snow had already fallen, we could see peaks white against a pale sky. Autumn leaves clung to the trees tinting the sides of rocky hills, water rushed out of its precipitous courses to feed the river. As we climbed the air became clearer, crisper, permitting the profiles of ancient defensive structures to be read in clear focus at distance. In the end I had felt obliged to leave Renardo the Citroën Estate as well and hired a Citroën *deux chevaux*, more for the fun of it than anything else. That's what I claimed—maybe it was the old mean me rearing its head. Had it ever lowered?

'You own all that and we're stuck getting around the country in a toy?'

'You know that's not true, Charlie. Back home a neat little car like this is favoured by . . .'

'By professors of anthropology. Think they're ideologically pure. They wear sandals too! Even a bark canoe isn't ideologically pure. Nothing is.'

We were laughing. Well, why not? I hadn't laughed when two days before I'd arrived at the Betti household to deliver the koala bear. Betti had not been there. Just the wife and the child. Child with brown startled eyes. Betti had been dead.

On my way from their apartment block I'd examined round the entrance. There were chips out of the stone where the sprayed bullets had struck. The assassins hadn't taken the chance of missing him as he stepped out on his way to the *préfecture*.

No prizes for asking why or by whom.

Madame Betti had been calm enough—surprised me how she was able to handle it. We talked for a bit while the child, Jean-Daniel, cuddled the bear all the way from the wilds of Australia, if you didn't read the tag. I asked about Garoud.

He'd been transferred. He was out of it. That was a relief for me, it was Garoud who'd worried me most when I first decided to return. It seems Betti had done his job getting rid of him. The price he had to pay though, had it been worth it?

'Look out!' A truck shot out of a side-road. Charlie corrected the wrong way, we mounted the footpath. The crazy bastard was laughing, tears running down his cheeks behind the half-glasses.

'You could have killed us.'

'But I didn't, did I? I love it . . . wilder, that's what it is. This is the way Rimbaud drove, I guess.'

'Doing battle with the Commies?'

'Not Big-Eyes, Essington. I'm talking about the poet Arthur Rimbaud. Be before your time.' He backed onto the road watched by a pair of bored women who must have seen a lot more interesting things than that in a long life. Charlie was having great fun with the dashboard-mounted gear-stick—symbol of French inventiveness.

We made slow progress through the mountains. The tiny car's even tinier motor laboured uphill but spun along fine on the flat, thanks to its huge flywheel. Charlie opened the sun-roof letting the crisp air compete with that supplied by the meagre heater.

There were all sorts of reasons for going to Entrevaux; reasons like nostalgia—that was where my troubles started, had I grown to love them? And I was fleeing before Karen arrived. She'd been insistent that psychic recuperation was not yet over when we'd spoken, Nice-Paris, on the phone that morning. I still held out high hopes. During the whole thing she'd never really turned nasty. But what did I know of the workings of a mind half as old as mine—one that had never been made to stand in line or to keep its shoulders straight. Was I starting to yearn for old values? Karen was the product of new stimuli, new ways of looking at things. She was part of the 'me' generation. Old-fashioned Essington Holt, he belonged to the . . . to the what?

Heading north was the right thing to do.

We had lunch at Entrevaux, sitting in the sun. Not too many cars or people about. I kept an eye out for the odd Slavic type in battledress, but they'd seen us coming, I expect, and clambered into their hidey-holes. Even from far off no cannon roar nor the rattle of machine-gun fire.

'Problems,' Charlie announced over coffee. 'We spend the rest of our lives here or keep on up to Geneva?'

I explained that I wanted to poke around for a couple of hours, that we still had lots of light to make it to Sisteron or, if not, at least to Digne. Charlie shrugged. I had an idea of what was at the back of his mind—a quick trip south along the way we'd come. He had got the hots for Dawn. It was a strange thing to witness, he had actually made some headway. I didn't think he'd worked on her hormones or anything but they'd got along like a house on fire. That had left me to entertain the beautiful Farah who did unconscious impersonations of Dela-croix odalisques. There were times when she looked a lot like my Dufy drawing as well.

With Charlie and Dawn it had initially been the worlds they held in common from the days of the loose coalition of the left: feminists, conservationists, ban the bombers and supporters of Aboriginal Land Rights. Nothing seemed to have happened but there was a fair bit of consciousness-sharing, if that's what you'd call it, going on.

The house where the guns had been stored was marginally transformed having lost the locked-up look. There were even optimistic signs of digging and planting along the narrow terrace on which it was located. A gaily painted Mini Moke was stationed beside the creek. I'd figured that the least effect Feathers' raid could have had would be a relocation of the arms cache. I guess I'd been right.

The new owner was English. He made junk sculpture. As luck would have it I caught him at it, working away and whistling. It was to do with shopping trolleys—pinched I would have bet. These were filled with rusted-out and broken styrene or tin food containers. (Shades of little Jimmy Winikie, I thought.) There were a few vacuum-moulded plastic bottles mixed in for good measure.

I pulled out the picture of Matt Smith/Milo Strossmayer to stem the flow of Frank Cummings' sales pitch. He didn't appreciate being brought back down to ground level. Charlie, maidenly shy, had said he didn't like intruding so he'd stayed on the far side of the river. I suspected he feared for his brand new Moroccan leather slip-ons. He was flipping stones across the water.

I had wet feet.

Finally Frank examined the photo. 'You've got to add a few years on,' I prompted.

'Could be,' he said. 'I had most contact with the agent. Only saw the seller once, when he came to move his junk. Boxes of it he had.'

'Frank, you're the artist, mate, you're the one with the visual memory.'

He shook his head, tapped himself on the temple: 'It's inside here . . . concepts.'

'Concepts! Shit, I have to find this man. Like he's dead now. But I want to find out about him, to understand him. He's a hobby with me, Frank . . . think of it that way.'

Then it occurred to me that Frank Cummings was scared. We'd scared him, Charlie and me.

'It's in your line, would you believe, it's about art, Frank.

About a picture by Dufy . . . Raoul Dufy . . . you've heard of him.'

But he was still scared. The first person ever to be badly affected by Dufy, by that bland talent.

'Do you reckon you bought it from him?' I tried again.

He pretended to look harder. 'Maybe, yes . . . maybe I did.'

'Well, Frank, the name? You must have swapped contracts with names and dates and gobbledegook.'

'Of course.' With dignity. Frank was a scruffy character, a bit of a roughneck really with his punched-in nose. His hair was about as long as the stubble on his chin. He was in denims—Union Jack T-shirt under the jacket. Like he might vote Tory against class interests.

'That social comment?' I asked, pointing to the shopping trolley.

'That's art,' he said. 'It is itself. No reference beyond that.'

'Half your luck. You sell it . . . that?'

'Actually, I'm rather well collected.'

'The collectors . . . you remember them? See that fellow over there . . . remember him?' I'd changed my voice a bit, gone quieter. It seemed to put the wind right up him. I thought that was best, maybe, to scare him shitless.

'He's a collector?' Frank asked. His eyes had gone deep and round, he was clasping his hands beneath his chin as though in the act of prayer. It was quite moving.

'He'll fucking collect you if you don't bring your head down out of the clouds and give me a straight answer.'

'Don't know why I bother.'

'Bother what?' Charlie asked. We were heading over a bit of flat country just short of Sisteron. You could see where the slabs of rock closed in to make it a fortified pass in the old days. They never built for the view, always for defence. The sun was already casting long shadows.

'Bother to bother . . . the brain won't stop.'

'It's racial . . .'

'Fascist,' I muttered.

'No, you're all the same. It's not that you're brighter. More like controlled stupidity. You won't let things alone.'

'You are a Fascist, you know that, Charlie? The nearest thing I've ever met to a real one. You think in racial theories.'

'And you're an obsessive. Carry that photo round, showing people. You're looking for a man who's already dead.'

'I want to pull the story together, tie it up.'

'Life isn't an English novel, Essington. That's where culture puts everything arse about. Life is scraggy, directionless, no neat ending. Same with the law . . . that's its central problem: the assumption that you can find a culprit, try him, declare him guilty or even innocent. Innocent! Think of that. The whole thing's a fairy tale with very complex rules.'

'And big prize money.'

'There's that too, Essington. Now that feller has agreed that he bought the house off the man in your photo . . . therefore Matt Smith was definitely Milo Strossmayer! Just as likely you could prove that because their names both have the initials M S. Coincidence doesn't make someone a Yugoslav gunrunner or responsible for the death of your Monsieur Betti. If you stare for long enough half the world looks like a photograph of the other half. Particles, little dots making patterns, that's all a photograph is. He recognized the face because he had a big bruiser like you standing over him. That's no guarantee of reality.' He was repeating Has's argument: don't hunt coincidences.

'What is?' I asked.

'Being . . . now, on this road. Those trees flying past. The water down there. None of that will drive you crazy thinking about it. That's the proof that it's reality.'

'I guess you're right, Charlie. Yet it fits. That guy's like a ghost. The time I saw him he appeared more or less out of nowhere. In exactly the same way he trotted off to nowhere. His mother either was or she was not. It's all like meaning in the eyes of that woman in my Dufy drawing. They seem full of it. But then you ask, full of what? When you come down to it they don't mean anything, it's in your head. That's art, I suppose.'

They could have missed the company, I don't know. But Mr and Mrs Next Door at Cap Ferrat had been pressing the instant I got back from Australia.

'Oh, Mr Holt.' They'd even taken the trouble to find out my

name—not so much trouble when you think of it. 'Our little baby has become good friends with your great monster in there.'

'With Desdemona?'

'Such a nice name.' There was no doubt about it, Mrs Next Door was well put together. I expect she took beauty treatments—whatever, they certainly worked. Better close up than at a distance. Her skin was like a pale polished timber and it won out over trans-Atlantic fripperies—the bejewelled cowboy boots.

Rebecca told me they were called Feldstein. They were Swiss. Rebecca didn't like the Swiss. Said it was because they murdered the French language. 'What do I do to it then?' I asked.

'You. Mr 'olt, you're not up to murder . . . not yet.'

'But I'll get there?'

'Perhaps you will.'

Henry Feldstein asked me over for a drink. 'Do bring the monster. We would like to meet him at close quarters. If he will not eat me or our little baby, Charlie, our little poodle.' The Redfern lawyer didn't like that when I told him.

'Eat you! It's a she, Mr Feldstein.'

'Does that make a difference?'

'No . . . I suppose not.'

'Around sunset, this evening. Are you free, Mr Holt?'

'Certainly, I've a friend staying with me at the moment though.'

'Bring her, most definitely.'

'It's a he, Mr Feldstein.' We were having gender trouble. 'Mrs Holt is away for a few more days.'

'Bring your friend, Mr Holt. It will be a pleasure. Mrs Feldstein and I look forward to it.'

We'd been back two days at this stage. Charlie had already been doing foundation work on the Dawn relationship.

Chapter 20

Papa Fisch ran the Fisch Galleries in Geneva's old town area plonked up on the hill above Lac Léman within whose waters large groper-like fish hang about waiting to swallow spilled gold bullion. There is an awkward relationship between the old town and the new, no natural continuity except a giant shopping plaza featuring the global names of high fashion—you walk in on the level where the discreet banks have their offices, you walk out into quaint cobbled streets. And what do you find there? Antique shops and art galleries. You get sick of it after a while in Europe; the commerce in the new, arts in the old. I'd vote for a more random mix, but I'm not the people of Geneva. Nor would I have run my yellow van all along the side of our innocent little grey *deux chevaux* just because Charlie had been trying to get out of a bus lane for several hundred hours.

Fisch Galleries was just along from the Cathederal—along the cobbles and down some steps. Mrs Feldstein had assured me we would find a warm welcome there. They'd made their pile and fled to the sun. Her father, Papa Fisch, elected to stay behind in his beloved gallery, surrounded by what he liked best, the art of the ages.

A stern-eyed woman occupied a desk squeezed in between carvings, vases, carpets and paintings. She stared at us, hard. That was the Swiss stare. Even the swans floating above the giant fish have that look about the eyes. Has all the gaiety been squandered in one gesture—the invention of the cuckoo clock? From then on it has been interest rates and discreet bank accounts. I got the feeling overcoats sold well.

We must have looked English-speaking. 'Can I help you?' Still the same stare. If she'd smiled she could have looked quite nice. Perhaps John Calvin brought the frown with him after his expulsion from Paris. '*Post tenebras lux*', he had cried, presumably from the old city's ramparts.

'That's light after dark,' Charlie had explained.

'You speak Swiss?'

'Latin, Bright-Eyes. I read it on a wall back there.'

I asked Cold-Eyes for Mr Fisch.

'In relation to?'

'Me being a friend of his daughter's.'

'Ah, Madame Beck.'

'No, Mrs Feldstein. My name is Holt.'

'That daughter.' Disapproval there.

I smiled, it's best. She picked up a phone, babbled into it in German. 'He will come.' Still no smile.

What the hell am I doing this for? I asked myself. Evidence of what a broken heart will do. Well, if not broken, damaged. Takes the mind out of a man.

'What mind, Ess?' I could almost hear Karen asking. Though not unkindly.

'Mr Holt,' Mrs Feldstein had exclaimed, 'if you are interested in art, if you are a collector, then you must not pass through Geneva without a visit to my father. His whole life is art.'

A very small man appeared out of nowhere. It was as though he had stepped out of the space of a large baroque canvas depicting Venus and Adonis. It was based on the famous work from the studio of Titian hanging in the Palazzo Barberini in Rome. (I knew that from books, used to yearn to see the original.) Only in this one there were more dogs. Papa Fisch looked about the same size as the dogs.

'Mr Holt, I believe.' Very correct. He was sporting hair hanging long over his shoulders from a bald dome. It was white, the hair. His skin was an antique parchment, smooth like that of his daughter. He had deep-set amused eyes. 'I am Paul Fisch. My daughter has rung me. She told me I might expect you.' Looked like she'd told him there was a prospect of making a sale. 'I must tell you it is a very great pleasure.'

I flashed the desk lady an 'I told you so' look. She had returned to her work, trying to stare out a piece of paper. I introduced Charlie Lawrence. We were invited upstairs. I don't think I ever passed a more interesting couple of hours.

Upstairs was a maze of small rooms—little people, little spaces. Why not, it makes sense. Big art was stacked all over the place. We sat in three chairs grouped around a one-bar radiator. That was after we had done the tour, culminating in a detailed examination of a Cézanne, a small picture, maybe ten inches by twelve.

'What do you think, Mr Lawson?'

'Lawrence.' Fisch had carried the picture along with us. Now it was leaning against a Gothic angel in polychrome wood—singing, hands clasped in reverence.

'I'm so sorry.' the old man stood corrected. 'It is my age. No, I tell a lie, names I have never mastered.'

'No worries,' Charlie hastened to reassure. 'I tell you, you're dealing with a philistine when it comes to painting, leaves me cold. Now your angel, that's a completely different matter.'

I might have been a philistine too but I was hooked. Art is one thing in museums—fine but cold, guarded; property of Big Brother. In your hands, on a domestic wall, it lives. It is an extension of day-to-day experience. Not just great art, all art. I was bowled over.

'You must be familiar with the head, the Cézanne self-portrait, in the National Gallery, London. It is not dissimilar, is it? I will tell you. Then we will see what you think. Then you may examine it again. That is not a valuable painting. Not at all. But it is unique and of great historical importance for it was produced in Russia a few years after Stalin came to power. There are quite a number of such pictures. Yet how many people know of their existence? How far are they spread through our Western collections?

'You know your history, gentlemen? Of how Joseph Stalin tightened his grip on Soviet life, of the problems that he faced in his economy . . . partly due to external pressure. Perhaps you also remember that before the Bolsheviks seized power many of the great collectors in Paris had been Russian. They took home with them magnificent works by the Impressionists and by the early moderns.'

It was a long story, convoluted. We got through a number of cups of coffee brought by a pasty-faced woman who might never have seen the light of day. She seemed part of the rooms, part of their crust of art and gloom. Then we started on the Armagnac.

At the centre of everything was a scheme to copy saleable works in the hands of the State. After the revolution that meant, with the years, more or less all works of importance and certainly all ideologically unsound modernist pictures. The copies were leaked out into the West as though smuggled, with a cover story that their sale must remain secret. To sell such art publicly while suppressing it would seem too obvious a contradiction.

The targets were ambitious private collectors. The kind of people who would pay anything for something exceptional, for something rare. The originals had long been stored away from public view, mostly at Leningrad—in the Hermitage Gallery there. More recently these paintings have been put on limited public view.

Fisch thought that those which had been copied were hidden away separately, safely. The quality of the forgeries was so good because in every case the model for the work already existed, no invention was required, every brush stroke was in its place just waiting to be duplicated. Somewhere in the Soviet Union a Cézanne, the sister picture of the self-portrait in London, waited to be rediscovered. In the meantime, the forgery which had come into the old dealer's hands must do.

'You see,' he had said, getting to his feet a fraction unsteady—we had been slumped too long, 'I purchased that painting for a considerable sum of money in 1931. I believed that I was buying a masterpiece that had been lost from our gaze. Instead I got a unique piece of history. I've had the pigments analysed, the binding oils—scrapings from the very edge of the canvas, from places obscured by the frame. Some of these materials would not have been available to Paul Cézanne. Some were specifically Russian—either they had trouble obtaining supplies or, more likely, they did not need to take a great deal of care. At that time it was the appearance and not the chemistry of the painting that was of prime importance.'

Interesting the way you pick up information. I'd had a little to do with forgery, even produced a few, but for an unsophisticated market. The Soviet forgeries were among the best ever.

The thing is that in most cases you wonder why anyone ever believed it. Your average forged work is well below par. It finds a home because of mugs rushing a bargain, human greed. And after that people get to believe in the reality of what they've bought.

To me Fisch's Cézanne was a little master-work—the artist portraying himself, collar turned up, staring out at us, the people of the future, through small dark eyes. His bald head read like an egg against patterned wallpaper. A mane of hair hung down behind. It occurred to me that in the region of the crown of the head the dealer and the portrait had a bit in common.

Other than visiting Fisch and paying too much for everything, there wasn't a lot to do in Geneva. Charlie wanted to go to the United Nations and look up a friend attached to the Australian delegation there. So, we braved the traffic again and got through with not a lot of damage to the little car—no thanks to the mean-eyed Protestant motorists. It finished up he decided to stay a few days. They'd been students together and the friend, a bachelor, was clearly looking forward to them going out on the town.

We were due to split up anyway, Charlie heading west to Paris. Me, I was intending to drive across the top of Italy, heading for Venice where all the houses were sinking. I was sorry to see the last of Charlie, he'd kept me laughing. He promised to be back, probably sooner than later. I said I'd ring from Venice, keep in touch. If his conference proved a bore why not come over and join me. You could see he liked the idea.

Me and the *deux chevaux* buzzed off over the Swiss countryside. Through neat, well-organized little farms wherever the earth was flat enough to till. I'd rung Karen at Cap Ferrat the day before; they were in residence, bags unpacked.

'So I'll see you.'

'Not too long, Essington.'

'I hope not. Be kind to the dog.'

'I promise.' That was a promise! Did it refer to the dog or it not being too long? I chose the latter, became elated, waltzed the grey comedy of a car. Mercedes and Ferraris honked their indignation speeding past. To be slow was unpardonable. Slow and erratic—I should be shot.

Neither faster nor straighter, up into the amazing mountains till we all plunged right into the side of Mont Blanc, through the tunnel to Italy, Milano and places east. Heading over Italy's only, if vast, plain spreading out either side of the Po—a stretch of land with too many people trying to do too much on it; never an uncluttered vista.

On the final stretch after a stop-over at Padua I lost third gear, had to make it straight through from second to fourth. Not so easy with limited power, but interesting. I didn't mind at all. It went with the car, a work of inspiration and invention—the sort of thing you keep going with fencing wire.

I left it in Mestre to get the gearbox fixed and crossed to Venice on the train.

You don't get stinking rich without relatives springing up from everywhere; getting a fix on you, both navigational and psychological. My mother had spent a lifetime thinking of her dead husband's sister sitting in splendour out on Cap Ferrat.

The letter had read: 'Dear Mr Holt . . .' It was an elegant claim to cousinship by one Andrew Bartlett who, with his friend Elizabeth, was spending time in Venice as a student. He was pretty keen to come over to the Côte d'Azure and look me up. Why not? Anything's worth a go. I'd rather turned the tables with a phone call. I had reversed the traffic. I was heading to look them up and, with any luck, by the time I arrived they would have found me a place to lay my head. Some place where damp wasn't too much of a problem.

'It's the ships that do it, those great throbbing motors. Energy waves spread through the water, hit the foundations, the entire city vibrates.'

'Any wonder it's sinking,' Elizabeth responded to Andrew's potted science.

We were eating ice-creams, sitting in the sun on the Fondamenta Delle Zattere. The ship was Russian, standing high out of the water, dwarfing the historical city: the anachronism. Seabirds fluttered about welcoming it, yet protesting at the same time. Sliding along the Guidecca Canal it obscured the practical housing developments facing us across the water.

Cousin and friend had taken Venice, its welfare, to heart. As though it was a dog they had picked up on the street after it had been hit by a motor car. Elizabeth looked like the kind of person who was headed for squandering her life on good works. She was nervous, beautiful in a haughty kind of way, her eyes popped like she'd been brought up iodine-deficient. Initially I thought her a fraction dotty. No, just intense.

'It's a scandal,' she maintained. Christ! If she went around the world getting outraged her adrenal glands wouldn't last the distance.

'All things fall and are built again.' Oh so wise: Andrew was showing us he knew poetry.

'Andrew, nobody's going to be able to build this again.'

I wasn't listening, not fully. I was watching. There were a couple of natives eating ice-cream over by the rail that stopped them falling into the choppy water. They were holding neck-reflectors in place, getting an under-the-chin tan. What they'd got so far was yellowish—more like jaundice than sun-bronzing.

We were all looking like people having a good time. On postcards, the envy of the world. The *vaporetti* and *motoscafi* pottered about, dodging the large international vessels arriving to do business. Every now and then a water-taxi or private launch zoomed past expressing a superior presence. No gondolas, not over that side.

The ice-cream was good. Likewise the coffee. Mine host was a large Austrian-looking man with curly red-blond hair. He reminded me of an owner who used to fly up to inspect cattle stations a couple of times a year when I was working in the Queensland Gulf country. The man I was watching seemed to sustain authority by some act of will. It did not come naturally.

Funny thing, the profile of a man sitting behind the proprietor's favourite viewing position rang bells. But I couldn't get a clear view. People kept on coming out, shaking the boss's hand, getting in the bloody way.

'Mr Holt.' I liked that. Made me feel mature. Elizabeth would have been about the same age as Karen—old enough to be my daughter. 'Mr Holt!' Elizabeth repeated. Mine host was now surrounded, a popular fellow. I turned attention to the cousin's girlfriend. She asked me: 'Have you considered contributing to the restoration fund?'

I must have looked quizzical.

'For Venice. There's a group in Australia. We've taken responsibility for a church . . . for saving it.'

I stared at her a minute. Her mouth was smeared with melted ice-cream. I felt like reaching forward, wiping it clean. 'Elizabeth, at my time of life you are starting to look around for anyone who can do restoration work. Not on churches, on yours truly.'

Andrew laughed too loudly. Trying to please Uncle. He'd actually called me Uncle at the start; we were cousins several times removed.

Elizabeth was not amused.

Mine host was crossing to where the coffee came from. I got a clear view and found the profile gone. It had happened before, a remembered face. People talk of *doppelgängers*— well some people do, pains in the neck—but it had always seemed to me that nature turns us out in sets with small variations alluding to individuality.

We separated at the Galleria dell'Accademia where Napoleon had shoved all the pictures. An orderly man, Napoleon. He'd even filled in a canal or two. I watched my young friends walk away. She had good legs, long and athletic; she walked as though she was on springs and elastic, like a dancer.

They had done a wonderful job, finding me an apartment at S. Gregorio up near the Chiesa della Salute. And had anticipated my wealth; the rent was astronomical. It was embarrassing being able to pay it. I sat there staring at the walls, listening to the silent world beyond them, measuring the cubic metres, filling them up with dollar signs.

Chapter 21

Sirens were blaring when I woke. I thought a nuclear power station must have blown its top. When I went into the street in search of bread, milk and coffee I found that boards had been laid to walk on—the pavement underneath was flooded. No wonder cats preferred to reside on the wooden Ponte dell'Accademia. I'd seen them the day before sleeping in boxes, piled on top of each other like caterpillars at a party. With the waters risen they could go up a step or two, providing the cat-minders moved the boxes.

It was raining; I found six or seven umbrellas just inside the door—discarded property of other short-term renters. I took a stroll, stepped into a gondola just short of Peggy Guggenheim's Gallery and crossed the Grand Canal to S. Maria del Giglio. I thought I'd poke over to S. Marco to take a look at the pigeons. The old Frank Sinatra favourite, 'Three Coins in the Fountain', kept running through my brain. Elizabeth told me later that would have been Rome. Not that she remembered the song.

People tried to take my photo, umbrella and all. It was a while before I was conscious of having spent most of my tourist energies examining passing faces. I still couldn't quite place the profile I'd seen the previous day on the Zattere.

Upstairs at the Correr Museum by the Piazza S. Marco, I met Andrew and Elizabeth as arranged. They knew a good thing when they saw one. I was that good thing. We had time to look around the exhibition hanging in the museum before heading off for lunch . . . my treat. It had been my treat the day before.

I'd seen the posters. It was a show from the Hermitage in Leningrad—modern French art. Unique. First thing that struck me going in through the door was a large Matisse dance painting made around 1910—strident colour, bold simple drawing.

We were a throng in there. Again I found myself examining people, though it occurred to me to keep a hopeful eye out for the original of the Cézanne head Paul Fisch had shown me in Geneva.

Andrew was lingering in front of a number of landscapes by Cézanne. He was enrolled at the art school part of the Accademia and hated it, thought it was out of date; they had to study drawing! In front of the Cézannes he was acting the student: deep, thoughtful—existential insights.

Elizabeth stuck with me, steering, pointing out things I should be thinking. Maybe I was getting horny, I felt constantly aware of her body. She seemed to make a lot of physical contact and when she spoke her lips almost touched my ear. I could feel her warm sweet breath.

I saw it as she pronounced the artist's name: Oula Strossmayer's Dufy! It was hanging there, large as art. I was transfixed. Couldn't believe my eyes. It was complete—the bust of Mozart, piano keyboard . . . was it a harpsichord? Strong vermilion.

I like to have faith in my visual memory—paintings, at least—I pride myself on that. I work on it when I get the chance. I read a picture from left to right, backwards and forwards, moving from top to bottom in the same way as you read a book. I find it allows me to see more, to pick up ambiguities, nuances of colour, expressive gestures. The Dufy was exactly the same painting, no doubt about it. I pulled out my wallet, extracted the snap I had of the Strossmayer version.

As I did that I was jostled, a group of people pushed past. Again I felt the long surfaces of Elizabeth's body, surfaces that didn't seem anxious to go away.

And initially I'd wanted to wipe ice-cream from her lips!

I went back over what old Fisch had told me about the Soviet fund-raising venture after Stalin came to power. If that story was true then there, in Venice, I was looking at the original of the Strossmayer Dufy. That was a twist. If it was the original hanging there, what was hanging back in Australia, in Feathers' office?

The Russians didn't have a second version of the Dufy Mozart painting—I knew that he had done several—they had the same one. No doubt about that. Right down to the details of the mind changing, the scrubbing out, the over-painting.

Fisch had said that they kept the originals—it wouldn't have made sense to do otherwise. That made Oula's the forgery. Had she known that all along?

Andrew caught up with us, breathless with a discovery he'd made about the semiotic significance of brush directions in Cézanne landscapes.

They fill their heads with shit, kids.

'That's great, Andy,' said Elizabeth, clutching his arm. I'd seen people do that sort of clutch before, steadying themselves. Her eyes were still trying to transmit messages my way.

I wasn't sure I was ready for those messages: the married man old enough to be . . . to know better.

Most Australian farms are the size of Venice. You needed that at least to support a family. We the visitors, are crammed in. We walk the streets, going from church to church, clutching our guidebooks. After a few days you get to notice that you've seen everybody before. You have. You've passed them in the streets going from the Scuola di S. Rocco to the Chiesa di S. Maria Gloriosa dei Frari. They have churches in Venice like an Australian town has pubs—on every corner with always a couple in between.

I had taken to walking on a percentage system, hunting the profile I thought I'd spotted when eating ice-cream on the Zattere. Maybe it had been a double, maybe not. If not then a gift from the Gods. In the apartment I put Milo's photo from the bomb death report up on the wall, something to brood over. Peter and Patrick, my friends from Chez Catz, had taught me not to believe the press. It's only written for money, that was their argument. Also I put up my colour shot of the Strossmaye; Dufy: the mysteries of life.

It kept on raining so the umbrellas were in my way along the narrow streets. Several times I pursued likely candidates past cake shops, fashion displays, exotic delicatessens. Each time it was the wrong man. I got wet feet. I tripped over cats. I got very little pleasure.

I rang Villa du Phare.

Karen was there with her mother. Mr Christophe had headed for the Dordogne where he claimed to have come from in the first place. Everybody has to come from somewhere. I'd thought that most of the European New Caledonians were out of the gaols of Paris. French counterparts of your dinky-di Aussie.

Karen was feeling a lot better, nothing around to remind her. Maybe, she said, I was right after all: better not to try and make babies, just let them come. 'It's more spiritual anyway, Essington.'

Elizabeth liked to call things spiritual. She could say it in Italian too. Elizabeth studied the language while Andrew studied art. There was a whole generation of us Australians dedicated to learning useless things—who was going to grow the food, keep the drains working?

Still, I enjoyed getting about with Elizabeth, and her grasp of the language was useful. The body contact sport was a bonus for the young at heart. She had made up her mind to show me how the other half lived in the sinking city—the other half was their half. We walked right over town to the Fondamenta Nuova where you catch boats to take you to the islands: Murano, Burano and Torcello. Not to mention the cemetery, S. Michele.

'Be prepared for a shock, your place is a palace by comparison.'

'A palace's rent.' She ignored that. Kept dragging me along. We were off the main tourist beat, there were less notable buildings and the streets were pleasantly empty.

'I wondered where people lived . . . ordinary people.' Then I asked: 'Where's Andrew today?' Intonation innocent.

'Drawing class, then it's the crit. The day of the professors. He has his work looked at.'

That was that; easy life, a professor's life.

I was standing by a small window, my head bent forward so it didn't hit the roof. Post-coital depression—I guess it was in the psychology books. Not that I hadn't given Elizabeth everything I'd got. Or she'd taken it.

She was making coffee, naked; proving those legs a reality. I had a pink towel wrapped around my waist. Modest Essington.

I gazed down onto a square. On the far side grill bars

cordoned off a disused church. The building threw a shadow cutting the square in two. Very neat, like an early Hitchcock shot. Two men stood talking to each other; one in the shade, the other in the sun. The man in the sun was agitated. He threw his arms about. He looked to be shouting but I could not hear his voice from up on the top floor. The window was shut.

Finally the victim of the shouting turned. He walked across in my direction. I caught the atmosphere, the conspiratorial subcurrents, another world beneath tourism.

'Coffee's ready,' Elizabeth announced. Even depressed I had to admit she looked fetching—her skin, and the white coffee-cups sitting on their saucers.

Venice is a heady place. A kind of antique fun-park gone short on fun. Even the water looks like it's due for a change.

I ate at a trattoria up my end of Zattere, around S. Gregorio. The waiter entertained me with a trick, balancing a fork on a match on the rim of a glass. I grinned stupidly. I found myself wondering if the cousin's girlfriend had any of the diseases that you read about in the newspapers every day. Then I ate my cake, tiramisu—a speciality of Venice the waiter said—basically sponge cake drenched in liqueur. It was all right. So was the meal. I guess I'd never grow out of wincing when I paid a bill. It was conditioning, like Pavlov's dogs.

I didn't ring Karen. Any distance had become too far away.

I was propped up in bed reading one of the books I found in the apartment. They were all about Venice, sort of narcissistic. I was reading about nuns threading pearls into their pubic hair as party preparation. Now, it seemed, was the dullest Venice ever had it. Yet quick enough for me.

Andrew rang. No, I was busy tomorrow. The day after? We'd see.

I walked over to the Fondamenta Nuova, over to Elizabeth's side of the town, only taking care to keep away from their square. I approached further down towards the Arsenal end. I was hunting for the face.

Then curiosity led me to take a *motoscafo* to the cemetery. It was a good day for it. Golden light, like a J. M. W. Turner painting—the sky, the sea, things all rolled up into a great golden ball. The boat drove right into the centre of it but the gold receded. It drifted out towards Murano.

I was left behind on the quay of S. Michele. The dead have a whole island—not a big one, but it is their domain. There is even a wall to keep them in.

The people who got off with me were bearing flowers, most of them anyway. They had a real reason for going there—so, bully for them. It was only when we'd gone in through the gate, entered the graveyard proper, that I got a sense of someone else among us as aimless as me. With that sense I got a shock that came on with the stages of recognition. It was the profile from the Zattere, it was Matt Smith out of the hills of Entrevaux, it was Milo looking like he did in the photograph of the dead bomber. He had his hands in the pockets of a cotton gaberdine overcoat. He was pretending interest in headstones. Pretending was the key to what he was doing. He was tailing me, it didn't take too much nous to work that out. Only he was making sure not to catch my eye. Instead he did a lot of peering at faded inscriptions as though he was an historian searching after clues.

With him on my mind it wasn't long before I lost direction, no north or south, just the sense of white stone—tombs and chapels—and Italian cypress planted in rows. Flowers brought over from the city to decorate the dead supplied the colour.

I passed through the arched gate in a wall and found myself cut off, alone in the non-Catholic section. There were the Stravinskys, Igor and Vera, side by side. Ezra Pound had a candle burning for his anti-Semitic soul while the great ballet impresario, Diaghilev, was honoured with an elaborate tomb-stone formed as a dome supported by pillars. There was a toe shoe tied to one of the pillars, signed, 'Santi Levy, 1986'.

And there was the man in the cotton gaberdine coming in through the gate. Paying no attention to me, doing nothing more than being there, keeping on my tail. For how long? Me, I'd been watching faces passing me in the narrow streets. Had he always been there behind, keeping me in sight? If so why me? How could he know who I was, that I'd been face to face with him before? I'd heard of photographic memories but . . . he'd seen me just once. And now I was out of place, out of context. The answer, the only one I could find, was that I'd been pointed out by someone. The question was . . . by whom?

The cemetery killed time, the trick was to avoid it killing me. I bolted for where we were again amongst people and then back down to the boat-stop, it was deserted.

A couple of minutes passed before he joined me, you could read the relief at finding his quarry in place, waiting like a good boy. I grinned at him. 'Excuse me.'

He raised eyebrows into that high forehead.

'How do you get back from here?' I asked.

'You take the boat.' There it was, the Canadian accent. This was no product of a fevered Holt imagination.

Just the pair of us waiting for the boat. Him staring fixedly into the shimmering light. He didn't appear inclined to chat.

You feel stupid butting in where you're not wanted, particularly in a foreign country. I was used to feeling stupid, had developed a thick skin. I wanted to find out how and why the pair of us were standing there.

'In for a long wait,' I prompted.

Not even a nod.

'Some cemetery. I wouldn't mind being buried here along with all the greats—the Stravinskys. Great general, Stravinsky.'

He didn't turn a hair, just stared at me with . . . was it contempt?

'And Diaghilev . . . did you see the ballet shoe? A cute touch.'

He took the two steps needed to close the gap between us. Both his hands were in the coat's pockets. Were they empty, perhaps?

'What do you want, Mr Holt?'

'My name, you know my name! Isn't this a small world.'

'"A great general, Stravinsky". . . you're not the type.'

'Quarter-back then,' I grinned, tried to make it look natural. I had my hands out of my pockets just like Mother told me to do.

He was cool, pretending to be at least half amused: 'And Diaghilev?'

'Let me guess, he played baseball . . . you can tell from the shoe.'

Now he looked weary, sick of the game. 'What do you want in Venice, Mr Holt?'

'How do you know my name?'

'You want what?'

'Would you believe, a holiday.'

'A holiday, coincidental. One minute you are poking about in the French mountains . . . were you on holidays there, as well?'

'As a matter of fact, yes.'

'Then, far away in Australia, you visit a Mr Has, ask him questions, investigative questions. Now here you are in Venice. You want to know how I know your name? Of course we have met before, we both know that. Of course I know who you are from then.'

'But to recognize me, pick me out in the crowd . . .'

'I didn't recognize you, Mr Holt. Our mutual friend Mr Has did that.'

'You mean he's over here as well. Why's that? Don't tell me, he's buying a palace.'

'He likes Venice, Mr Holt . . .'

'It's Essington.' I held out my hand.

He produced his, and in it a neat-looking little snub-nosed .38.

Funny thing, the next thought I had was of the Betti kid holding the koala bear, those surprised eyes looking up at me over the top of the synthetic fur.

There was a lock of thin, greying hair hanging forward over Milo's brow. Something like a grin distorted his mouth. He'd taken a step backwards, just out of reach. I guessed he'd heard about the fiasco outside the silk shop on the Rue de France.

That was my magic moment, and possibly my last. I knew that I was gazing into the eyes of the connection. This was the man who knew it all. Possibly the legitimate heir to Oula Strossmayer's property, son of the original Oula. I felt sure, in the light of the death report, that he was involved with the pan-European far right movement that had managed to blow up a car in Nice. Who were the dummies who'd got themselves killed to launder a few identities? Had they been mug recruits for the movement or simply innocents set up to be driving the car?

And Milo was the man, clearly the brains, behind the gunrunning from Entrevaux to where? It didn't take much intelligence to guess that it was into the north of Yugoslavia through Venice and Trieste.

This son of the committed Oula Strossmayer had finished up with the revolutionary gene in his make-up as well. Only with him it had shifted one hundred and eighty degrees. His revolution was against the Communists. There was something about his eyes I noticed now I was looking into the dumb tube of steel pointing at my stomach, something to suggest that he'd be holding a gun against the state no matter what.

Still, I wasn't a state, and he was holding one against me too. I already knew what it felt like to get hit. This time there wasn't a chance of it being a graze. Don't bugger about, Essington, I thought.

I smiled. Good humour, they say it spreads.

He was asking about the origins of my interest, about who I worked for, demanding that I come clean. It was too late to explain that the whole thing was a confusion, their confusion, to tell them that they'd have to go back to basics, get hold of Feathers, ask him their questions. Or the mace man, Randall. Yet I felt that as long as he didn't know the answers he wasn't absolutely certain to pull the trigger. For that long I'd continue to share the sensations of the living.

The cemetery island of S. Michele is a quiet place. The dead don't raise their voices. A shot from a .38 would carry right across to Venice proper. It could even penetrate the erotic imaginative recesses of Elizabeth's mind up there in the miniature apartment. That was if the window was open, if she happened to be at home and not out learning her verbs. A dead Essington would count for nothing in the history of all those churches and palaces over there. So, keep the bastard at it, guessing.

I started telling him a little of what I knew. Trying to make it sound deep, mysterious. Trying to keep the pressure off that trigger. It was to do with documents, I explained. Hidden in the back of a painting. That was what I had to bargain with.

Milo was asking about the list. Asking about names. It was the names they wanted.

What list? Which names?

The smile—was that too kind a word?—faded.

He explained that he was interested in documents that had been in the possession of Oula Strossmayer—but made no mention of a blood tie. In particular he was after a list of names. That was what had put me in the firing line, the list Brkic had burnt. And he'd known what he was doing when he put it to the torch, or so it seemed. I'd let Has know who held the papers packed away with the cutting featuring the Canberra lawyer's name. That, it seemed, was a stupid thing to have done. The list that was destroyed had status, it was the thing that got people excited, it was what they were after. They'd figured that Oula must have had it. So, anybody who got hold of Oula's effects was likely to have got the list along with the rest. That anybody was yours truly, the old Essington. Not that I could work out why a slip of paper written in a strange alphabet upset their apple-cart. Strange people, the Europeans, their lives are an endless settlement of old debts. Nothing gets cleaned up, put away for good. The settlement of one conflict forms the basis for the next. It's their habit.

All right, I said, I'd tell him everything. And I did, spitting out the words as payment for seconds of life. Wishing that the mourners would come back down from the dead and wait to catch the boat. Company was what would save my skin. Most of what I had to say only confirmed what he knew already. You could see the bored look about the eyes. But when I got to the axe murderers of Millbourne I could tell that I'd engaged his interest. He wanted me to go over that bit again.

Why me? I kept on asking myself. Why has all this happened to me? Just because I was innocent, unconnected? Does God hate the innocent as much as that?

He was worried now, worried about Barney, about little Jimmie Winikie. An eyebrow shot up, two vertical creases cut into his forehead. He swept back a lock of hair. A questioning vacancy clouded his gaze.

I moved, shifting weight; that brought him back. He stabbed the air with the barrel, making the point of its capacity to deal out death.

'Up till then they'd said it was you lot who'd finished off the old woman.'

'They?' he asked. 'Who'd said?'

I told him about Feathers, about ASIO; if he wanted to kill someone why not look in that department? Those bastards weren't spending what looked a lot like life's final moments stuck on a Venetian boat-stop with a gun hovering in front of them.

Boring, one-track mind—he was back on about the list. That, clearly enough, was top priority. And I didn't have it to deliver. And if he believed that then he might just as well blow me away to hell.

He stepped back further, I watched as the trigger finger tightened. My mind closed in hatred about the image of my school-friend, Gerald Sparrow. Where was he? Why wasn't the bullet about to tear its way through his patriotic frame? Then I was sucking in air as though that might soften the impact. Milo had the gun raised. I shut my eyes, opened them, his hands were in his pockets. He had closed the gap and taken my arm in a farce of comradeship.

Looking about, confused, I saw my salvation. Four middle-aged men, each dressed for the dead, had joined us in the wait for the *motoscafo*.

At the Fondamenta Nuova, the instant the rope was caught, tied, and the gang plank laid, I cut and ran. Fast, past the shop-fronts of the monumental masons who faced the cemetery, the repository for their art works. I crossed a canal bridge then headed in toward S. Marco.

You can run out of luck, hit a dead end, there's lots of them in Venice just like there's sudden areas of deserted stone paving where an executioner can practise his art unprotested.

I didn't look behind but ran, unthinking, through the labyrinth. Suddenly I burst through a narrow arch into a square. Several women carried bags of shopping. Two labourers were digging a hole. The church was locked away behind a grill—I recognized it. I took bearings, crossed the open, negative, architectural space; entered a door.

From the darkness of the passage I looked back over the square in time to see my would-be killer sprint the same track I had just taken. He looked around him, trying to pick up the scent.

Shaken and out of breath I climbed the stairs to the top floor. I knocked on the door. Elizabeth opened it.

Chapter 22

Curious, stimulation comes out every which way. Elizabeth seemed to enjoy the older man. It must have been to do with her daddy. That second visit she was slower, more playful; very playful indeed. She wore a broad-brimmed hat at a crazy angle as she perched up on top of me, arms back, hands clasping her ankles. She rocked backwards and forwards. Her bulging eyes were really quite attractive—expressive—but what did they say? She smiled down on me the way St George might have regarded the corpse of the slain dragon. Every now and then she would roll forward balanced on her knees like a jockey entering the straight, lean right down and suck my ear lobe. It was better than getting shot.

I froze when I heard the door.

'Only Andrew . . . not to worry, he's camp.'

'Lizzie?' His voice. 'Oh! . . . Sorry.' He must have retreated into the kitchen.

I heard pots and pans.

'Coffee anyone?'

'Just a minute,' Elizabeth called over her shoulder. Then she stepped up the pace.

It had always seemed unlikely that Dufy would give away an important early work, something he had already kept for a couple of decades. Give it to a girl who was his model, maybe his assistant from time to time. It would have been more realistic to think of him being generous with a recent work, a piece with which he was not a hundred per cent happy.

The exhibition at the Correr Museum had resolved that problem: the picture that had found its way into Oula's hands had not been the real thing. I wondered if the drawings were also of unsound provenance. The answer came up that nobody would have gone to the trouble of faking them. If they'd been of the same subject as the painting, then maybe yes, to help with the authentication. But the Hindu Model paintings came well after the Mozart bust ones. There was no reason for the Russians to produce forgeries of Dufy's work dated after their revolution. Other fakes, how would they have got into the hands of that old woman out in the New South Wales bush?

I rang Fisch. After a bit of an argument his hard-eyed assistant put me through. She was protective, that was the problem.

I told him about the Dufy out of Russia.

'That is interesting, Mr Holt. You see, as I recall there were miscalculations and naïveties. Although I do not know the picture . . .'

'A Mozart bust, early.'

'Ah, yes. But still, Mr Holt . . . you see it would not have been worth the effort. The price would not have been so great.'

'I get your point. They would have done better sticking to the big names.'

'They were out of touch. Because it was considered bourgeois, because they were disapproving of it; they must have been unable to understand the works they made or the value system into which they were injecting it.'

Made sense to me.

'A Dufy, you say?'

'That's right, Mr Fisch.'

'There was a story but I am not so sure I remember it right. A second-hand story.' It seemed that Fisch dealt as much in them as he did in paintings. 'Can they be trusted? You might know, Mr Holt, that Dufy visited the United States in 1949 to consult doctors about his arthritis. One of these people he had already met in the late thirties . . . a collector who had visited him in France. Dufy was a great success with the Americans, but not the artists; he attacked them. He said that the trouble with American artists was that they couldn't see what was around them until they saw it in a picture.' Come on Fisch, I thought. He continued: 'You see, Dufy had diagnosed the disease that was eating away at modern art.'

'Interesting.' I hoped I sounded impatient. Perhaps Fisch was well into his daily bottle of Armagnac.

'The doctor who had already visited Dufy before the war was

218

later to become a client of mine. He had a story that relates to what you are talking about. This was of Dufy buying a forgery of one of his earlier works to get it out of circulation. The strange thing was that he was not so keen on his more exploratory early pictures anyway, he considered them too aggressive, too attention seeking. Then he discovers one of them forged!'

So there was my answer. Dufy had discovered the forgery himself and purchased it to put the thing out of the way. I'd heard stories of other artists doing the same thing; even with the genuine article if they considered it substandard, liable to damage their long-term reputation. Dufy buying back the forgery made sense of the gift to Oula: he'd given her a painting that had no real value. Could be that he told her as much. He'd given it for the gesture's sake, as a memento. Never dreaming that she would cling to the thing, cart it with her half-way around the world.

An innocent, on arriving in Venice I'd sent a postcard to Villa du Phare, telling them my phone number and postal address in S. Gregorio. The information was passed on to Gerald bloody Sparrow by Rebecca—the two of them miraculously smashing through the language barrier. I was back in circulation. People could line up again to destroy my life.

Karen said she wouldn't have given the bastard a dried pea let alone my address. But she had been away over at Aigues-Mortes at the time, showing her mother the sights.

'And?' I asked.

'Essington . . . I'm sorry. I know I'm being a bitch.'

'Karen, something's going to come undone. For Christ's sake try. I mean it's just a case of grabbing your mind, fixing it to something. Why not to me?'

I didn't do a lot of good. She finished up weepy. I got snappy. The phones returned to their hooks. Outside, the sad night streets.

On top of that—while I was still confused—I got a call from a man claiming to be Has. He wanted to see me. Wanted a chat.

How'd he get the number? From Richards and Partners. I

deserved better than Feathers. Now the bastards knew where I lived.

I didn't have much. I packed my bag, put it by the door. If Has knew where I was I could expect a caller—sooner rather than later. The question was, why had he bothered to ring me? It was like a warning.

Answer: because, like Milo, he didn't really know what I had. Well that was answer number one. Answer number two might well have been that they were outside waiting for me to run. I'd be easier to take in the street. In the apartment they'd have to dig me out.

I rang Elizabeth. No reply. She'd felt like that type of person: not around when needed. Mind you, it was her right. So, I was the old Essington on his own.

If I stayed put I'd be safe enough I thought, irrationally. The unknowable was how much noise they were willing to make that close to the Yugoslav border? I had a pretty good idea that Smith/Strossmayer was hanging about, preparing for something. Everything pointed that way. He was waiting for an action a lot bigger than nailing me. I was a petty accident along the path of history. It was the kind of garbage those creeps believe—history. Not unlike Feathers and his mate Randall. It made them feel big, history. In Feathers' case not big enough to be in Venice following through. It seemed like he'd stuffed up my life then turned his mind to more important things. The ASIO attention span was limited, they'd demonstrated that before.

For relief I tried the number of a hotel in Paris out near the Porte de Clignancourt, on the wrong side of Montmartre. Karen had given it to me. It was Charlie Lawrence's last known abode. The switch put me through, he answered straight off.

No, he wasn't getting amongst it. He was bored. If anything was happening he wasn't finding it. They were all wrapped up in their own problems. 'And you?' he asked.

'Pure joy . . . the endless party.'

'Half your luck. Tell me, Maestro, when are you heading back *chez vous*? I'm itching to see that Dawn again.' Every man to his taste.

'Soon as I can pack my bags.' Did I sound edgy?

'You're all right, aren't you, Essington?'

'We'll see . . .'

'What's that supposed to mean, for God's sake?'

'It means . . . if I don't turn up, Charlie, start looking.'

'Holy Jesus! Essington, if you need help, say. I'm on the next plane.'

I said I thought that would be too late. But there was no putting off Charlie Lawrence. So I told him where I lived, how to get there. Someone to pick up the pieces.

There was a well in the middle where the two buildings met. Not with water. All the rooms that needed pipes were set around it. It was also a cat club. I couldn't work out how they got there but the woman in the apartment next door fed them promptly at twelve each day.

I was a couple of floors up. The cats were all out to play because it was night. The apartments across the well from me were in the other building. Their door led onto a street behind mine. If you wanted to go from one door to the other it was a long walk around.

I had no difficulty clambering down into the well; the pipes provided enough footholds for an octopus. Standing among cat shit and the smell of leaking gas I set to tapping lightly on a window made of crinkly glass. I guessed I was tapping at the casement of somebody's bathroom.

I tap-tap-tapped. There was a light somewhere in there but I got no response. Tap! Tap! Louder. More urgent.

What a joke, me down where the cats hung out. Could I make it back up? What the hell to do?

Someone, a couple of floors up, shut a window. The way people do—an expression of something. I started banging on the glass, really rattling the sash. It was jerking about in its frame when, as though a miracle had taken place before my very eyes, the thing swung open.

Up I went and over, dropping to the floor on the far side like a baby elephant. I knocked over a stool with a whole lot of stuff on top. The door into the rest of the place was ajar; I stepped through it into the light. I was in a little hall by the front door. I went through the next doorway to the source of the light. There was the crack of a pistol shot, a point of fire ripped through my flank. I fell back hitting my head against the door jamb.

I couldn't have been out long. Coming to I got the picture back: a wizened little man in paisley smoking-jacket over pyjamas. He had been frozen in a position of extreme fear against the room's far wall, pistol pointing at the doorway. Now he was fussing over me, dabbing my face with a wet towel, the gun was on the floor by my side. He'd given himself a bigger fright than he'd bargained for.

'My, my, my,' he repeated. A pince-nez hung around his neck by a gold chain. Looking down I saw I was losing quite a bit of blood from the wound but I knew nothing was damaged. I would have looked worse than I was.

After consciousness it took a while for the brain to actually tick over. I gave it the time. He was forcing a glass to my lips, brandy. I sipped a wee drop, lunged, got the gun, sat up with it pointing at the old man. He was having a bugger of a night.

'Oh my God!' It was a north-east American accent gone creaky as though it lacked oil. He started to tremble violently, wrapping thin arms around his torso for comfort. There were the strands of a white beard-moustache outfit framing a mouth frozen into an idiotic grin.

'Steady,' I said. 'It's all right.' I looked about me: books. Heaps of books. They were on the floor, spread over table tops, couches. There were shelves of them up the walls, floor to ceiling. Chances were that the report of the gun would have been deadened by all that information. Could be they were a collection—thus the gun. A foolish insurance policy. I wouldn't have known, not about books.

'The bottle.' I gestured towards the brandy. He obeyed.

'And glasses.' The one he had recently raised to my lips had spilt, then been trodden into the rug as he stepped back. He picked up a couple from the one area of the room not devoted to the printed word, from where the bottles were.

On our fourth brandy he settled down. I'd spun him a tale within which I was the victim—the ultimate victim. He got over his fear, became concerned again. Cloth he'd used to dab me back to life was stuck between my belt and the wound, stemming the flow of blood.

The old boy was already a little drunk. He prepared coffee while I guarded the telephone—I didn't want frantic calls for help and I was mistrustful of the motives behind his eccentric, forgiving behaviour. How could a man so recently at gunpoint take up the cause of his would-be assailant? But I'd found a genuine soul, a being who lived by his own rules, who was as quick to shoot as he was to save. Somebody after my own heart. Only all shrunk up, the fluids sucked out of him by books.

After coffee we clinked our glasses preparing to drop a fifth brandy down the hatch.

Professor Blakey was reluctant to accept the handful of lire notes I'd shoved into the drawer beneath his telephone to cover a burst of calls. As far as buying the pistol was concerned he wouldn't hear a word of it.

'We are honourable people,' he protested. 'There's another world above commerce and usury.' Could have been he was the man who kept the candle alight on the grave of Ezra Pound over there on S. Michele. He pressed the point: 'If you tell me you'll return that gun it is sufficient.' That mistaken view of human nature clearly afforded the old boy a good deal of pleasure.

Five star hotels—I rang around. I found him finally at the Cipriano. You couldn't get better, Blakey assured me. Yes, they had a Mr Has. No, he did not wish to be disturbed. And I didn't wish to leave him anything that could be traced.

A young Italian friend of Blakey's had no trouble entering my apartment. He found the contents of my case and everything else strewn about. The door had been open, lock busted. He hadn't seen anybody hanging about when he went up there. He thought it looked like a thorough search with some damage done. There went the deposit component of the advance rent. And for what? There had been nothing for the bastards to find.

The same young man, Giovanni, managed to cajole the switch at the Cipriano into letting him speak to Has. A matter of the heart he had explained in Italian—the words sounding like a song. I was drifting into these people's debt. I'd called the lawyer's office in Canberra three times through the Venetian night, trying for information. My hosts gave me the benefit of their local knowledge and their mastery of the language. Blakey had armed me. Now, with my case returned, I was able to change out of blood-stained clothes after being patched up with materials Giovanni had obtained on a shopping trip.

We were well into the day and Elizabeth was last on the list. Although groggy with sleep she made a point of writing down the things I asked her to do. Could you rely on a girl who couldn't get herself out of bed in the morning?

Finally Blakey, with a bit of help from his books, wrote out a long list of family names in the Serbian Cyrillic script. They were to be my stock and trade.

He was plucky, Blakey. I recalled the fear written across his shrivelled features at the moment he shot me. Yet in the light of day he was enthusiastic, plotting action, offering assistance. And he cut an elegant figure: Anglophile tweed suit, check shirt, woollen tie. On his head he placed a deerstalker.

Giovanni was a fund of information. They were a curious combination: Blakey who had squandered career years on one of the Ivy league universities, teaching things about the language of the Magyars—those who had threatened the power of Venice in the thirteenth and fourteenth centuries—and Giovanni, the waiter, who knew his native streets. Confident of their loyalty I updated my story, filled in gaps and details, right up to crystal-gazing about my meeting at midday with Has on the Zattere. My problem was, how to get out of it alive? Perhaps that was the problem for me with Venice as a whole. There must have been a whole Croatian network spread through the city. It was an ancient connection, Venice and that coastline around the top of the Adriatic. The city's eastern associations were historically stronger than those it had with the modern state of Italy.

Whatever the contrary arguments, I'd made up my mind to get to the centre of everything, to resolve the questions that made my brain ache. And there was Assistant Commissioner Betti. A touch of justice wouldn't be out of place on that one. Not that I anticipated passing judgement and carrying out the sentence. The most I thought I could hope for was a chance to talk my way through it, then get the bastards to leave me alone.

All right, at the back of my mind, but right out of the way, there was the wild fantasy of me, the avenging angel. No more than wild fantasy. My real chances were simple—an exchange followed by a semi-planned departure. The currency I had to use was the counterfeit list of names.

Chapter 23

I caught the *Motoscafo Circolare* from the stop outside the Gesuiti Church across to the Giudecca where I took up position, clutching Blakey's binoculars while sensing the comforting weight of the pistol in my pocket.

I was keeping an eye on the nominated table, the one directly behind the spot where the owner seemed to like to posture, smugly dignified if not one hundred per cent at his ease. That had been the table where I caught a glimpse of Milo Strossmayer not so long before. I figured it was a place they hung out, little chance of them getting the location wrong.

A brisk wind was blowing, the Giudecca Canal was choppy, so much the worse for my plans. A man rowed for recreation in a sleek varnished craft. He was having problems, catching crabs.

I could see from right out beyond the façade of S. Giorgio Maggiore—one of the masterpieces of the sixteenth-century architect, Palladio—the incongruous funnel of a gigantic pleasure cruiser fated to pass between me and the outdoor coffee bar that was my target. How long would it take? No way for me to judge. My watch was saying eleven fifty-one—nine minutes to go. Assuming he was punctual.

There was a negative space where the bar structure poking out into the canal met the stone face of the Fondamenta. That was to be filled by a water-taxi if things went to plan. Nothing went to plan. Looking up I could see a plane coming into the airport on the mainland. I thought of Charlie, to arrive now would be bad timing.

It had been Andrew who answered the phone when I called up Elizabeth to get a bit of help. He'd hauled her out of bed for me. Had he been a fraction more reserved than when I last saw him? Than when I savoured his coffee, us evolving into an awkward threesome? Elizabeth's whispered information about Andrew's sexual preferences aside, and I had to hand it to him he was cool, had he perhaps got more rich cousin than he'd bargained for? If he was put out, if he got at Elizabeth, then what I'd arranged could fall to pieces. I was grasping at straws. Andrew and Elizabeth were two of them. For her a straw might have been too weighty an image—more like thistledown.

The ship was rounding S. Giorgio, past where its marina was tucked behind a sea-wall. Still no Has. It entered my head that I stood out like a sore thumb having let the next *Circolare* pass, headed up towards the railway station. I panned the glasses along the length of the Zattere: from the wall at the back of S. Maria della Salute right down to where the big ships tie up beyond S. Sebastiano. Then I panned them back again till they locked into a view up along a side canal leading over S. Gregorio to the Peggy Guggenheim Gallery. Four men were walking beside the water. The binoculars brought them close. They were coming directly at me. Then the ship moved across my vision and I stood up to walk, as casual as possible, in the direction of Zitelle, the next stop along.

While I watched, Professor Blakey and his friend, Giovanni, were doing their bit keeping the table occupied. When last spotted they were engaged in conversation with mine host. I had to assume that their presence would hold the place until Has specifically requested it. The last thing I wanted was some indignant tourist plonking himself down and staying put.

Would it look set up? How many people were watching? How many guns would there be dragging good tailor's cloth out of shape?

The *Motoscafo* emerged from the canal leading to the Arsenal where the great Venetian war fleets had once waited an admiral's orders. Slowly it crossed to S. Giorgio before coming on down to me. Training the glasses back all I could make out were people—no likenesses. Had it really been Has walking towards me before the ship passed? Too late for doubt, midday was striking. I boarded the boat, electing to stand for the short trip. I found myself gripping the pistol butt in my pocket.

First thing I saw was the diamond on his finger, I remembered it from Canberra. And he remembered me, he was standing, smiling, had he gained height or was that an effect of my fear? He wore an overcoat and a Homburg hat, both black; they made him appear old-fashioned, like somebody in the photos that Oula Strossmayer had hidden behind the Dufy. On his face the expression that had won my trust . . . the eminently reasonable man.

Would that I could look so straight. I sat by the rail, facing in. He raised no objection to a reallocation of the seats. It was in my plan to sit close to the water.

A waiter swooped. I ordered Campari while scanning faces at other tables. No sign of Milo. But any number of the customers could have been people trained for an attempt at the destabilization of Yugoslav power in Croatia. Of course, that was paranoia, by degrees the entire world looked to be shifting to their side. It was paranoia and fear.

'United with your team, Mr Has?'

'Teams!' He gestured generously with both hands, then he laughed. 'Is life a football match, Mr Holt?'

'It's all we've got . . . breathing.'

'A very Australian point of view.'

'Maybe it is.' It was my turn for the grand gesture, I indicated the crowds on the Zattere. 'Are you trying to tell me all these people are just waiting to die for a cause?' Confidence was returning, Has dropped back to his normal size, the small man yet thick-set. I stared at the cleft in his chin, at his old man's skin.

He rubbed his hands together, that was my answer.

'Or kill for one,' I added. 'This is going to sound weak-kneed to an old warhorse like yourself, Mr Has. But I gave a kid a koala bear the other day—sweet sentimental me. Can you guess whose child it was? Well you wouldn't, would you? He was called Betti, a friend of mine. Poor bastard was trying to keep all the private armies in check.'

Has 'tsk tsked' with a moist lip movement. Could have been the Croatian love call.

'The tragedy is that I believed your potted philosophy. I fell for it. And the Jewish stuff as well.'

'I am flattered. But why shouldn't you have believed it? I told you the truth. My mother was Jewish. All the more reason, Mr Holt, to guarantee survival.' When he smiled the broken

228

nose seemed to twist to one side. 'Unfortunately I have made the very serious error of believing you. The innocent out of his depth.'

'It's not an act, Mr Has. Let me assure you of that.'

'That, I choose not to believe.'

My Campari arrived. Given the situation it looked a fraction piss-elegant. I greeted it with regret. He had ordered a hot chocolate. It arrived capped with stiff cream, the type they squeeze out of nozzles.

'The fact is I am an innocent,' I said. But I wasn't backing down. 'You people have been working to change all that. What I can't understand is why. I was suckered into all this by what I believed to be friendship. So, tell me. Why?'

'You take the question out of my mouth. It is exactly what I have been unable to determine. You must understand that the innocence has become tedious. Yet the question hangs: Why, Mr Holt?'

The whole bloody thing, like always, going around in circles.

'Tedious enough to prompt your rat-faced mate to try to put me out of the way. At the cemetery too . . . that's where he caught up with me.'

'Another of your faults. You see too much. You know too much. Always on the spot. Just why is that? As for our friend that you encountered out there at S. Michele . . . rat-faced? Hardly. I would have thought him a pleasant-featured person. You see, that was a particular error. Your being here, watching us. Always in the streets, searching, and at this time. Why at this particular moment, Mr Holt? This is our moment, you see that. Our moment in history. For a long time, some say for too long, we have prepared for this time, prepared to make our move. And you are here.'

'But he wasn't sure was he? Not certain, Strossmayer? Didn't know what to do? Bungled it, missed his moment. Why do you think that was, Mr Has?'

'Because, to speak plainly . . .'

'I wouldn't expect anything less of you.'

'Flattery. The truth is we know who you are but not why. You do not seem to be a part of any organization, but you meet with people who are. You keep us confused.'

'You, though, you're the brains, right? Yet you're stupid enough to be interested in me?'

His face set, we had got to the nitty-gritty. 'I seek to know what it is that you have got. Declare your interest. At the start I thought you were a part of that ASIO circus. You and the fellow, Gerald Sparrow. Then, with your European connection, we began to think again. Also, and here I flatter you, with your surer touch, it seemed totally unlikely.'

'Thank you.' Even in the firing line I could appreciate an anti-Feathers remark.

'No,' he continued, 'I mean it. That is precisely why we are taking you seriously. It is my belief, our belief, that you possess a document that could do great damage to our cause. Something with the potential to create for us considerable embarrassment. At the beginning, as perhaps I have already indicated, I would not have believed this to be possible. Otherwise I would have given the matter more of my attention.'

'What form would that have taken, I wonder?'

'Attention, nothing more.'

'And that's what you were searching for last night, after the phone call? Would you mind if I send you the cleaning bill.'

He smiled, but no humour in it: 'That you should be so lucky. Yes, Mr Holt, searching, but we did not find what we were looking for.'

'The list?'

'Exactly.'

'You know why? Why you didn't find it? Because it wasn't there, Mr Has.' Even I could see that the scrap of paper torched by Brkic in Sydney's Serbian Club was my tenuous connection with this life. That's why I carried an invented version of the same thing in my pocket . . . on the off chance. But was there really any way out of the mess into which I'd been shoved? Give them the paper, where was the incentive for them to allow me to drift towards the twilight of my life? 'Mr Has, that's old stuff, the list, who's going to be interested? Why are you interested? If I understand your political position right you'd all be on the same side. You and the people named on that piece of paper. A lot in the grave by now, natural causes or put there by members of some other faction.' I'd gulped the drink, called for another. Has seemed to be checking the layout, eyes communicating . . . with whom?

'Mr Holt.' We were being very formal. I remembered talking to the undertaker, arranging my mother's funeral, that had been the same: stiff, correct, unconnected. 'You misunderstand the importance of the list. Every name on it would be wanted in most countries of the world, particularly now, today, when there is an upsurge of hysteria about war criminals. Why this should be I cannot tell. Perhaps just that these men are becoming old, soon the Lord will remove them from the possible grasp of human justice. Is it justice at all, forty years, more, after the events? We find that Klaus Barbie becomes the star of the French press, keeping the journalists occupied, the newspaper-owners rich. His trial is theatre, permitting fools to enjoy the luxury of indignation.' He was scraping about in the bottom of his cup with his spoon, picking up the last morsels of cream.

'We would like to avoid offering the world its free entertainment, Mr Holt. We would wish to spare any of the people listed on your document unwanted fame. Offer instead a quiet, a dignified end, sanctuary.'

'All your old cronies. Fade away like they say old soldiers do.'

'Mr Holt, when these people are caught, brought to trial, or even if things progress no further than the stage of accusations, a great deal of damage is done. Good men have their reputations ruined. The further away we are from the events of the Second World War as it is called, the more imprecise people's memories become. In Austria, a president's power is eroded, in some provincial town in France the name of a mayor is removed from the town hall, a family is forced to sell its farm, to move far away. Rumour breeds rumour, it spreads like a disease. Good, even great causes are damaged. No, Mr Holt, a list like the one that came into your hands is best destroyed.'

'It is destroyed, nothing to worry about.'

'And I don't believe that.'

'Or do you want to use it as a hit list? Is that what you have in mind?'

He threw up his hands warding off the suggestion.

I looked about me. No sign of the water-taxi . . . but Milo

Strossmayer established two tables away and signalling to a heavy-featured man who looked like a first cross between *Homo sapiens* and a tank.

Staving off the inevitable: 'I've got a couple of questions.'

Leaning forward: 'But, Mr Holt, we do not have time for games, not even your charming ones.'

'Hardly games! That's not what I'd call illegal shipments of arms! And, Mr Has, we're all short on time.'

'What questions?' Impatiently now. 'I must warn you, you're in no position to bargain, nor do I feel inclined. You have no way out of this situation, out of Venice for that matter.'

'I slipped through easily enough last night.'

'Luck, Mr Holt.'

'I'm a lucky fellow.'

'I think you will need to be. All right then, test me with your questions.'

Come on Elizabeth. 'Maybe statements, Mr Has.' He was paying more attention to Milo than to me. 'Why come to me for the list? I never had it.'

'That, I choose not to believe.'

'Then would you believe this, Mr Has, that I'd made a kind of vow to myself to fix up about Assistant Commissioner Betti.' My empty heroics, a product of anger, frustration. Where the hell was the water-taxi? And if I'd got away, the question would surely have remained: Where to? Essington had done it again, rushed in, gone off half-cocked. Funny isn't it, the way a plan can seem fine until it's put into practice.

'You are wasting my time, Mr Holt. I am not sure that you realize you are a minor affair, a side-show. Do not put too high a price on yourself. One of life's mistakes. Hand over that list and then you are free to go. No one will harm you.'

It would have been true, well perhaps. But I was stuck there. The deal had been that I drop the list written out by Blakey onto the table then go over the side to where Elizabeth should have been waiting in the boat—those water-taxis were sleek and quick. But, of course, the whole plan had been a crazy fantasy, too neat, a filmic illusion.

The names that Brkic had burnt, they were the people that the Americans and the British had done trades with—information for disappearance.

Where the fuck was that boat? Elizabeth? I guessed at that moment she was sitting on somebody's face, the whole thing escaped from her mind. And me, high and dry. Or she was just a little late.

I saw Milo stand, then he joined us. So did the tank man and someone else.

'Come along,' Milo said, 'and don't try anything foolish will you.'

'Stuff yourself, why should I? I'm staying put.'

'Not to be recommended.'

'And why would that be?'

'Because there is a man up there in that building.' He was pointing to the top floor above the restaurant which was the up-market relative of the outdoor area where we were seated. 'He has your head in a telescopic sight. He is ready to drill a hole right through it. In fact, I think he would prefer it that way.' The third man—he was very small, almost a dwarf— thought that was very funny. He laughed so hard he had to extract a large white handkerchief from his pocket to wipe his eyes. A human touch.

'Good for him,' I said, fighting to preserve a veneer of calm. I rose, went along quietly. Only then did I hear the approaching boat motor, see Elizabeth standing, trying to take in the scene. Too late.

To keep myself going I leant over towards Milo. 'I'm going to kill you for Betti,' I said. But I didn't believe it. Once it was said the echo sounded hollow and left no vibration, wasn't picked up on the air.

They'd decided on my apartment. I was frog-marched up the stairs and in. No key required with the busted lock. The door, giving directly onto the kitchen, hung open, pretty much the way Giovanni had described. Milo and his mates hadn't actually got around to taking the place to pieces but they hadn't been gentle either.

The dwarf-like man propped a chair against the door to hold it shut.

Blakey's stainless steel .22 had been lifted out of my pocket along the way. Another lesson for him about human nature. Now it was placed with tantalizing carelessness on the kitchen bench.

The tank man with the heavy features must have been the executioner. Up close I could see he'd powdered out a birthmark that covered a quarter of his face. Milo and number three who looked like a midget version of Tito—the same open appearance and heavy brow—had got hold of my arms. I looked on my way to an old-fashioned beating.

Has intervened, indicating the layout—the kitchen window opened into the well. Other people might hear, wouldn't that be too bad. A certain sadistic chill had colonized the kindly Mr Has of Has and Danilović.

We moved into the sitting-room where the window faced the street. The shutters were closed. They closed the door into the kitchen as well. With everything shipshape I took a wallop to the solar plexus. Just for starters. Nobody asked me about anything. He hit me again; his eyes glazed over, then he just kept on punching. Has stood back to watch the show.

There has to be a first time for everything.

I lunged about, the two men attached. Then I started taking blows to the face. It was too much. I felt like I would explode from within. He must have opened up the bullet wound again, I caught sight of blood oozing onto my shirt. Then from some new cut it began flowing down into one of my eyes.

My strength was going, consciousness became ill-defined. Then the blows ceased.

'The list, Mr Holt,' Has demanded. Now he was holding a gun—snub nose, exactly the same as Milo's.

I heard it from a long way off as though it belonged to someone else, to someone in another building, even another life, but I recognized it as my voice. It sounded thick and slow. 'I'll give it to you but there're copies. Any number of them.' Was I shouting? 'So . . . what do you fucking want?' I reached into my shirt pocket for the list Blakey had written.

'Copies!' Has smiled. 'I don't think you have followed me, Mr Holt. It's the names that I want. It is immaterial who else has access to them. Those people are to be silenced. They represent a danger to us and to our cause. War criminals we do not need, they are—how should I say—bad public relations. We would like to bury the past. A new Croatia will have a clean slate.'

I half hung between my handlers. Has unfolded the sheet of

paper. His smile faded by degrees then every facial muscle went rigid.

'What is this rubbish?' he shouted. 'You play games? Take me for a fool?' But 'fool' was obliterated by a shot. Has fell to the floor. I lunged backwards, Dwarf-Man still attached. A volley of shots followed. The Tank pitched forward on his face. The magic apartment killing mine enemies—worth the rent. I threw myself at Milo who was aiming at the empty doorway. I had his gun hand but it was hard with the dwarf around my neck. The three of us crashed to the floor as Milo's gun exploded right against my cheek.

A figure dashed into the room, at least that's what I sensed. Another shot, Dwarf-Man dropped away. Me, I concentrated on Milo but I was fading.

'Hang on, Essington!' Surely Charlie's voice. He'd made it, unwanted.

Another shot.

I'd had Milo in a bear hug, his body arched against it, resisting. Suddenly, with that final shot, I was clinging to a man tied together out of pillows and collapsed in my arms: Milo Strossmayer with the soul gone out of him.

Has was crawling about on his hands and knees. He was groaning loudly.

Charlie was about as white as he could get. The pistol, Blakey's pistol that they had left on the kitchen bench, hung from one finger by the trigger guard.

'That was the first flight I could get on,' Charlie said. Then he leant forward and began to vomit.

You can't please all the people all the time, but my God I'd tried. More fool me. Recovering, I made resolutions. I'd been making them all my life. I promised myself the new resolutions were going to stick.

I ditched the *deux chevaux*—nobody had got around to touching it, anyway. Poor little thing was at the bottom of the car class system and used to bigger wheels throwing mud all over it.

Charlie and I flew home. I'd already broken resolution number one. I'd given the green light for Andrew and Elizabeth to visit. Immediately they decided on straight away. The bastards couldn't wait. Wasn't Karen going to love Elizabeth?

Funny thing was, she did.

I was Ulysses, I thought. I was going to draw the bow, re-establish my position. Charlie was going to show Dawn that a man could be gentle. I could see that resolution in his eyes when he mentioned her name. They're the sorts of thoughts the homecomer entertains. Then, when you arrive, as often as not you blow it. Only a word, one word, sets up the old pattern. Difficulties you vanquished in your imagination are more stubborn in reality. And the world once it changes is always from that moment on utterly changed.

So we settled back, a *ménage à combien*? Three, four, five, six. Me playing Mr Moneybags, always picking up the tab and yet, through the magic of arithmetic, never slipping back.

It was all right. I was forgiven. But nobody was quite as pleased to see me as the dog, Desdemona. With Karen it was: 'Hi, Ess.' A breezy kiss. Smiles . . . even gaiety. Things would be OK but never quite the same again. Dawn had become emotionally proprietorial. She'd take me aside, discuss Karen's problems like they were stock diseases. The big change was that from then on she wasn't into destroying bedrooms with me anymore. Wifely duties she would perform, but more as duties. So the game was new, the rules changed.

And Charlie's passion for Dawn? On her side it was ideological. He was a black (technically anyway); for her that equated with feminist. They had something to fight for. Where the body was concerned it was strictly hands off.

The Christophes had had their fun and departed. I knelt at the foot of my bed and prayed for God to send rats to eat out his car's upholstery.

'What pleasure have great princes?' I read that somewhere. Not that I was a prince, not the old Essington Holt. But I was a long way up the stack out there on Cap Ferrat. For guidance, I thought a lot about Blakey who had demonstrated that he had connections: his side of the story was the one the police bought. There wasn't any other side—Has died in hospital never uttering a word. Blakey's was one of life's solutions: transfer your love to a place and have young friends.

And have young friends . . . We were all out on the terrace. The sun cut through the leaves of the eucalyptuses, beyond whose silhouettes the Mediterranean was the sparkling azure it's supposed to be.

I'd been drinking too much since leaving Venice.

Mr and Mrs Feldstein were either putting things into or taking things out of the Ferrari. Their poodle was at the fence, yapping. Desdemona loped down to chew the fat with it—sociable creatures, dogs.

It was Sunday. Despite that, Karen and Dawn decided on a trip into Nice to arrange something at the shop. They were taking the Citroën Estate. That would leave Charlie, Farah, Elizabeth and Andrew. And me.

The Citroën gave a little roar of life which beckoned Elizabeth and Andrew down the steps in pursuit. They thought a trip to Nice might be just the thing. Then Charlie, he squeezed in too.

The car passed out through the grill gate.

I turned, Farah was still there, sitting looking out to sea. 'They left you behind?' I said.

'I stayed. Anyhow, there was no room.' She regarded me, serious. There was depth, almost magic, in those dark eyes. I poured another drink. She took Perrier water.

'What now?' I asked.

'Now, Mr Holt, you show me the house.'